Knight Secrets

C.C. Wiley

LYRICAL PRESS
Kensington Publishing Corp.
www.kensingtonbooks.com

LYRICAL PRESS BOOKS are published by

Kensington Publishing Corp.
119 West 40th Street
New York, NY 10018

All Kensington titles, imprints, and distributed lines are available at special quantity discounts for bulk purchases for sales promotion, premiums, fund-raising, educational, or institutional use.

Special book excerpts or customized printings can also be created to fit specific needs. For details, write or phone the office of the Kensington Sales Manager: Kensington Publishing Corp., 119 West 40th Street, New York, NY 10018. Attn. Sales Department. Phone: 1-800-221-2647.

Lyrical Press and Lyrical Press logo Reg. U.S. Pat. & TM Off.

First Electronic Edition: March 2017
eISBN-13: 978-1-5161-0100-9
eISBN-10: 1-5161-0100-6

First Print Edition: March 2017
ISBN-13: 978-1-5161-0103-0
ISBN-10: 1-5161-0103-0

Printed in the United States of America

I am grateful for my husband and family's love and support. Thank you for your endless patience.

A huge thank-you goes to my friend and super beta reader, Susie Fourt. You're the best! And many thanks to my dear friend and critique partner, Kimberley Troutte, who always talks me through the crisis. Thanks for reminding me to breathe.

Chapter 1

England, Summer 1415

"Riders!"

The gateman's urgent pronouncement echoed over Margrave Manor's bailey yard. Lady Clarice of Margrave looked up from the bed of herbs and wiped the sweat from her brow. The women beside her in the vegetable garden of meager crops paused in their work, weeds bunched in their fists.

"Maud," Clarice said. "See what has Nobbins in such a panic."

"Yes, my lady."

The servant rose slowly from the raised beds scented with flowers and herbs. Her longtime friend straightened her lower limbs with care. Once Clarice's nursery maid, Maud had become her closest companion over the years. Her heart ached with knowing their remaining time together was limited.

Clarice nodded to the women beside her to return to their labor. "Wait, Maud." She shook the dust from her skirts. "Stay here and rest whilst I question him."

"But 'tis my duty to protect you."

"Nonsense. You know as well as I 'tis a rarity for a stranger to pass this way." Clarice snorted with derision. "More than likely that ol' fool Nobbins snuck into the cellar and helped himself to the honey mead." She tapped her temple. "Visions from battles of old."

The clang of the watchtower bell tore through the air. "Riders!" Nobbins shouted again, his voice croaking with age. "Lower the portcullis."

The two women flinched as iron posts struck cobblestones and locked in place. Color drained from Maud's weathered cheeks. "My lady, I think 'tis best if you come away until we are certain the strangers are gone."

Clarice glanced toward the gate, ignoring the servant's insistent tug. "No. I—"

"We must heed Lord Margrave's orders."

With each pealing cry of the bell, a nervous shiver dug into Clarice's stomach. "I'm aware of my father's warnings, but—"

"Then promise me you will bide here until I learn who comes," Maud said.

Before Clarice could voice her argument, the servant rushed from the garden with a swiftness that belied her increasing years. Ripping off a handful of fragrant catmint leaves, Clarice worried them between her fingers and turned to comfort the women of the woods who had come to gather herbs and vegetables. They fluttered about like a flock of pigeons, running to hide behind the vegetation.

"Shush," she snapped. "Stay calm. You'll be safe here." Clarice prayed she was correct.

Torn between fear and curiosity, she palmed a rosebud and waited. Who rode to the manor? What news did they carry? The order to always remain hidden echoed in her mind. Her father and stepmother would be furious should they learn she had disobeyed. The land outside the wall was a dangerous place for a young woman without an escort. More important, Maud would be beside herself with worry.

What harm is there in a quick peek?

The temptation to know who had arrived at their desolate country manor became too much to ignore. Clarice let the rose petals fall to the ground and dashed toward the outer wall. The wooden panel door, hidden in the aging stones, protested against her shoulder until it gave way. Slipping through the narrow passage, she craned her neck to see beyond the wall. Her lungs caught at the sight of the advancing riders.

Destriers charged the arched bridge leading to the manor. A dust cloud swirled into the blue sky. Every hoof strike made the ground tremble. The air hummed with the jingle of iron rings and the creak of leather. Sunlight glinted off helmets and breastplates. Red and white banners led the way, announcing their allegiance. But they were still too far away for her to discern their symbols.

As the riders drew nearer, Clarice's fingers tightened around the edge of the door. Unable to turn away, she fought to draw in a breath. The men on horseback numbered at least threescore, and more followed behind. Soldiers reined in their mounts, shouting for the others to fan out to protect their flanks.

'Tis King Henry's banner of the red rose.

A destrier, dark and monstrous in stark comparison to the other horses, broke free from the field of men. Sitting tall in the saddle, the rider moved as one with his mount. The visor remained down, protecting his face. Auburn curls cut wavy lines against his broad shoulders.

"Hold!" Nobbins yelled from the gate. "What business 'ave you with Margrave Manor?"

Clarice leaned out, straining to hear the exchange over the roar of blood pulsating in her ears.

"I am the lord of Sedgewic. Upon the king's command," the rider barked, the timbre of his voice hoarse and grating. "We demand to cross this threshold."

"Present your orders. This gate won't open until you do."

Although the rider made no outward appearance of anger, nor did he order his men to advance, the air trembled with the man's impatience.

Slowly, as if fighting the decision, Nobbins lowered a bucket from the small opening in his watchtower. The lead rider withdrew a packet from his tunic and inserted it into the bucket. It inched up the wall, the rusting cogs complaining, counting out each crank of the handle until both missive and bucket tipped through the narrow window.

Moments passed. The gate remained down. Horses stomped the earth, feeling their riders' agitation.

Clarice could not turn away. She hoped, in some small way, that her presence at the wall helped Nobbins to keep the soldiers at bay.

The lead soldier struck the portcullis with his sword. The power behind his swing caused the iron to clang. "Open this gate." He pointed toward the mass of soldiers behind him. "Or know the king of England's wrath."

"My lady—"

Clarice clutched the wooden door to steady her balance and tore her attention from the intruders.

Maud stood behind her, bent over, gasping for air. She held out the missive. "You shouldn't be here. Come away quickly."

Clarice swallowed and broke the king's seal. The words, written with a heavy hand, blurred and danced before her. "They carry King Henry's orders . . ." She glanced up. "They are to search the property, from cellar to attic, for my family."

Maud gasped, clutching her throat. "Lord and Lady Margrave? Your stepbrother, too?"

A sinking feeling formed a knot in Clarice's middle. "What has Robert done now?"

"My lady, please." Maud shook her head, doing her best to usher her charge to the shadows. "Come away. Hide before 'tis too late."

"This is madness," Clarice argued, digging her heels into the earth. "The Margraves have always enjoyed a place at the royal court. My father is one of Henry's trusted advisers."

Despite the heat of the day, a cold dread seeped into her back. A surge of anger slashed through the growing fear. Squaring her shoulders, she choked down the panic lodged in her throat and forced authority into her orders. "We shall inform the king's good men that neither my father, stepmother, nor their son, Robert, has been in residence for over a year. Make haste," Clarice fluttered her hands as if shooing a stray chicken. "Tell Nobbins I order him to draw up the portcullis."

"But how will we defend ourselves?"

Clarice lifted her sleeve, wiping the perspiration from her neck. "Our numbers are few. Would you pit two men and a handful of women against those soldiers?"

"My lady, I've heard stories of the destruction the king's soldiers leave behind."

"Indeed, but their fury will be greater if we do not bid them enter. What would you have us do? Pray that the portcullis will hold against their weapons and brute strength? For how long?"

"Lord Margrave's orders—"

"'Tis no time to argue." Demanding shouts continued to echo across the bailey. The dull thud of wood striking iron caught Clarice's breath. They were using a battering ram to gain entry. Her heart thundered against her bones and she rubbed the ache in her chest. "My father is not here and we haven't the defenses to hold against the king's force. Instead, we will be hospitable and pray they will leave peaceably."

Maud grasped her arm. "What of the women of the woods?"

Clarice's mind spun, searching for answers. How had she forgotten the small group of women huddled together in the garden corner? Their faces were milk white, their eyes wide with terror.

"Here." She grabbed a basket of beans and young onions, shoving it toward the women. "I fear your pitchfork and trowel will do little to sway them from their purpose. Go through the garden gate and head to safety. Be sure you aren't seen."

The women bobbed their heads. "Shall we send our men?" one asked.

"No, 'tis best we try for peace. Be sure to hide what livestock you have and store the food away from the buildings should the soldiers decide to scorch the earth."

Clarice flinched as the shouting at the watchtower grew. "Go. Make haste while you can."

She watched them run through the garden. An eternity later, they slipped through the hidden gate. Oh, how she wanted to flee with them. Instead she waited, giving the women time to get away from the wall. Then she pushed past Maud, striding toward the watchtower. "Nobbins," she shouted. "Open the gate before they tear it down."

"My lady—" Nobbins had climbed down from his tower. His cheeks flushed, he met her in the bailey. "But, my lady—"

"Do it," she ordered, gripping his forearm. "Let us pray we are in time."

Nobbins's rheumy eyes widened. Turning on his heel, he trotted to do her bidding.

Clarice braced her feet, defying the weakness that made her knees tremble. Relief came with the complaints of the cogs and wheels as they drew up the heavy iron chain. The portcullis began to rise.

But 'twas too late.

The first wave of foot soldiers advanced before the iron bars raised to its full height. The weathered oak panels of the inner port shattered on impact of the battering ram and the soldiers flooded the bailey.

Tom, the stableman, attempted to take a stand. Met with a fist to his head, he fell to his knees. The soldier struck again. Tom's mouth gaped and blood spilled down his chin as he tipped forward.

Stunned by the violence, Clarice stood in the open, unable to move, unable to stop the sob bubbling up. She clawed blindly as Maud tried to drag her away.

"Do you think to stop them by yourself?" the servant hissed, yanking Clarice toward the shadowed corner of the garden. "They don't know nor care who you are. They'll strike you down the moment you stand in their path."

Foot soldiers marched through the bailey, swords drawn. They made short work of destroying the doors of the outer buildings. Then they turned their attention to the livestock.

"I let this happen." The contents of Clarice's stomach churned. "I've put us all in danger, haven't I?"

"They were entering, like it or not." Maud cupped her charge's chin. "Promise me, now more than ever, you will heed your father's orders and stay out of sight."

"I—" The sounds of devastation drew Clarice's attention. "No. No." She leaped to confront a soldier who was stealing the manor's milk cow. "Stop!"

Nobbins shouted, lunging toward the men, drawing them from the garden and away from the women. His rounded stomach met with a fist. Sucking in a breath, he struggled to remain upright. The soldiers braced their weapons, barring him from advancing. They jerked his arms behind his back, restraining him with a length of rope.

"What would you have us do with this one, Lord Ranulf?"

The lead rider remained seated atop his powerful horse, towering over all. His helmet on, the visor covered all but his eyes. "Where are the lord and lady of Margrave?" he demanded.

The gateman shook his head. "You'll not find 'em here. I'm kept on to mind the manor." He glared up at his captors. "And keep thievin' bastards out."

Clarice ached to know the demon on horseback. To see his ugly face. To make him pay. Maud's whispered reminder to stay hidden to protect the others kept her crouched in the garden. She slipped deeper into the shadows.

The commander braced his leather-and-steel-clad forearm on his saddle and lifted the visor to reveal a stony expression. Auburn curls captured the sun before settling over his broad shoulders. His jaw flexed, making the livid pink scar on his temple jump. "Lord Margrave is wanted for treason. I suggest every Margrave soul show themselves." His deep voice carried over the bailey. "Or I'll order the buildings torn down, stone by stone. This estate will be burned to the ground."

"Treason?"

"I beg you." Maud hissed, placing a warning hand around her wrist. "My lady, our people will fare far worse if you present yourself now and give the soldiers reason to harm you."

"My father would never commit treason against the throne. He would never shrink from his duties. Nor will I." Her fingers curled into tight fists. "These are my people. My home."

"Think it through," the servant hissed. "There's nothing we can do for your father at this moment. But Nobbins and Tom? They would give up their lives to protect you. Do you wish for their deaths?"

At the shake of Clarice's head, Maud nudged her lady toward the tower doorway. "Now do as I say. I'll keep you safe. 'Tis my vow to Lord Margrave."

"My father—" Clarice fought the rising panic.

"—would want you to heed my guidance," Maud finished for her. "This is your home. But you must keep yourself hidden until the soldiers take their leave. 'Tis the only way to ensure the safety of the others. Your father will sort out the rest in due time."

Clarice searched for the stableman. The ground was stained with his blood, but he stood propped up by the milkmaid's shoulder. She glanced over to the spot where Nobbins had confronted the soldiers. Her throat burned and her chest tightened, squeezing. He had put himself in harm's way to protect her from her foolishness to save a cow.

Who was she to think she could persuade the king's men to turn away from this madness? Her father had placed Nobbins in the watchtower to keep intruders out. And keep her in. She should have kept to the shadows and let him do his duty.

She searched her old friend's face. "But what of you?"

"They won't want a broken-down woman. I'd be too much of a bother and mayhap die on the road." Maud led her through the tower entrance. "Go, my lady. Hurry and hide."

"No, I—" Clarice stumbled over the threshold.

"Hush, now." Maud put her weight against the door to push it shut. "If you must know, I intend to convince them that the plague has struck. That will explain why the family is not here, and why there are so few servants for them to corral." She paused, determination glittering in her old gray eyes. "Stay here 'til I come for you. Ignore the stench if you can."

Clarice pressed her cheek against the stone doorway. "And what if your plan does not work?"

"Then all is lost."

Nestled off to the side of the tavern, the king's men huddled in the enclosed alcove. The door to the small chamber remained hidden under a stained tapestry. If not for the swan emblem they each carried in some form or fashion, no one would know they had banded together as brothers. Knights of the Swan.

The amber glow of one small candle in the middle of the table did little to improve the light. The flickering shadows kept the room's inhabitants concealed in the shadows. Ranulf scanned the group of men. Some were familiar to the royal courts. Others were not. 'Twas a rarity for the brotherhood to meet together. Over the years, he had learned to recognize the voices and faces of fellow brothers. The others would remain unknown to him until the time came for personal contact.

Ranulf passed a thumb over his ring before placing a fisted hand on the table for all to see. He watched as each member brought out his own talisman. Whether simple or elaborate—an embroidered patch, a ring, a brooch, or a dagger from the Holy Land encrusted with an emerald—each bore the symbol of the swan. Ranulf noted there were a few missing. Logistics, ongoing missions, or death was the only explanation for their absence. Rarely did a man retire from the brotherhood.

King Henry's mother, Mary de Bohun, understood the intricacies of the royal court. Before her death, when Henry was still a child, Mary had gathered those she trusted to watch over her children. Using the emblem passed down through the de Bohun family, the swan had begun to appear in various ways. The first of them was Mary's silver ring, created with the tips of a swan's wings entwined, the head tucked in with a small emerald that winked from time to time.

When contact was required, the message for swans was passed. Many times, growing up, he and the young Prince of Wales had used this as a means to send their own private messages to each other. Ranulf often wondered if Mary de Bohun had intended for this band to continue once Henry sat upon the throne. Of course, given the circumstances, she could not have foreseen her son would one day be king. Born as a means to protect her son, the Knights of the Swan now stood in service as the king's secret guard.

A faceless brother leaned toward the center of the table. He kept his voice low as he peered into his mug of ale. "'Tis certain. One of our own intends to end England's claim to the French shores by cutting off England's head." He turned with a grunt. "A true pity you failed to find the bastard."

Ranulf stiffened, fighting the urge to rub the aching scar at his temple. Annoyance at his failure to locate the Margraves escalated with each moment. Not one among the handful of Margrave servants could tell him what he needed to know. Although the old woman had said the plague had taken most of the people, he had his doubts. His knuckles whitened. He would know the truth soon enough.

"Maintain watch," the brother said, pointing a finger in Ranulf's direction. "Wait for the vermin to slither out of their holes."

Ranulf uncurled his fist, wrapping it around his mug. "The devils will have their heads impaled on pikes before they see their foul plan through."

Impatient to be off and about his task, he shifted his gaze over the small group. Their allegiance to King Henry and England strengthened their resolve to do whatever it took to protect the Swan.

Chapter 2

Clarice stood inside the main hall as little tremors took possession of her legs, her spine. She gripped her elbows. The life she had known, torn asunder by uncaring destriers' hooves and accusations of treason by King Henry's demon, no longer existed.

Lord Ranulf. That name was seared into her memory. He was the one who had led the charge against her home, sentencing her family to destruction. His voice had been muffled by the visor and might be difficult to recognize should she hear it again, but the rest of him she would recognize anywhere. Of that she had no doubt.

Nearly a week had passed since the soldiers had carried away anything of value from Margrave Manor. Maud had set fire to the mixture of soiled linens, rancid tallow, and the latrine chute's refuse, keeping her safe from the soldiers. Surrounded by the stench of death and the possibility of plague, they had steered clear of the tower. Instead, they'd made use of their time, destroying whatever they touched. Thanks be to the saints, they had left Maud unmolested and refrained from burning the buildings and fields to the ground.

Clarice dug her nails into her elbows. Maud may have protected her from the king's men, but watching the soldiers lead the servants away had left her with a gnawing ache of helplessness. She prayed for their souls and that God would watch over them. And cursed the king's devil who had destroyed her home.

The cold stone of the hall seeped through her clothing, burrowing its way into her back. A gentle breeze caught the lingering scent of Maud's inventive use of the latrine chute and a torch. It had taken the better part of a day to remove the smell from the keep. Mayhap in time, it, too, would fade with the memory of seeing her home invaded.

Tears filled her eyes. The last few days had taken their toll, the heartache too much to bear. Dragging in a raw breath, her chest shuddered under the weight. With the new day came more trouble. *Saints help me, my family has returned.*

Today, at the break of dawn, Robert had charged through the unguarded gates on his stallion. The horse's ribs heaved as it fought the excessive sawing of the reins. Her stepbrother's coal-black hair glistened under the sunrise as he stood on the stirrups, scanning the bailey and buildings. Snarling when no one ran from the stable to offer aid, he tore off his leather gloves and tossed them to the ground.

Soon after, a carriage had rattled over the bridge. At first she had not recognized her father, Lord Nicholas Margrave. His clothing and hair disheveled, he sat upon the box instead of riding his prized horse. Utilized as a packhorse, Buttercup trotted alongside, looking miserable and weary. When the horses stopped, her stepmother, Lady Annora, pulled back the curtain and stared up at the tower.

Clarice shuddered at the memory of the disapproval written upon their faces. Their piercing gazes had searched the shadows from which she had watched them cross into the bailey.

The family had been in residence for a few hours and already the air in the main hall throbbed with fear and outrage. "Christ's blood," she muttered. "I'd rather be left alone to grow old in this musty manor then spend another moment with my . . . family."

Ranulf peered over the boulder. Margrave Manor was little more than a bailey and keep. Decaying vegetation filled the moat. Empty fields lay fallow from neglect. The large, dirty gray structure stood as a crumbling effigy of the past. 'Twas as if Nicholas wanted to forget it existed.

King Henry's men had taken over where the Margraves left off and made the manor uninhabitable. Remnants of the garden lay trampled by hooves. The portcullis remained raised. Fragments of the main gate hung in ragged angles, rendering Margrave's country manor defenseless.

Ranulf offered up a curse against Lord Nicholas Margrave and his family. It had not been his intention to visit the English countryside twice in less than a week. Yet his duty was clear. He would expose those who wove the threads of this latest plot against his king. He was certain others were involved. He could feel it in his bones.

All who were a part of this ill-gotten plan would suffer. As a knight of the Swan, he had vowed to protect the king or die.

A movement amid the trampled vegetation caught his eye. A young woman strode along a stone path leading to the tower. Her arms were wrapped around her waist, exposing the gentle curves of her body. The flow of raven hair swayed in rhythm with her hips.

"Hello, mysterious lady. Who might you be?" he whispered. "I wonder how you slipped past our search."

In truth, the report of a deadly pestilence had caused the men to move more swiftly than usual, cutting short their visit. His frown deepened. She moved down the path with ease and did not show signs of illness. He knew he should have insisted on another sweep of the manor before they left. "Plague." He gave a derisive snort. "Indeed."

He edged closer to get a better view. The maiden paused in front of the tower entrance, looked around furtively, then slipped through the doorway before he could see her face.

"God's bones," he muttered. "I wager 'tis Robert's latest conquest." He could not comprehend the depths of their idiocy. Despite the young Margrave's infamous reputation, the women of the court continued to throw their virtue at the man's feet.

He tore his thoughts from the woman and continued to watch the bailey.

"So, they have all come home to roost, have they?" Ranulf slid his hand through his tangled crop of hair. The thought of Robert of Margrave set his teeth on edge. The man was annoying, like flies lured in by a dung heap. But Nicholas Margrave's treachery against King Henry would not be ignored. Justice must be served.

His focus narrowed. The air crackled, charged with the sensation felt right before a heavy storm. "'Tis time to draw them out. Then wring their fool necks."

Determined to uncover what he needed and return to the Cock's Inn before nightfall, Ranulf hitched up the baggy tights he had borrowed from a fat peddler and led the horse and cart toward the manor.

Clarice clutched the skirt of her woolen gown and strode up the narrow tower stairway. The urge to scream out her frustrations boiled in her empty stomach. She slammed the chamber door shut. Birds nesting under the eaves shot into the sky.

After all these years, she had come to accept that her stepmother and stepbrother did not love her. She had convinced herself that her father cared for her in his own way. But with the gloomy days came the unrelenting voice in her head that would not be quiet. Why did they hide her away in the country? Robert was wrong. She did not carry a soul of violence. *So then why lock me away where they could forget me?*

The desire to know a better life, where she was truly loved, whispered in her heart. Try as she might, the ache to experience life beyond the Margrave walls refused to be ignored. But a woman alone, without money or protection, would not survive for long. At least she knew this demon. Soon her stepbrother and stepmother would leave. And so would Father.

She clutched her stomach. *What a wretched fool I am. How could I forget about his troubles?*

There had to be a way to prove his innocence.

Maud hobbled into the chambers. She stood in the center of the room, her grizzled hair loosened from the ever-tidy bun, her hands hidden under her apron. "My lady—"

"Whatever is the matter, Maud?"

"Someone comes."

Chapter 3

"The king's men?" Clarice forced down the panic clawing its way up her throat.

"A peddler. See here," Maud pointed her gnarled finger out the chamber window. "His cart is fair to heaping with all manner of supplies. He nearly scared my hair to white when I saw him standing there. Not a sound was a' comin' from him or his horse. 'Tis like he's an archangel sent from heaven."

"Don't forget, Lucifer once held a place in heaven, too." Clarice glanced down at the man. He led his cart past the point where once their gateman had stood sentry. Thanks to the king's wrath, there was no one left to guard the entrance. Not that there was anything left of value anyway.

"Do you recognize him?" she asked. "He might be one of the king's men in disguise. Lady Annora was certain they were followed."

"No." Maud peered around her. "Looks like Fat Thomas's mare pulls the cart, but I've never seen that peddler before." She wedged her body near the window. "Hmm. Fat Thomas never cut a figure such as that."

"And how would you know of Fat Thomas's figure?" Clarice pressed.

A rosy blush crept up Maud's neck. "Mayhap the peddler heard of your family's misfortune," she said, ignoring the question.

Clarice frowned. "We've never had peddlers venture this way before." When he looked up, she snapped back out of sight. Careful to keep hidden, she watched him caress the animal's neck. He was unusually tall, with broad shoulders. The hood of his voluminous cloak covered most of his face.

A gust of wind caught the edges of the head covering, revealing a hint of bronze-colored hair. He caught the hood and tugged it forward. Despite his lowly position of peddler, he boldly continued to gaze at her window.

"He's a persistent one." Clarice smiled at Maud. "Do you think Father and the others are done shouting and are aware someone has entered our gates?"

"I fear it 'twould not be my place to say, my lady."

"Mayhap, I . . . we . . . should go down to speak to him. I hid a few coins under my pillow. 'Twould be a blessing to have a morsel or two to stave off our hunger." Clarice hesitated. "I suppose since my stepmother is in residence, she should be the one to barter with him."

"'Tis not for me to judge," Maud said, turning to smooth the thin bedding over the mattress.

Clarice rested her hands on her hips. "Since when has that stopped you?"

Her servant and friend gave an indignant huff. "Lady Annora may be my master's wife, but in my heart 'tis you who is the lady of Margrave Manor. I'd rather take my orders from you."

"Hush! You best not let her hear you." Clarice checked to see if the peddler remained below. He rewarded her with a slight nod of his head. Spreading out his hands, he motioned to the cart. "It appears the stranger intends to stand there until someone comes out to speak with him."

"'Tis a certainty."

"If we go quietly we might convince him to part with something." Clarice grimaced. "If we hurry, we'll agree on a fair price before Annora steps in and causes us to pay more than we should."

A growl emanated deep within the empty cavern of Clarice's stomach. She must hurry before the peddler turned away from the household. "Maud, you don't need to go down there. Stay here. Save your joints."

"Forgive me for reminding you yet again," Maud said, catching Clarice's wrist. "But remember that no outsiders are to know you are the lord's daughter. Promise me you'll at least keep your face covered." Her hold tightened. "Swear it."

Clarice nodded and blew out the candle. She caught up the cloak hanging from a peg. Her shadow danced crazily as she raced down the stairs, then came to a skidding halt.

With the hood of her cloak positioned to keep her identity concealed, she pulled her shoulders back, straightening her stance. Raising her chin, she called out, "You there. Stay where you are."

The peddler bowed, touching his forelock in respect. Though he kept his head lowered, his gaze traveled up her plain homespun skirt to the edge of her cloak. She gripped the hood to keep her face hidden.

"Mistress? Forgive me. I heard the manor might 'ave need o' supplies." His deep voice resonated with power.

"Yes." Jumping as a crash erupted from the main hall, she turned, her stomach pitching. "We must make haste," she said, taking a step closer.

Lady Annora marched down the steps. Her stout body pumped across the bailey, her ample breasts straining against the material, threatening to escape the gown's bodice. Robert strode by her side. Their outraged voices carried on the evening air.

"Who is she speaking to?" Annora clutched at Robert's arm. "She knows never to speak with strangers."

"I don't know, Mother," he said. "She needs someone to take a hand to her."

Clarice glanced at the peddler. She flinched as her stepmother continued to blather on. "Grain," Clarice said, raising her voice. Saints, but she did not want her faults aired within the stranger's hearing. "And meat."

"What, mistress?" the peddler asked, distracted by the spectacle.

Determined to have something in her stomach that eve, Clarice hurried toward the cart, calling out as she neared, "Grain. Eggs. If you please."

"Hold! You there. Peddler," Annora said, her pudgy hands fisted on her rounded hips. "I am lady of this manor."

Robert came up from behind Clarice, wrapping his arm around her waist. "Mayhap we should let her deal with the peddler, Mother. 'Tis clear she's eager to serve."

Clarice ground her back teeth, fighting the urge to elbow him in the stomach. She dared not lose her opportunity to gather foodstuffs for Maud.

Her stepbrother let her go with a shove and her braid swung out from between the folds of the cloak. She stumbled before the peddler caught her, righting her balance.

"Best be careful, m' lady," the peddler whispered.

Clarice's skin warmed where he touched her waist. She ducked her head, keeping her face covered with the cloak. "My th-thanks, kind sir."

Robert slid beside his mother. He lifted her hand, letting it rest in the crook of his arm. "My lady, 'tis obvious we've interrupted a clandestine meeting among the servants." Bending a deep bow, he turned. "I fancy a haunch of salted beef or pork. See what you can work out with the man." He flipped a single coin to the peddler. "This should take care of her inadequacies."

Clarice's face heated from his verbal slap. To her dismay, the peddler followed the arc of the glittering coin before giving chase. She had hoped him cut from a different cloth. *Does no one have honor? Does it even exist?*

In an exaggerated leap, he reached and missed. Stumbling in his efforts, he narrowly missed falling into Robert and Annora and had barely righted himself before receiving their first wave of tongue-lashings. His busy hands dusted the young lord's tights. While they were still in a jumble, he continued to scrape an awkward bow, offering his apologies, and cracked Robert in the jaw with the back of his head.

Tangled in Annora's skirts, Robert teetered and fell with a dull thump. A muffled groan erupted from where he sat in the dirt.

A bubble of laughter leaked through before Clarice could cover her mouth. She cleared her throat before another burst forth.

The peddler kept his head down in deference and held out his hand. "Terribly sorry, m' lord."

Robert swatted at the help and scuttled out of reach. "Hold, you lumbering ox."

"Enough," Father shouted, striding toward them.

Maud followed close behind. Her little feet flew across the trampled grass.

Father pulled up in front of them. His glance skittered off Annora, still panting from her unaccustomed exertion. "Take your mother," he said, shoving her into Robert's arms.

"What would you have me do with her?"

Smoothing his hair back, Father's voice rose with each clipped word. "Remove. Her. From. The. Yard."

Robert held out his forearm. "Come, Mother. The lord of Margrave desires to deal with the peasant himself."

The scowl etched in his face deepened. Father motioned to Maud, who strayed not far from his side and nodded in Clarice's direction. "You'd do best to do what you're told." His attention returned to Maud. "And you," he said, pointing a narrow finger. "See that you manage your charge."

"Yes, my lord." Maud bobbed a curtsy and turned. "Come, my dear."

Reluctant to do her father's bidding, Clarice cast a longing gaze toward the peddler's cart. Her stomach growled in rebellion.

Ranulf tore his attention from the young maiden and did his best to ignore the tingling sensation from where he had held her. He kept his face covered as he searched his bags for food: a haunch of salted pork, a bag of grain. On a whim, he added a bunch of carrots, two eggs, and one onion to the pile.

He hated having to wait upon the man suspected of plotting against the king. *Saints!* Although his orders were to watch for Margrave's cohorts, Ranulf itched to get it over with and deliver him to the king.

The felon faced any number of punishments including hanging, emasculation, disemboweling, beheading, and drawing and quartering. The king could employ any combination of his choosing. A grizzly sight Ranulf never became used to seeing.

The accusations of treason had rung false when he first heard them. The man had been the king's confidant and adviser. He had witnessed their friendship in court and on the march. What had caused him to turn on his monarch and country? Although Lord Margrave had had the unfortunate luck of marrying a harpy, he always carried himself with a quiet spirit. He was a warrior who had lost his desire for battle, a man beaten into submission. This was not a man with the stomach to commit treason against his king.

Lord Margrave waited for everyone to leave the bailey. Once they were out of sight, he dusted invisible dirt from his tights. "Where is Fat Thomas?"

Ranulf raised a quizzical brow. "Fat Thomas?"

"That's his horse and cart."

"Oh." Ranulf nodded. "He's feelin' poorly. Stayin' at yonder inn."

"Hmm." Margrave pinched the bridge of his nose. "I saw what you did."

"M'lord?"

"I suggest you not make a habit of it. Your betters won't take kindly to poor treatment. Before you know it, there'll be a noose bearing your name." He rubbed the back of his neck and slapped his thigh. "Enough said. I must tell you, I've very little coin with me, but I understand our larder is nearly empty."

"So 'tis rumored, m' lord."

"The water of the rumor mill runs fast." Nicholas frowned. His gaze landed on the broken gate.

"One hears things now and again." Ranulf tapped his temple. "A smart one knows when to listen."

Margrave clapped him on the shoulder. "Never a truer word spoken. I'm told the king's men confiscated all the livestock. Have you access to a hen or two?"

Ranulf paused, his grip tightened around the bag of grain. Margrave knew they had lost a few skinny animals but had no concern for the men who stood against the king's soldiers? He shook free of the outrage, evening his voice. "Fat Thomas keeps a roost of 'em at the inn. Will bring 'em back soon as I'm able. Plannin' to stay for a while?"

"I've nowhere to go but here," Margrave said with a wistful smile. "Until my end has come."

"Swans?" Ranulf offered, then wanted to kick himself as soon as the word left his mouth.

Margrave blinked. "Swans?"

Ranulf had to see where 'twould take him and so pressed on. "'Ave you need for a brace of swans?"

"'Tis a luxury I cannot afford."

"These are special. 'Eard it said they come from the king's own aviary."

"The king, you say?" Margrave shifted, trying to peer into Ranulf's face. "One never knows. Mayhap I'll send word for swans." He nodded and spun on his heel, then paused. "Have we met before?"

Ranulf squatted to check one of the horse's hooves. His back to Margrave, he inspected the frog for stones. "No, m' lord," he said over his shoulder. "I'm sure if we've met 'afore, we'd both recall."

Silence crackled in the air between them. "I suppose so. Though 'tis odd. There is something quite familiar about you."

Ranulf tensed. He kept his hand out of sight, moving it ever so slightly to the short blade hidden inside his boot.

Margrave cleared his throat. "No doubt a tired old man's eyes playing tricks on him. See you return with a hen or two. Speak to Maud when you do." He jerked on the bottom of his surcoat. "I'll leave you to your labor."

Ranulf touched the peak of his hood in salute. "M'lord."

Left to fend for himself, he bent to ready the cart. The silver ring emblazoned with the swan emblem swung away from his neck on a leather thong. He slipped it under his tunic as he stood up. The cool metal stroked his flesh, reminding him of his purpose.

His trip onto Margrave lands had not gleaned near as much information as he had hoped. More questions came to light than answers. Why in all that was holy had he offered the assistance of the Knights of the Swan? 'Twas that relentless gnawing doubt. He could not ignore it. If not Lord Margrave, then who led this plot?

Catching movement out of the corner of his eye, he wondered at the identity of the raven-haired wench. He had hoped her curiosity would get the best of her and she would return despite her orders.

Finally, the pile of foodstuffs lay on the ground. Even with the lightening of the load, he doubted the raw-boned horse could carry his weight and reach his destination without faltering. He could not bring himself to ride in the cart and decided to walk beside the animal.

The reins hung in his hand as he pondered the position in which Margrave found himself. Hearing the patter of feet, Ranulf spun around. He crouched low, prepared for attack.

"You there."

Ranulf jerked his hood forward and straightened when he recognized the wizened old servant, Maud. "Yes?"

"His lordship sends a message to you. Says he'll take those special swans. Decided when the time comes a brace of them birds just might save his soul." She held out a coin for him. "I know 'tis odd, but he says to give you this trinket as a payment for your time. I know 'tis not of usual coin, but mayhap you will find a use for it."

Ranulf lifted the silver disc and nodded. "Tell your lord it may take a fortnight, but I'll come by swans one way or another."

Maud snorted and shook her head, grumbling under her breath. "Brace of swans. What am I to do with swans, I ask you?"

"Wait." Ranulf dug in a pouch hanging from one of the wagon pegs. He held out a tumble of multicolored ribbons. Fat Thomas would make him pay dearly for these. The wide smile on the servant's wrinkled face was enough to show 'twas worth the price. He grinned. He had gained an ally in the manor.

"Oh my, I cannot take those."

"'Tis for your troubles. And the young maiden."

Maud put the ribbons to her cheek and let the cool satin tickle her face. "She'll be pleased. She doesn't receive gifts such as these."

"Times are 'ard."

"Times are always hard for that one."

On a whim, Ranulf pulled out the loaf of bread he had intended for his next meal. "Please, take it."

"An angel, for certain," she whispered. Without another word, she lifted her skirt and trotted off toward the door in the tower.

Once over the bridge, he widened his stride to reach Cock's Inn. Margrave had passed him a coin with the shape of a swan stamped on one side. He had acknowledged the need for swans. Swans. The code word used by the Knights of the Swan. Could it be that Lord Nicholas of Margrave understood the trap was set? No matter; he would send the message on to Henry and wait to learn his liege's desires.

His plan set in motion, Ranulf's thoughts were no longer on the pending meeting with Margrave, nor how he would come by a brace of swans on short notice. Instead, they lingered on the maiden.

Though she did not speak it, 'twas clear she held no warmth for Robert.

Chapter 4

Clarice ran the satin ribbon against her cheek. *Astonishing.* A gift from a peddler. Half a loaf of bread rested on the side table. *Amazing.* To hear Maud tell it, a miracle had occurred.

The meager fire in the hearth stirred as the door to Clarice's chamber was thrown open.

"A word with you, my dear," her father said, striding in.

Thoughts of the peddler slipped away as easily as the ribbon through her fingers. Clarice fought to keep from commenting on Father's unkempt appearance. His hair, always kept tied with a leather thong, hung loose about his neck. Black ink marred his fingers. A bit of red sealing wax stuck to the cuff of his wrinkled white linen shirt. Mud coated his polished boots and he carried a thin, flat packet under his arm. After fiddling with the string tied around the end, he placed the packet near the foot of her cot.

Ever the lord surveying his lands, he gazed out the chamber window. Legs braced, as if preparing for battle, he took a deep breath. "I fear I've failed you."

"You fail me not." Clarice rose from the bench to stand beside him. She looked out, wondering if he saw the manor as she did. Though this was her home, it, too, was her prison. Her heart skipped a beat. Would their trouble with the king change her father's mind? He would feel the need to protect her. Mayhap they would flee the land together. Oh, what she would give to leave. Despite her fractured relationship with her stepmother and stepbrother, she would ask to join them.

"A man should know what takes place under his own roof," he whispered. "Blindness has besmirched my good name and now my life."

"Father—" Clarice began.

He gripped her arms. Desperation glittered in his eyes. "I intend to repair the damage."

"'Tis Annora who—"

His hold tightened, silencing her response. "Have patience with your stepmother. She is distraught and cannot help her sharp tongue. The one good thing of this hideous predicament is that you are safe here. Only a handful of people know you are my daughter. You'll be safe once I leave," he repeated.

"Father, if you are to flee England, I should go with you."

His jaw worked, clenching and unclenching. "You are safer here."

"Perhaps you haven't noticed but the gate is damaged and no longer stands."

"I will see it repaired."

She jerked her arms free "Every time you leave me behind . . . you break my heart." Her limbs trembled in anger. "I am a dutiful daughter. I deserve better."

"I've hurt you?" Father stiffened, as if she had struck him. "I never intended . . ." He swept up her hands, holding them to his chest. "I vow, Daughter, if you do as I say, I will remedy your ill-treatment."

She searched his face, looking for the truth buried within his promise.

"I've sent word for help." He continued, his grip tightening on her fingers. "Once I prove that my guilt lies in being a damn fool, I will be free of King Henry's ire. We'll be back in his good graces."

"How long—" Clarice started, but stopped when he released her.

"I'll send for you when I am ready to depart." He kissed her forehead before leaving her chamber. His steps were not as heavy they had been when he'd entered.

The shadows in Clarice's chamber grew and faded into the darkness of night. She lay on her little cot, her head resting upon the meager pillow and wondered when her father would return.

His promise to send a messenger with news of their preparations for travel never came.

Restless, she kicked out her feet. The packet Father had carried into her chamber earlier that day had fallen to the floor. Tempted to see what it contained, she nudged it with her toe.

Casting a glance toward the door, she listened for footfalls that did not come. "Who's the fool now?" she muttered. "No one is coming for you tonight."

Unable to ignore her curiosity, she moved closer to examine the packet. The looped string caught all four corners. Although tied in a knot, it was loose enough to lift with her fingertip. 'Twould be simple enough to peek inside. If intended for another, she could repair it without anyone the wiser.

After slipping the string over a corner, she unfolded the linen wrapping. Candlelight danced across a dagger's steel, her image reflected across the blade's edge. The hilt, bound in leather, fit perfectly in her hand.

A smile lifted the corners of her mouth. At least for that night, she would sleep with it by her side.

When dawn broke across the cobalt sky, the first piercing wail rang through the bailey. Grim-faced, Maud soon appeared at the chamber door.

Clarice led her to the side table and poured a cup of watered wine. She shoved it into Maud's hands. "Drink."

Maud shook her head. "You must come at once. Your—stepmother—"

"Is that who raised such a hue?" Clarice gave a disgusted snort. "What is that woman demanding now?"

"No, child." The servant set the cup on the table and gripped Clarice's hands. "'Tis your father."

"The king . . ." Clarice's legs threatened to turn to water. "They've come for him?" She tore her hands from Maud and headed for the stairway. "Why didn't anyone summon me?"

"Wait—"

Worried for her father's safety, Clarice raced into the main hall. She followed the sound of weeping echoing against the empty walls. It led her to the master's library. She skidded to a halt when Robert appeared and blocked the doorway.

"Let me pass," she said, wincing as his fingers dug into her shoulders.

"No. I cannot."

"I must speak with Father."

He drew her close. His arm draped over her shoulders. The scent of stale mead filled her nose. "He's dead."

"Wh-what?" she stammered, clawing at his hands as she leaned past him to see inside the room.

He shut the door, but not before the image of her father hanging from the rafters was imbedded in her mind. Clarice cried out in horror.

Robert pulled her to his chest and stroked her back. "Not to worry. Your life will soon return to what it has always been. I'll see to it. I promise."

Clarice stared out the narrow window of her chamber. The sun bled out its final rays before setting for the evening. Torchlight danced across the lawn. Under the cover of twilight, the mourners moved in silence. By eventide, they would lay Father to rest in a remote corner of the garden. He would have an unmarked grave to hide the sinner who took his own life.

She scrubbed her face with the back of her fist. Damn the empty space where her stepmother's heart should beat. Earlier, a tearful Maud had brought Lady Annora's latest decree. "Clarice is not to set foot outside her bedchamber until all the mourners depart through the manor gates."

Although her prayer had always been for her lot in life to change, never had she prayed for Father's death.

Maud's account of recent events replayed in her mind. In the taking of his own life, Lord Nicholas of Margrave—her father—had committed a sin so great, the church would not bury him with their blessing. Despite censure and rumors of treason swirling over her husband's name, Annora had commanded the old servant to find someone to mourn his demise.

Maud had ridden to the Cock's Inn. She'd found a few travelers willing to leave the crowded room. It took little effort to convince them to abandon their spot on the hard wooden floor. Given enough coin, they gladly wept copious tears for the lost soul.

Clarice offered up her own prayer as the coffin passed below. "I love you, Father," she whispered. She added the often-repeated request: "Take me with you."

Remaining at the window, she watched the flickering torchlight wind down the path. The meager flames wavered against the evening breeze.

She searched for her stepmother's form among the followers and found only paid mourners. Just as she had suspected. Lady Annora had left her husband's side long before they tossed the first shovel of dirt. Clarice uttered a curse and added Robert's name to the list of absent family members.

The chamber door swung open and the sweet perfume of violets wafted in. Recognizing the cloying scent, she glanced over her shoulder.

Annora stood in the doorway, dressed in a soft black woolen gown and matching cloak. Her fawn-colored hair was neat and tidy, not a strand out of place. The soldiers may have left the Margrave's manor house and accounts in desperate condition, but she had managed to protect a few jewels. The amulet she always wore on a heavy gold chain remained safe around her neck. Rings encrusted with rubies and sapphires winked in the waning light. Only the darkened smudges under her eyes spoke of recent heartache.

She huffed at Clarice's silence and stepped into the chamber. "Come, my dear." She held out her hand to draw her near. "Turn away from the window."

"A moment longer." Clarice continued to follow the faint glow of the torchlight. "They have not yet laid Father to rest."

Annora wiped at a tear. "You would ignore me? I strive to protect you from your loss and this is how you thank me?"

Half-turning, Clarice saw the pain on Annora's face. Her resentment melted. "Please, I ask for your forgiveness. 'Twas not my intention to cause you harm."

"Of course you didn't." Annora's thick fingers smoothed the sleeve of Clarice's gown. "You never intend to cause pain, do you?"

Encouraged by the sudden tenderness, Clarice caught her stepmother's hand. "I ask that you would grant me a request."

"Of course, sweeting, if 'tis within my power."

"Reconsider my confinement. Allow me to go down to the garden and join the procession."

The woman's stout body jerked as if splashed with ice-cold water. She yanked her hand away and stepped back. "No, you will stay here."

"For pity's sake, can you not allow me a small comfort for at least today?"

"Pity!" she sputtered. "Share with me what comfort I gain this day."

"I thought we might console each other in our loss," Clarice answered softly. "You, Robert, and I are a family. 'Tis all we have."

Annora's hand stole over the gold chain swinging between her breasts. She clutched the glistening stone to her heart. "I fear little comfort can be found here. Too much has been promised. Too much has failed."

Swallowing her pride, Clarice offered, "Perchance Robert and I—"

"Robert agrees," Annora cut her off with a smile. "Already a day has passed since your father's death. 'Tis not the time to indulge in self-pity but to make amends to King Henry. As it is, my son has had to travel beyond Henry's reach until I can find a way to make up for your father's missteps."

Clarice could see an idea spring to Annora's mind. Her skin itched where her stepmother's gaze traveled over her body from head to toe. She wished her father were there to sway Annora from any ill-conceived scheme she might devise.

"Henry is young. Virile," her stepmother went on.

Clarice's eyebrow arched in consternation, trying to follow Annora's hidden meaning. "So I assume, from Robert's many tales. Yet I have heard he has turned from his devilish ways since donning the crown."

"Nevertheless, Henry might close an eye to religious chastity and accept a small token of our . . . loyalty." Annora tapped her lip with her fingers. Excitement sparkled in her eyes. "If he accepts, it will prove he has forgiven the Margrave name."

"What gift might we offer the king? You know the soldiers left nothing of value."

Annora stepped closer. As soft as a whisper, the single word was spoken. "You."

"Me?" Amazed at her stepmother's audacity, Clarice tensed like a hare caught in an archer's sights.

"'Tis time you accept your fate." Annora's desperate voice tore across the barren room. Its volume bounced against the rafters. "With your father's death, he has betrayed us all."

"There must be another way."

"A pity to lose one's head on a chopping block over such a trivial matter as your virginity. 'Tis a good thing we kept you safe within these walls." Annora lifted a loose strand of Clarice's hair and held it up to the light of the remaining sunset. "In truth, I would rather keep my head and make the necessary sacrifice."

Clarice blinked back tears and glanced at the open window. The flickering light had all but disappeared.

Annora proceeded with relentless determination. "Our precarious position with the crown forced your father to take his own life."

"I still do not believe Father would take his own life, nor ever betray his king. Please, M-mother, allow me to discover who spread this venom."

Her stepmother whisked her skirts out of the way and swept across the chamber to stand by the hearth. Annora trailed a finger over the stone mantelpiece as she spoke. "'Tis a laughable notion."

Clarice followed her, relentless in her pursuit. "I will find our justice, but do not think to sacrifice me to the king's bed."

Annora paused, turning slowly on her heel. Her eyes glittered with animosity. "Did you know, 'twas your father's decision to keep you hidden behind these walls? Not that I minded, Clarice," she hesitated, examining a smudge of soot on her fingers, "have you never wondered why there was no family Bible on display?"

"I thought perhaps 'twas in safekeeping."

"Without proof, no one will believe you are his child unless I say 'tis so."

"Maud will—"

"The word of a servant?" Annora shook her head, dipping her hands in the bowl of water warming by the fire. "Accept it: You have nothing with which to bargain. Nothing that will open doors."

"But—"

"No." Her stepmother held up her hand for silence. "There is naught you can do on your own. You'll stay behind these walls until I deem it time to present you to the king's mercy. Then you'll wield your maidenhead like a finely honed weapon. If you behave yourself and luck is with us, he'll take you to his bed. If you please him, our place in court will be secured."

Clarice fisted her hands to keep from throttling the woman. "I will speak to the king, but I will not spread my legs for him to plunder."

"I don't understand why you are so distraught." Annora offered a cold smile. "I hear the king can be quite generous."

"You are mad," Clarice sputtered. "I never—"

"When the time is right, once assured you have pleased him, I will bring forth irrefutable proof that you are Nicholas Margrave's daughter. If you've done well, he might even forget you are the daughter of a traitor."

Desperate, Clarice cast a wide gaze around the cobwebs hanging from the ceiling. Would the woman never listen? "As you said, no one has knowledge of my existence. Why would the king want me? Or believe what you say is true?"

Annora paced the floor, her gown swishing with every step. "Patience will be necessary. We'll wait until Robert gives his signal that he is out of harm's way," she said with a giddy lilt to her voice. "Then we shall strike."

"Patience," Clarice repeated. Her father had put that same request to her on the night of his death. They asked too much. Her body shook with rage. "Though I am certain 'tis no concern of yours, Maud and I have very little to survive the winter. There is only a small amount left from the supplies Father purchased from the peddler."

"You will do as you are ordered," Annora hissed. "You owe it to your family."

Clarice jerked as if struck. "I did nothing more than desire your love and affection."

"Rubbish! Had you not maimed Robert in your jealousy, he would already be a part of the king's army."

Annora now stood so close that Clarice could taste the violet scent permeating the air. The stench mixed with the accusation was enough to make her ill. "We were children. He should never have climbed on the roof to kill the birds."

"Robert may have been out on the gable but 'twas you who pushed him. Made him fall and injure his arm."

"Lies—"

Annora waved away her protest. "'Twas a grievous injury. If he could have fought by the king's side, he would have managed to hold the king's favor. Despite your father's treasonous behavior, Robert would have convinced Henry that we remain his loyal subjects."

The gold chain hanging around her neck twisted in her plump fingers. "Because of your selfish actions, your stepbrother has no military presence to prove our loyalty." Her lips trembled as she spoke. "Our house in London is already confiscated. Now, with your father's disgraceful death, this manor house and land will be out of our hands."

Clarice looked about this hated room. Hidden in the country, Margrave Manor had been easy for her stepmother to ignore. Without funds and labor, the buildings already showed signs of decay. "Let them take it," she said, putting a brave face on it. "I've had my fill of this place."

"Oh, I think not," Annora said. "You will not be able to live with your conscience when Maud is cast from Margrave lands. Homeless. Penniless."

"You wouldn't."

Annora waved with a careless flip of the hand. "A few well-placed whispers of treason heard often enough soon becomes truth. Your father is proof of that."

"Maud can come with me. To a convent," Clarice offered.

"'Tis a sad circumstance, my dear, but no convent will want you when they discover you are without funds."

"Father would have set aside a dowry—"

"One would think that, wouldn't one?" She picked up a discarded flower, twirling the dry stem between her fingers as she pressed her point. "As I said, Clarice, if I get what I want, I will produce the proof of your birth to our king. When you fulfill your duties to your family, I will see that you are comfortably settled."

The mutilated flower fell to the floor and turned to dust under her heel. "Or I will conveniently forget it with very little effort. Count yourself warned, my darling. Do not deny your duty. 'Tis the only answer left if we are to be saved from the king's wrath."

Clarice stared in disbelief. "I refuse to play the harlot."

Annora's eyes narrowed above her rounded cheeks. As she backed out of the chilled room, she bit out a final instruction. "Fight me on this and I will start the whispering. Your beloved servant will be dead before nightfall. Cooperate, bring pleasure to your king, and she might live out her days in the quiet countryside. 'Tis on your head. You have until tomorrow to decide."

"Stop!"

"You think to sway me from this plan?" Annora asked. "Begging does not change the heart. This I learned from your father. Despite my sacrifices for him, did he offer a shoulder of comfort for me? No. Not once. His adoration was always for his angel. For you. Never for Robert. Never for me." She turned, her fingers whitening as she clutched the door. "At long last his beloved angel will no longer haunt my dreams."

The turning of the iron key cut into the echoing silence.

Chapter 5

Clarice placed a precious log on the glowing embers. The shadows on the wall stretched as nightfall took hold. Standing near the hearth, she warmed her hands. *Oh, if only the peddler would hasten his return.*

Once he crossed the gate's threshold, she would send a message with Maud, asking for his help. Their time was growing short.

Already a week had passed since her father's death. She feared her stepmother was going mad with frustration. Despite the woman's efforts, Clarice remained firm in her refusal to play the king's harlot.

Footsteps shuffled across the stone pavers, stopping outside her chamber door. She tensed. Did Annora come with a new plan of how she would deposit her in the king's bed? Despite her effort to remain calm, her legs trembled as the door opened.

"I've victuals, my lady."

"Good woman," Clarice said, stumbling back. "I fear tonight you have taken five and twenty off my years here on earth." She rushed to take the tray from Maud's hands and inhaled the comforting aroma of a thick, hearty stew. "God's spirit! You are too good to me."

"Hush now, my lady, 'tis a trencher of day-old rabbit stew, not a side of venison."

"What brings you here at this hour? You should be abed and resting."

"How can I sleep with our lives in disarray?"

"All will be well soon enough," Clarice said, juggling the tray with one hand. "Come. Sit a moment." With her free hand, she patted Maud's shoulder and started at how bone thin it had become. "Tell me, how did you come here without being noticed?"

"Lady Annora has retired to her bedchambers." She wrung the threadbare apron in her hands. "'Tis Lord Robert. He has returned."

Clarice set down the tray on the bench by the fire. "That must mean the king's ire is not so bad."

"I overheard the two of them talking. They will find a way to rid you from their lives should you refuse them again."

"Maud, are you sure you heard correctly?"

"My knees may be weak, but I know what I hear."

"Father spoke of France being a haven for those who threaten England's crown. I will plant a word of it in their ears." Clarice ripped off a small chunk of bread for herself and held out a larger piece for Maud to dip into the trencher. "I wager they will be gone by morrow's eve."

"They argued this night. Harlots of London were mentioned."

The stew-soaked bread lodged in Clarice's throat. "What?" she croaked, dodging the woman's well-intended blows to her back. "Are you certain?"

"'Tis certain as the hair on my head is gray. Go, child," Maud said. "Hide yourself in the glen until they leave."

"And what would happen to you?" She covered Maud's overworked hands. "I won't leave you to their wrath."

"Lord's mercy, I could not go with you if I wanted to. My legs are too old for travel."

"Then we shall do as I said before and wait for them to grow bored. They'll not wish to remain here indefinitely. Not while the king's wrath continues to hang over their heads and there's a new life for them to create elsewhere."

Maud twisted her work-swollen fingers together. "God, forgive me. I fear I've waited too long." Agitated, she rose and paced the chamber. "I thought his mind was breaking, that he was overwrought. I didn't understand the danger." Her lips trembled as she whispered the last. "But he knew, didn't he?"

"Who?" Clarice peered at her old friend. "The peddler? Don't worry so. You'll add wrinkles to your face. What would he think when he returns?" she teased. "He might forget where he keeps more of those beautiful ribbons."

"No. I . . ." Maud snuffled a tear and gulped the air as if 'twas her last before plunging into a nearby stream. "I dare not tarry any longer." She reached into a deep pocket sewn into her skirt and pulled out a shiny object.

"What is this?" Clarice stared at the key Maud pressed into her palm. She brushed her finger over the smooth, rounded edge that stuck out on one side. "It looks like the head of an ugly bird."

"'Twas Lord Margrave's," Maud said. She flipped the cloak hanging on the hook and shoved it into Clarice's arms. "Now do as he wished. Run; seek out King Henry."

"You would have me follow Annora's plan?" The thought of betrayal plunged into her chest. Its icy hand clutched her heart. "As much as I would like to clear Father's name, I will not run to Henry's bed."

"No, child, not to his bed." Maud closed the few steps between them. Determination glittered in her aged, watery eyes. "To his throne to seek his help."

"Impossible." Clarice waved her off. "You know I'm not allowed outside these walls. And even if I did escape, there is truth that my chance of survival would be grim. Let alone gaining an audience with the king."

"But, my lady—"

The truth of her desperate situation peeled back the thin layer of bravery, revealing the foolishness of hope. "'Tis as Annora said. Even if he would deign to forgive our family, I don't have proof of who I am. I'm an unknown. And an unknown gaining a royal audience is unheard of."

"Attend my words," Maud urged again. "I thought it madness at first, but I cannot ignore your father's wishes any longer. If even a hint of suspicion surrounded his death, I was to give you that key. You must leave Margrave and find a red wolf that will lead you to the king. Show the key to the wolf. He'll understand its meaning."

"A red wolf?" Clarice patted Maud's gnarled joints. "Even if I knew where to look for such a wolf, I wouldn't leave you."

Maud grabbed her shoulders with surprising strength. Holding them tight, she said, "Yes, you will." She placed her palm against Clarice's cheek. "You have no choice."

Clarice dropped the last remaining stick of wood onto the pile of embers in the hearth. She held the oddly shaped key up to the light. A bird's head formed the top. She shook her head and dropped it back into a little satin pouch hidden under her gown.

If the key did indeed hold great importance, her father would have given it to her the last time he had visited her chamber. And why place it in Maud's care? It took the better part of the night to convince the poor dear that Clarice had no knowledge of wolves, let alone one specific red wolf. Even if her father had mentioned one, she did not have the slightest notion in which direction to begin her journey.

With dawn nearing, she blew out the candle before the last little chunk melted into a puddle of wax. After tucking the woolen blanket around her feet, she curled into a tight ball.

Waiting for sleep to come, she worried how the old servant would fare with the day's work laying heavy on her thin shoulders. Regardless of Maud's arguments, Clarice's resolve remained strong. She would not leave her behind to fend off Annora's wrath, nor the king's edict should her stepmother's threats prove true.

The slow grind of metal turning back the bolt chased away all thoughts of warm toes and a cozy fire. Clarice blinked the weariness from her eyes. Moving her hand under the wad of cloth she used to pillow her head, she touched the blade her father had left behind.

The door opened.

Unaided by candlelight, the intruder inched through the entrance, then across the room. Toward Clarice's bed. The rosy glow in the hearth flickered. His demon shadow, painted on the wall, bent and swayed with every step.

Her grip tightened around the hilt of the knife. 'Twas Robert. She had always been able to feel his presence whenever he tried to slip into a room without her notice.

"Clarice. Clarice," his singsong chant began. "I know you're here." He chuckled at his wittiness. "'Course where else could you be, eh?"

She held her breath until her eyes watered. She dared not scream for fear Maud would come to her rescue. The frail woman would never outlast his strength. Not even with his weakened arm.

"Come here, sweet sister. Let us comfort each other."

Clarice dropped silently to the floor and slid under the cot. The sound of his steps moved closer.

"'Tis cold in here," he muttered. "Let me warm the chill away."

She wanted to shut her eyes, will him gone, but that would be a deadly mistake. Maud had reported she'd overheard Annora and Robert arguing about drinking to excess. If he'd had too much, he would be in no mood to leave empty-handed.

"Come, Clarice," he called out again.

His boot caught the side-table leg and he stumbled. Fear closed around her heart as he snapped up the blanket and peered under the bed. The shadows cast from the fire behind them danced under his cheekbones. "There you are." He grinned, his teeth flashing like a cunning fox. "You must realize you can never hide from me."

She could smell the fresh polish on his leather boots, the lingering scent of stale wine. "Go away, Robert. You have no business here."

"Is this anger necessary? I desire to speak with you. As family," he said.

"'Tis not the time. Not here. Not alone."

"You injure me with your wrath. How can your words be so ugly when they are surrounded by your beauty?"

Before she could respond, he snagged a fistful of hair, jerking her head forward. Startled, she let the blade fall from her hand as she grabbed at the pain in her scalp. Too late, she realized her mistake. She slapped the floor, searching for her knife.

"You don't have ol' Nicholas to protect you now," he taunted, hauling her to her knees.

"You cannot mean to do this." Gritting her teeth, she slid her hand over his fist, settling around his wrist. "You are my stepbrother."

Sweat beaded on his forehead. His eyes widened and narrowed as he swayed to gain his balance. He ignored her efforts to pry open his hand and ran a finger across her lips. His wine-soaked breath wafted past her nose as he whispered, "What is it that makes my mother hate you?"

"Please, Robert. 'Tis a few hours until dawn. We will speak of this on the morrow."

His hold on her hair tightened. A sad smile creased his lips. "I am lord now." With a twist of his wrist, he pushed her toward the cot. "'Tis time you learned your place."

Clarice's fury uncoiled. Her elbow connected with his throat. Caught off-balance, he grunted as his back slammed into the table.

She scrambled on hands and knees, searching for the dagger. *Find it! Find it!*

The fall of his approaching footsteps drowned out the thundering in her ears. Her lungs burned. Robert's fingers dug into her ankle, moved up her leg. She glanced back. The hilt lay hidden under the bed, barely out of reach.

He stood over her, chest rising and falling in fury. The rasp of metal slid against the velvet-lined scabbard hanging at his waist. With the dark shape of steel in his hand, he raised it and lunged.

Clarice gasped at the explosion of pain in her arm. She rolled to her side, knocking into his leg. His knee buckled.

She crouched in the shadows, aware of the sticky warmth spreading over her sleeve. Despite the fire racing through her arm, she tightened her grip and surged forward.

The hiss of air from her dagger slicing in a high, arching sweep caught Robert's attention. He turned as her blade bit into his leg. His howl of pain ripped open the night.

The howl turned into a curse when Clarice kicked the soft spot behind his knee. Flailing his arms, he lost the battle for balance and fell. His head struck the side table like a ripe melon hitting the ground.

Clarice dragged air through her lungs, forcing them to fill and release.

Breathe. Live. Breathe. Live.

Chapter 6

Clarice's fingers trembled as she checked the saddle once more. After tightening the girth, she cast a wary glance outside the stables. Moonlight quivered between the branches, but nothing else stirred. With a gentle hand, she led Buttercup, her father's palfrey, toward the remains of the Margrave gate.

A rustle in the bushes made her muscles freeze. Her heart thumped as rapidly as the rabbit that came bounding out of the shadows. She slid her palm over Buttercup's velvet muzzle. "Come on, girl," she whispered.

They stayed to the edge of the bridge. Her fingers cramping around the reins, she glanced back at the bailey. A shiver ran through her body, threatening to take control.

Her stepmother would be furious when she discovered Robert, bleeding from his injuries and bound to her cot. The cut on his leg had not bled near as much as the wound on his head. Unable to leave him to die in a pool of blood, Clarice had done her best to staunch the flow with a bed sheet. She quickened her pace, fleeing the tower and the thought of Robert's condition.

Once free from the wall, she found a stump and climbed up on Buttercup's back. The simple act of leveraging her body into the saddle tore into her arm. A wave of nausea mixed with the searing pain. She gasped, waiting for the throbbing to subside, then nudged the horse's flanks. Together, they slipped into the mist.

The cloak drawn tight around her body, she kept to the shadows and turned in the direction her family had traveled without her year after year. She must reach the king and clear Father's name. Though how she would ever manage that when no one of influence was even aware of her existence, she did not know. But she had to attempt the impossible. If she were to succeed, she needed to put distance between herself and her family. She tamped down a sob that burbled up her throat, just as she had so many times since Robert had entered her bedchamber. To remain hidden behind Margrave walls no longer offered the illusion of safety. She knew the truth. For a woman, alone and without protectors, the dangers inside and outside the walls were equally fatal.

After donning a pair of leggings, she had bunched up her gown to hide it under an old cloak she had found in the stables and bound her breasts. To aid her disguise, she had cut her hair until it stopped short of her shoulders. She swiped at the jagged strands of hair sticking to her dampened cheek. The edges of her cloak gripped in one hand and the reins in the other, she prayed for courage.

Clarice glanced back. Had anyone followed? Seeing no one, she nudged Buttercup with her heels. "Make haste."

The air, heavy with early morning fog, enveloped both horse and rider as they traveled along the path. Tiny clouds formed by their heated breaths trailed behind them.

Soon, the day's first light exposed the surrounding countryside. The horizon stretched in front of her, the trail vacant of other travelers.

Her concern for Maud grew. She ached for her friend and cursed the old woman's stubborn streak. Annora and Robert's anger would create a harsher existence for Maud. 'Twas one of the reasons Clarice had remained agreeable for so long.

She knew firsthand of her stepmother's vengeance. Even at the age of nine, she had experienced the depth of the woman's animosity and resolve.

It had been ten years ago and still she could see Robert's shocked expression, hear his wail of surprise. She shuddered with the memory of that horrid day.

It had started as a simple child's game of hide-and-seek, with Father searching the manor for them. It had been Robert's idea to crawl out on the roof. A perfect place to hide. But then Robert had started kicking at the baby birds nesting in the rafters. They were so small. So innocent.

Even now, Clarice's stomach knotted at Robert's cry as he fell from the roof.

Panicked by what she had done, she had hidden in the nursery and covered her ears with her hands. Father no longer searched alone. Her stepmother's angry threats broke through the open window.

Yet hope remained. The chest in the corner drew her attention. Although the day had not started out as she had anticipated, excitement had bubbled inside her, just as it had the first day she had stumbled upon the false wall and the hidden contents. Buried beneath household cast-offs was the chest, covered in layers of dust, brimming with secrets.

Caught in her own misery, she had almost missed the soft whisper of the nursery door swinging open.

"Daughter, what have you to say for yourself?"

"Father." It had been too late to dive for cover behind the small cot. Clarice had ducked her head and stood her ground. "I did not wish him harm."

"Your stepmother is sorely vexed." Father rested his hand on her shoulder. "Best keep yourself hid until our departure. We're already in the midst of preparations for our return to London."

"Please take me with you. I swear I won't be underfoot. And it won't cost you a penny to dress me. See?" She held up a delicate confection made of fine white linen, shot with blue and silver threads. "Wait here," she said, ducking behind the dressing screen before he could refuse her request

Father paced the chamber. Head down, hands behind his back, his stride had brought him to the small chest she had dragged from the boarded-up masonry. He bent to retrieve a sleeve of shimmering yellow poking out from under the heavy lid. His knees seemed to crumble under his weight.

"Father," she cried, "please, tell me what is wrong!"

"Who gave you permission to wear this?"

Clarice would never forget how he had growled like one of the wild animals that prowled the glen surrounding the outer wall.

"I-I'm nearly grown and want to go with you. I—"

"Answer me. Where did you get these garments?"

Her hand had trembled as she pointed to the chest. "I found it. In there."

His long fingers stroked the satin material. "Should never have kept them," he had muttered. "Knew nothing good would come of it. But I couldn't let her go."

Clarice knelt and cupped his chin. "Who, Father?"

His smile wobbled. "An angel, little one. 'Twas so long ago. Oftentimes I have wondered if she was the remnants of a fantasy." He smoothed the flyway strands from her cheek. "Then I see your face."

Emboldened by his gentle caress and determined to try once more, Clarice touched the back of his hand. "Please, Father," she had whispered. "May I travel to London with you? I am all of nine years and have never seen beyond the horizon."

Before she had his answer, the door crashed against the wall.

Annora had filled the doorway, legs spread and arms akimbo. Her reddened face crumbled as she attempted to hold back her tears.

"Nicholas, I told you to yell out or send a runner if you found her." She rushed to his side, tugging on his sleeve. "Robert is surely dying whilst you stand here wasting time."

Father let his arms drop from Clarice's shoulders and stepped away to comfort Annora. "Calm yourself."

"He needs a physician, not an idiotic village midwife."

" 'Tis his arm he landed on, not his head. The woman will know whether moving the boy will cause more damage than good."

Annora's concern for her son scattered. "What is that, Nicholas?"

Her father moved to block her stepmother's view of the old chest. He had attempted to tuck the gold material out of sight, but 'twas as slippery as a moonbeam and refused to be hidden.

Annora stepped forward, snapping the material from his hand. The fragile silk caught under the weight of the lid. She tore it from the trunk.

Her father's heartrending moan had been as audible as the ripping of the shimmering gown.

"You." She shook the tattered material in Clarice's face. "How did you come by this? Speak up."

"I found it, Stepmother. I never meant—"

Annora turned and searched her husband's face for an answer. "How could you?" She swiped at the tears on her cheek. "You said you rid your life of all her possessions, yet I would recognize her stitchwork anywhere."

Father had folded his fingers over Annora's hand. "A lapse of memory. It means nothing. You are my wife now."

"Yet here they are." She pulled away and shook the limp fabric at him. "It's been nine years, Husband. Her mother is long dead."

"Annora. Please. Forget this nonsense. Go." He pressed her toward the door. "Have the wagon brought around. Perhaps your sense of urgency is correct. We should transport your son to a surgeon immediately."

Her back rigid, Annora had nodded and walked to the door. She turned, her words etched with warning. "Do not forget to burn the clothes this time. Everything."

The door closed on the view of Annora's retreating backside.

Clarice had ducked her father's hand before he could pat her head like one of his obedient hounds. The cold, empty feeling had trickled in, gnawing at her heart. "You are leaving me here again, aren't you?"

"'Tis for the best." He had hefted the trunk onto his shoulder.

"Those belonged to my real mother, didn't they?"

Father dropped his chin and walked away.

"Wait! Please. Don't go!" The too-large gown, tangled around Clarice's legs, mocking her for wanting to be loved. She had fallen to her knees and wept for the mother she never knew.

Now, ten years later, Clarice could still hear the bolt to the nursery striking home. Her heart still ached with loneliness. She flinched at the sting of tears. Although she held no love for Robert, she had never meant to cause him harm. Only send him away.

She gripped the wooden pommel, slumping with the realization. Dear God, had the wound she inflicted upon him today been a mortal one? If so, her soul might forever be marked with his blood. 'Twas as Annora had predicted: She was homeless, destitute, and without protection.

The weight of Father's blade thumped against her thigh, reminding her that she was no longer defenseless. The truth became clear. She had found freedom and she would fight to stay alive. Although she had allowed others to command her nonexistence, never would she give anyone that right again. Once she fulfilled her vow to discover the truth behind her father's death, she would make a life of her own. A place where she was loved.

With each step, Buttercup carried her closer to finding another life outside Margrave Manor. Clarice touched the pouch hidden under the oversize leather tunic. Thanks to the purse she had lifted from Robert's waist, she had a few coins to help her along the way.

She shifted her seat and winced. The injury she had sustained throbbed with each step the horse took. By midday she cursed her own idiocy for not packing a morsel of food. By the time the sun had lowered, all thought of eating had dissipated. Instead, wave after wave of nausea coated her tongue.

Weary of traveling the whole day without rest, she searched her surroundings. Dappled shadows, thrown off by the setting sun, danced under the canopy of trees.

The dusty road swam in front of her eyes. She shook her head and licked her dry lips. A safe haven to rest was what she needed. She would have preferred to stop at a village. Yet there was not one building in sight to offer protection from the elements. The clearing was little more than connecting paths and a patch of sweet clover growing nearby. An outcropping of boulders might form a decent windbreak, protection for her back, at the least.

She swatted at the hair sticking to her overheated face and pain seared a path from elbow to shoulder. The ground lurched toward her. She glanced down at her arm. The strips of cloth no longer staunched the wound from Robert's blade. She needed someone who knew the ways of healing unguents and a needle. That would take time and money, both in short supply. She had no choice. If she attempted to ride further, she very well might fall and never get up again.

"God save me." She groaned as her feet touched the ground and gave the saddle an evil look. "Never fear, Buttercup. 'Tis certain I can unsaddle you."

Clarice swore there was a hint of mocking doubt in the mare's eyes.

"With just a bit more effort," she muttered, "the job will be done."

The saddle and blanket began to slide over Buttercup's rib cage. Clarice lunged forward, catching the horse's tack before it hit the ground. The mare shook her head. The metal rings sewn on her bridle filled the clearing with a pleasant jingle.

Ignoring the leaden weight of her legs, the pain in her arm, Clarice set to gathering the dry wood scattered along the fringe of the clearing. By the time she had a small campfire she could barely lift her arm. The binding wrapped around her breasts bit into her flesh. Sweat formed over her lip as she dragged the saddle and blanket closer.

Those tasks completed, she leaned against Buttercup's sleek neck. The horse looked up from the clover and nickered as if to urge her to keep going. Clarice's forehead rolled against the mare. Thoughts of rest filled her mind as she stumbled toward a soft grassy spot.

She nearly missed seeing someone standing on the rise of the knoll. The stranger bounded down the hill. Arms swinging and pumping, he propelled his body over the crest, yelling gibberish as he sped toward her.

Chapter 7

"Sir R—ulf!" the stranger yelled. "I'm co—"

The small clearing blurred, her exhaustion winning out. Clarice shook her head, struggling to understand what the stranger shouted as he ran pell-mell down the hillside. Her heartbeat drowned out the pop and crackle of kindling as the fire caught. She shot glances at the surrounding rock formations. Shadows jumped from behind every tree. Her muscles screamed against her demand to draw the blade from her belt. Afraid he intended to plow her over, she braced for impact.

"Wait, I—" He tripped over a tree root and struck the ground. A rush of air slammed from his lungs. "Wha-mph." The momentum carried him dangerously close to the fire.

The world tilted. Through sheer will, she righted it and nearly jumped out of her ill-fitting boots when the stranger groaned.

His eyebrows arched as he peered through dust-covered lashes. "You're not him." He wiped the gritty dirt clinging around his mouth and cleared the dust from his throat. Despite his effort to lower his voice, it cracked as he spoke. "I pray you forgive me—"

A healthy pink spread over his smooth cheeks. The man was only a boy. Clarice staggered forward. "Are you injured?" She held out her hand and did her best to smile when he grabbed hold. Her grip tightened. "Can you stand?"

Wide-eyed, he nodded.

"Good." She drew him up, but his head barely met her waist. "What brings you here?"

He shook his head and tried to withdraw his fingers from her grasp.

"What? You wish me to believe you've lost your tongue?" Her

skull throbbed as she bent to peer into his dirt-smudged face. "I don't believe I can do that."

Narrowing her eyes, she cocked her head, as if looking at him from a different angle would clear her muddled thinking. A preposterous idea gathered form. Had she heard correctly? Her uneasy stomach twisted. Had he yelled for a red wolf? Her pulse raced at the possibility of the first clue in solving the puzzle of her father's death.

"Who do you seek?" she demanded, pressing her dagger against his neck. "Tell. Me. Now."

His Adam's apple jumped with a nervous leap. He blinked and gulped again. Tears began to form.

Clarice feared that to acquire the much-needed answers, she would be forced to harm him. The blade was sharp and honed to a fine edge. If he held any intelligence, he would not dare make any sudden movement.

"Name's Hamish," he croaked.

She pressed the weapon closer, praying he believed her threat. "Where will I find this red wolf?"

Hamish stared up at her and did not flinch when sweat trickled down his neck.

"You'll not leave this spot until you reveal this creature's whereabouts," she insisted. Her voice sounded odd in her own ears. Her tongue, thick and heavy.

A drop of liquid fell to the ground. And then another.

She frowned. Each russet drop darkened as it mixed with the dirt. The blood was not his. She made sure to turn the blade's sharp edge away. *Then whose?*

Her thoughts muddled, she fought to stay on her feet. Each labored breath filled her ears. The dagger wavered. Her mouth dry, she licked her lips. *Rest. A few minutes.*

She shook free of the whisper. If there truly was a red wolf, she had to find it. For Father. For truth. To find . . . what was it? *Love?* A giggle bubbled in her throat. *Love. A fairy tale for dreamers.*

Clarice wagged her head from the rambling thoughts. "We wait here together—" Her mouth felt stiff. "—until you tell me of the red wolf."

"He'll cleave your head from your shoulders," he shouted in her ear.

She jerked with a start. Her legs crumpled beneath her. Clarice rolled, trying to keep from cutting the boy, and they went down together. He cried out when she landed on top of him.

"Shh." She pushed away the surge of darkness. "Give me a—"

Ranulf watched Aldwyn's ears twitch. He listened, searching for what distressed the battle-strong horse. Muffled cries came from the direction of the nearest crossroads. Wary of marauders, he loosened his sword from its scabbard. There would be hell to pay should someone dare use his lands for evil.

He nudged Aldwyn forward. The curses became clearer as he rode up. Ranulf swore he recognized the voice. That boy had nearly run under Aldwyn's hooves as they were leaving Castle Sedgewic's bailey yard. It had cost him nearly an hour's time to locate the castellan and deliver the child into Mistress Erwina's care. She had assured him young Hamish would not escape her watchful eye. She had enough chores to keep the boy from following through on his nonsense of becoming the lord's squire.

When the muffled cries turned to wails, Ranulf dismissed all caution and charged over the knoll. He reined in his mount as he bore down the crest.

Two bodies lay in a tangle. One lay atop the other. A cloak-covered head drooped from a set of lifeless shoulders. A set of short, pudgy legs stuck out from the pile.

Hamish struggled to push the limp body away. "Get off me. Goat-brained idiot."

Ranulf shook his head. Now that he knew the boy would live, he was ready to string him up by his little thumbs. How the child had made it to the crossroads before him, Ranulf could not fathom. The meeting with his informant had taken longer than expected, but had been necessary. Hamish must have slipped from Erwina's grasp the minute she turned her back.

Short of breath, Hamish paused, as if weighing his options. "Wake up," he yelped, kicking out his legs once more. "Get your arse off me."

Giving a soft command to Aldwyn, Ranulf dismounted and moved toward the boy. Wary there might be more marauders hiding in the brush, he kept his sword in hand. He grabbed the back of the cloak and lifted the body lying atop the boy. Surprised by the marauder's slight build, he tossed him to the side. The lifeless form skidded across the dirt and came to rest against a nearby tree.

"I thought I gave you an order to stay home," Ranulf said.

Hamish blinked and then shut his eyes, squeezing them tight. "But you need me here." He squinted through narrow slits. "If I had not discovered the trap before you came this way, 'tis you who might have been attacked."

At a loss for words, Ranulf held his pounding temples. His fingertips trailed along the raised scar cutting into his hair. Delays from all fronts had torn his plans asunder. He had a mind to ignore the child, mount up, and ride away.

Instead, he let his hand drop and looked down. Dread coursed through his veins as he stared at his fingers. "Yours?"

Hamish looked at the smeared blood. His eyes widened in fear. Gulping, he rubbed his throat.

Ranulf followed the boy's dirty fingers. They left a streak of dirt across a fold in his plump neck. A tiny scratch nicked his skin. 'Twas not deep enough to cause the stain on the boy's tunic.

"The stranger asked about you," Hamish said.

"What?" Ranulf glanced at the still figure lying by the tree trunk.

"Asked about a red wolf." His sherry-colored eyes shifted up to Ranulf's head and pointed to the red hair that curled out of the chainmail hood. "Figured that might be you."

"You know me as Sir Ranulf, your lord of Sedgewic." He ruffled Hamish's wave of nut-brown hair. "And as your lord, I demand you stay put when ordered."

Hamish pressed his lips together in a stubborn line.

Ranulf turned his back on the urchin. He could ill afford another delay. He did not need to worry about a sprout who had the tendency to get into trouble at every turn. A vision of the tiresome child by his side while in battle was enough to turn his red hair gray.

He glanced over at the lump resting at the base of the tree. Narrow shoulders and twig-thin legs stuck out from under the cloak.

None too gently, he rolled the stranger over, nudging back the hood. A cap of short black curls sprung out from the folds. The contrast of raven lashes resting against the unnaturally pale skin startled him. Not a stub of whisker grew on that smooth jaw. Judging by size and frailty, this youngster should still be attended by his nursery maid.

Ranulf flipped the voluminous fabric and discovered a gown buried beneath the layers. The tail of the skirt, knotted to ride high over a set of leggings. *Correction: she.*

"'Tis a maiden?" Hamish leaned over to see for himself. "Is she dead?"

"Not yet, but she'll soon be if we don't get her help."

Hamish studied the body lying at their feet. "Why should you care? She tried to kill me."

Ranulf looked over to see Hamish rub his neck. Mayhap now the boy would understand why he could not be his squire. The king's business often brought danger.

"Might have killed you, too," Hamish said. "Should cut out her heart and be done with it."

Ranulf shook his head at the bloodthirsty boy. "We must discover what brings her to me."

"*We*," Hamish crowed. "That means you and me."

Patience fading, Ranulf waved his hand at the pest. "I've no need for your company."

He wrestled with the change of plans. She had asked about a red wolf. A select number knew his name spoken among the king's secret order. Fewer still knew the Knights of the Swan existed. First the swan and now the red wolf. Twice, in less than a fortnight, he had heard these coded words.

He was more than a night's ride from the port of Southampton. He had information to share. The king would decide how he wished to pursue Lord Nicholas of Margrave and his family. Once that task was completed, Ranulf hoped to sail out across the Channel and reach France with the king's fleet. However, until he knew why this young maiden had asked about him, he had no right to leave England, not without answers that might well save the king's life and throne.

Chapter 8

The clatter of horses' hooves echoed over Sedgewic's wooden drawbridge, drawing the attention of the castle folk. One of the guards dove out of the way of Hamish's mount. The palfrey flared its nostrils, shaking its mane as if to say it had had enough of its rider.

Ranulf reined in Aldwyn beside them. The desire to thrash the boy pushed to the surface again. The orders were on the tip of his tongue. Then he saw Mistress Erwina, the castellan of Sedgewic. Tears of joy coursed down her pale, weathered face.

"My lord," she said.

"Don't let him out of your sight again, Mistress. You there, Micah," he snapped at the stableboy standing nearby, ready to take his horse's reins.

Micah ran over and bobbed an eager nod. "Yes, m'lord?"

"Easy," Ranulf ordered as he bent to place the girl in Micah's arms. He kicked out of the stirrups and dropped down. "Hand her to me. Gently."

Muttering his thanks, he turned and began the long climb up the stairs to the main hall. "Make way," he barked at those foolish enough to stand in his path. "Mistress Erwina, you'll find me in my bedchamber. Bring what you need for tending wounds."

"But my lord, do you think 'tis wise—"

He ignored the irksome woman and made his way to the one room in the decaying castle fit for habitation: his personal chambers.

After placing the injured soul on his bed, he turned and opened the shutters to let in the sun's early morning light. He sat on the edge of the mattress and slowly peeled back the bloody cloak.

Close on his heels, Erwina rushed in, her arms loaded with towels and bandages. She tossed instructions over her shoulder, ordering the servants to heat the room and send up more water.

"Goodness. Goodness," she clucked like a hen after chicks. A crease formed between her brows at her attempt to take over the care. "Your lordship, if you please."

Ranulf grunted and blocked her hands. "Go slow. 'Tis not a fresh wound but dried to her clothing."

"How long has she been in this deep sleep?" Erwina asked, wringing out the water from the cleaning cloth.

He shrugged. "From the story Hamish told me, he said she attacked him and then fell atop him. We rode through the night to get here."

"'Tis a blessing the wound started to seal." Erwina set the bowl and medicinals on the small table beside the bed. "Any more jarring and she could have bled to death."

"'Tis that bad?" He glanced up, catching the censure in her tone. Ranulf pushed back the young maiden's hood. Short tendrils of ebony wrapped around his fingers. The silken strands caught the morning sun. His hand hovered, resisting the temptation to touch the glistening cap.

"My lord, if you please," Erwina said, nudging him out of the way. "If you cannot help, I must request you depart this chamber and send another in your place."

He tore his attention from the maiden, squaring on Erwina. "She held a blade to the boy's throat. Would you wish the same?"

"Hmph." Erwina waved her hand. "She's no bigger than a fairy. By the look of her, she won't be causing trouble for a while."

He scowled down at the girl, so pale and small. "No matter. I will stay until you are finished."

Erwina's deep exhalation became a statement that her patience drew thin. "I beg your lordship's pardon, but you can see she's in capable hands." She paused in the removal of blood and dirt. "My lord, because you are here, there are other matters of business that must needs tending."

"Hamish? The rascal can stew in his own mess for a time."

She lifted her eyes from their patient. "I suppose, given the state in which you rode through the gates, that you missed the additional men filling the bailey?"

His head jerked in the direction of the old garrison building.

Erwina supplied the answer to his unspoken question. "The king's army rode in last eventide, stationing themselves in the stables."

His gut clutched, burning a path into his throat. Why were they here unannounced? Eyes narrowed, he waited, listening to the sounds below.

"'Tis nothing to fear. Ol' Scoggins recognized them and bade them enter. Go." She fluttered her hands at him, shooing him toward the door. "Though I doubt the girl will have the strength to cause trouble, I promise to call out."

The object of concern lay on his bed, her face gravely pale. The urge to run a soothing hand over her brow rose in his heart. He started to reach out, but a shout from the bailey below broke the siren's call. Ranulf frowned, curling his fingers into his palms and turned away.

The old woman was correct. 'Twould be a while before he heard the young maiden's tale. In the meantime, he had a castle to protect.

"You'll find a guard stationed outside the chamber door."

Clarice refused to open her eyes. Someone, watching and waiting, observed her as she slept. She bit back a sob, pressing it against the back of her throat. The more she fought, the more powerful it became. A thin stream of air seeped through her clenched teeth.

Memories of her flight from the only home she had ever known came in pieces. Darkness trailed behind Robert's attack. It slithered through her thoughts, tugging her into a deep abyss. In the silence of the room, the fear of her wickedness leaped out at her. Had she killed her stepbrother? Could she do something so vile and not recall it?

The pounding in her ears rose to a deafening roar. Flashes of the night came back to her. The boy at the campsite. Had she harmed the child in the woods?

Tossing the blanket aside, she rolled onto her shoulder and gasped. Pain shot down her left arm. It trailed to her fingertips, throbbing through her nails. Fire was everywhere, eating her alive with its flaming tongue.

"Hush, child. You'll find safety here."

A cool, papery hand settled on her forehead.

"Where am I?"

"Speak up. These ears are too old for mumbled gibberish." The watcher shuffled about the room. "Name's Mistress Erwina. I am castellan here. Take care of everyone in Sedgewic." The sound of heavy keys sliding against a metal ring punctuated her pronouncement. "And now I'm here to tend to your wound. Tell me, dear, what is your name?"

Clarice froze and waited.

"No sense in trying to ignore me," Mistress Erwina said. "I'm not going away until you do." The woman tapped an impatient beat on the wood floor. "I already know one of your secrets."

Restless, Clarice shifted under the weight of curiosity but kept her silence. She squeezed her eyes closed and willed the woman to leave.

"I'd wager you are wondering if I can keep your secret."

"What secret puffs you up like an adder?" Clarice muttered into the pillow.

"Hmph. Rude girl. Believe I'll let you stew a while longer." The woman moved about the room, rearranging the furnishings, stoking the fire in the hearth.

Clarice startled when the metal tongs clanged against the grate. A shower of sparks shot from the logs.

The woman—Mistress Erwina—dropped the tool in place and returned. "Tell me, if you can," she said. "Which of your secrets do I know and the lord of Sedgewic does not? At least," she added with a wink, "not yet."

"Sedgewic?" Her stomach rolled, twisting in knots. That name represented the moment her mundane life had shattered and forced her out of what she had believed was safety. "How did I come to be here?"

"Don't you remember?" Mistress Erwina fluffed and patted, straightening the bedding. Each movement, exact, without waste. "Ah, I suppose not. 'Tis another bit of information I possess and you do not." She clapped her hands together. "Well? Do you wish to guess? An exchange of secrets, hmm?"

Clarice lifted her uninjured shoulder, feigning indifference. She picked off a downy feather from the mattress. "It matters not."

Mistress Erwina trailed her finger along the bandaged arm. "Think it matters not that you carry a wound on the back of your left arm? 'Tis I who tended to that wound. Took several stitches to draw your flesh together. 'Tis fortunate you thought to bind it tight. And more so that I have a steady hand."

"I suppose you wish me to reward you."

"Yes." Mistress Erwina bent forward. "I would know your name and how you came by this."

Clarice slid her gaze to the bloody piece of embroidered material held out under her nose. Father's standard of three interlocking wreaths. Now, barely discernible under the dried blood. The family edict to keep her identity hidden raged in her head. She swallowed to loosen the knot of tension growing in her chest. "And what will you do with this knowledge?"

Mistress Erwina placed the ruined embroidery on the side table. "Years ago, I searched for answers to questions that stole my sleep for many a night." She tapped the edge with her fingertip. "I believe you have those answers."

Clarice bit down on the fear that threatened to choke her.

"I see you tire from our chat," the castellan said, straightening her back. "Mayhap by morn you will be ready to speak."

"By morning, I daresay, I will no longer be here."

"No. You are still weak and need rest," Mistress Erwina cautioned. "Sleep is what you need. We'll speak afterward."

"Am I not free to go?" Clarice struggled to sit up. Fire seared through her arm. It wrung the air from her lungs. "This cannot be."

She tried not to flinch when Mistress Erwina braced Clarice's uninjured shoulder and held her there until she gained her balance.

"You threatened injury to a favorite of his lordship's household servants," Mistress Erwina said. "Give him and yourself some time. At this moment I daresay he hasn't the patience to deal fairly with you."

"I must leave at once," Clarice croaked. She licked her lips. Her mouth was as parched as a dry riverbed.

"Hush, child. There is a guard on the other side of yon door. He is under orders to stop you." Her cool fingers smoothed the tendrils from Clarice's fevered cheek. "Stay and rest a while. We'll sort things out. For now, I've another knot to untangle." She turned to walk away, muttering. "Although how I'll ever convince the lord not to allow that child to disrupt his life again, I'll never know.

She stopped to cast back a stern gaze. "I know you think me ill willed, but I'll help you if I can. Your secrets are safe with me. For now."

Clarice pushed weakly against the weight of the bed furs. The effort stole her ability to rise. Helpless, she watched the door ease shut, sealing her in another prison.

No! "Not this time." She swung her feet over the edge of the great bed and clung to the thick mattress. Her ears buzzed like an angry hive. The floor pitched under her legs. The walls heaved until she slowed the drag of air into her lungs. In time, the blood returned to her limbs and the buzzing stopped.

Once able to focus on her surroundings, the warmth of the room struck her as unusual. Would a prisoner such as she often receive the luxury of a large fire or a soft pillow on which to rest her head? Even as the daughter of the manor, she had never known such grand accommodations were possible.

In the past, her orders had been to keep to the tower whenever her stepmother and stepbrother arrived at Margrave. There she kept herself hidden in her bedchamber until they took their leave. This, her father promised every time the tumblers turned, was done in the name of safekeeping.

Now she knew the truth. Safety resided in the same place as love. It existed only in fairy tales and dreams. Once, she had dared to envision a knight who would save her from the tower. But that was when she was young and still believed in such.

Clarice ran to the door and pounded, shouting for the sentry to release her. After a time of no response, she pressed her damp cheek against the door and worked out a plan to escape her new prison.

Chapter 9

Arms crossed, Ranulf rested his back against the stable entrance. Merry shouts lifted up to the rafters, threatening to shake down the aged timbers. Someone had fashioned a trestle table out of spare lumber. A side of wild boar rested on two rough planks. His stomach grumbled when the air, scented with smoked meat and warm mead, reached his nose. He did not care to count the cost to his storehouse until after his guests had taken their leave.

His attention drifted over the room until he came to rest on a familiar back. Broad shoulders towered over the regiment of men. He knew of two men who would feel comfortable making camp in his dilapidated stables. One stood before him. The other was sure to be nearby.

He advanced into the stable, and the troop of men quieted as he filled the space. Purposeful strides brought him within inches of their leader's wide back.

Ranulf placed his hand on the meaty shoulder. "You dare make camp without permission?"

The man flexed his muscles and swung around. His fists curled into tight balls. "The king's men go where they will it."

Ranulf sighed. Some things never changed. Nathan Staves always did like to lead with his fists. Ducking the blow, he caught the knight's jaw with an undercut of his own, knuckles scraping against the coarse red beard.

The towering man squared off and charged, throwing his massive weight of muscle and bone at his attacker. Ranulf dodged him at the last moment. The timbers holding the weight of the roof shook from the impact. Leading with his head instead of his brains, Nathan struck the post. His thundering motion stopped and he toppled over, as if cut off at the knees. Bits of thatch slid down from the rooftop, showering dust through a hole in the ceiling.

"Damn," Ranulf muttered. "Someone will have to repair that, too."

"Enough, Nathan," Sir Darrick of Lockwood called out. "Continue this nonsense and we shall yet sleep under the stars."

Face flushed, Nathan shook his head and pushed the tangle of hair out of his dazed emerald eyes. "Ah, Darrick." A lopsided grin stretched as he struggled to prop himself up with his elbows. "He knows better. Had he been a man of honor, the esteemed Sir Ranulf, lord of Sedgewic, would not have jumped out at me from behind."

"Honor, is it?" Ranulf offered his hand to the man on the stable floor. "What manner of knight enters a man's castle without notice?"

"A man's castle?" Nathan repeated, his eyes now focused and alert. "We thought 'twas a deserted ruin until ol' Scoggins showed his ugly face at the gate."

Ranulf's smile slipped, and he withdrew his offered hand. The man had a vexing way of making him lose his temper. "Darrick has the right of it. Get your arse off the floor."

Sir Darrick let his gaze drift upward to the ruined ceiling. "If we may dispense with the pleasantries you exude for one another, I suggest we carry our reunion somewhere less—drafty."

"Right as usual." Ranulf hid his reflexive cringe by dusting off the imaginary dirt from his sleeve. "Although soon you will find that this is one of our finer buildings."

"A great leader sees to the comfort of his men." Darrick nodded his appreciation. "I noted the fresh mortar in your masonry. Bringing an ailing castle back to its glory is a massive undertaking."

Ranulf managed to tip his head. In the short time he had been lord of Sedgewic, he had come to think of the falling-down heap as his own. It fit him well. He understood the damage abandonment created.

After waiting for Darrick to leave orders with Sergeant Krell, one of the oldest soldiers he had ever known, Ranulf led Darrick and Nathan across the bailey yard and past the stonemasons. The outer wall was no longer the pile of rubble 'twas when he first inherited the castle. It now stood strong. Despite the decay, he had begun to think of the king's gift as a blessing instead of a curse. With every improvement, he staked his claim on the lands. He would not release it without a fight.

"Ranulf, pray tell me what you did to irritate our king," Nathan prodded. "Mind you, I ask to ensure I don't make the same misstep. Banishment would be far more pleasant."

Darrick laid a hand on Ranulf's stiffened shoulder. "'Tis only jealousy. In time, we, too, will receive a boon from our king."

"Jealousy?" Nathan grabbed at his chest and stumbled, feigning a stab wound. "I would rather be landless than have to rebuild a hovel."

"Enough," Darrick said. "One day you'll go too far."

Ranulf shook his head. "He speaks what others are probably thinking."

Nathan had the good sense to flush with embarrassment and stammer out an apology. Ranulf grunted. The hotheaded knight meant no harm. There had been a time when he, too, had not been ready to take on the responsibilities of a castle. The back of his mighty steed, Aldwyn, had been his home. The simple possessions required were his broadsword, a strong suit of armor, and an occasional willing wench to warm his bed.

Sir Darrick reached out, staying Ranulf by his arm. "A word."

Nathan stopped beside them. A knowing look passed between the two men.

Gnawing irritation boiled under Ranulf's skin. He held out his hand and Darrick dropped a silver swan into his palm. Ranulf closed his eyes, hating to see the sign that Henry didn't trust him to complete the task. *Why is the king involving more of the brotherhood?* He opened his eyes as Nathan dropped another silver swan into his hand.

"By all that is holy, you are not needed." He gripped Nathan's wide wrist, forcing his palm open so that he could return the swan to its owner. "I can fulfill my vow without your help"

"Our king disagrees." Nathan hissed. "Margrave remains free. The threat continues."

"'Tis not for our pride," Darrick reminded Ranulf, "but for King Henry's life."

The simplicity struck Ranulf, clearing his head. "I know this. I spoke with Margrave and could have taken him into custody, but I have a plan to clear out the rat's entire nest. Not just one."

Nathan arched a brow. "Go on."

"Come," Darrick said, stepping between the two men. "Show us where we are safe to discuss this in private."

At Ranulf's reluctant nod, Nathan grinned back. "Bites you in the arse, doesn't it?" He added an explanation, "Three heads, three souls, all working together again."

Ranulf forced his fingers to uncurl and willed them to stay peaceful. "This way," he said, pointing to the main hall.

They moved as one, already the seams of a team, sewn together by duty.

When Nathan Staves lagged behind them, Ranulf could not help the question. He had to ask. "Darrick, what in Christ's blood did he do to be included in the brotherhood?"

Nathan brought his head between them and slapped their shoulders. The heavy, ham-sized grip nearly brought Ranulf to his knees. Refusing to let the knight see the weakness, he tightened his muscles, just as he did when he prepared for battle.

"'Tis bloody good to work with you, too," Nathan growled.

A plaintive wail came from the castle hall, drawing all three men up short.

"In the name of all that is holy, what is that?" Darrick asked.

"If you'll excuse me." Without further explanation, Ranulf took off at a run toward the main building. He had been a fool to leave one guard to protect his household from the stranger. Maybe he needed help after all. He thundered up the stairs, taking two steps at a time. The report of boot heels told him his friends were right behind him.

The men reached the hall as Erwina and Hamish left the stairs and turned in the direction of the cutlery. She pinched the child's ear as she led him away. Ranulf swore under his breath and relaxed his grasp around the hilt of his sword. He had intended to be there when Sedgewic's castellan doled out the punishment, but it looked as if she had it well in hand.

"Did the boy commit murder?" Darrick watched the two retreat from the hall before turning on Ranulf. "Whatever his crime, surely you don't approve of beating a child."

"Beat a child? Don't be ridiculous." Ranulf knew that under Darrick's cool mask of indifference was a heart that existed for righting the injustices on the defenseless. "'Tis more than possible Mistress Erwina will drag him to the kitchens, where she'll stuff him with meat pies."

"Meat pies, you say? Wild boar?" A hungry look in his eye, Nathan rubbed his stomach, reminding Ranulf that they had yet to break their fast.

He looked for the two serving girls usually found tucked in the corner by the great hearth. Just as he thought, they had been hiding near the fireplace. They stared with longing toward the hallway that led to the kitchens, no doubt planning a way to earn their own punishments.

"You there," he called out. "Fetch Mistress Erwina. Tell her our guests have need of food and drink."

Bobbing a curtsy, Faith and Mercy ran to the kitchen, their shiny blond ringlets bouncing with each step.

The wail began again. It came from the bedchamber overhead and wove down the stairway, lifting the hair on Ranulf's arms.

"Many thanks for your hospitality," Nathan said, tugging on the neck of his tunic. "But if that boy is crying out while eating her meat tarts, I think I shall plead mercy and try my luck with our troop's own larder."

Distracted by the frantic cries for help, Ranulf shrugged and walked toward the stairs. He waved his friends on. "If you will excuse me, I won't be but a moment."

Ranulf kicked shut the warped door with the heel of his boot. His eyes adjusting to the dim light, he noticed the empty bed. The anger he had worked so hard to keep in check began to build. He spun around at the sound of a muffled hiccup. The bedeviling wretch lay huddled on the floor beside the doorway. Curled into a ball, she shivered pathetically in the dark bedchamber, a wide strip of linen wrapped around her upper arm.

"Christ's blood." He marched over, intent on yanking her up by the neck and propelling her to his bed. But instead of scratching and clawing her way free, she lay still. 'Twas as if all the fight had left her, a notion that irritated him like a poisonous plant rubbed against the skin. "This is intolerable."

He smoothed the damp hair out of her face. His own tanned skin stood out against the soft glow of her cheek. He grunted, forcing the tender image away. Mindful of keeping the bedsheet wrapped around the small frame, he lifted her from the floor and deposited her on his bed.

After pulling the coverlet up to her chin, he carefully withdrew her hands. Fresh wounds marred each knuckle. Her slim nails were broken and jagged, bleeding around the tortured edges. He dipped a clean rag into a bucket of cool water to wash away the stains on her hands.

"Who are you?" Her voice was a caress of velvet across the skin.

He paused in his task and turned to see chips of deep sapphire observing his every move. "I think I am in a better position to request the same from you."

He stifled the shiver as soon as her jeweled eyes glanced away. The need to bring a sparkle to them surged through his veins. Hopeful he was mistaken in her attempt to harm Hamish, he decided to offer his information first. After all, his singular concern was to discover where she came from and send her racing back to her nursemaid's skirts. It did not matter how he gathered the information. The quicker the better. King Henry's patience would last only so long.

"A bargain." He used the gracious smile he had perfected years before. "I'll tell you what you need to know and you'll tell me what I ask. Fair enough?"

Blue sapphires slid over him again, leaving a heated path in their wake. He shifted uncomfortably. Though he had many faults, sexual depravity was not a common companion of his. Though some would disagree, desiring someone so young was wrong. Depraved. 'Twas not so long since he had lain with a woman. He lifted his eyes and locked onto her gaze. Their depths were shadowed with secrets and pain.

He sat down on a chair near the bed and leaned in. "Who hurt you? Where is your home? Ah, you shake your head; how naughty of me. I forgot our agreement."

He hated having to force a captive to reveal her secrets. But the mantle of protecting the king weighed heavily on his shoulders. 'Twould prove most enjoyable to have this over and done with.

"I believe I promised to go first." He settled into the chair, his back pressing against the oak spindles, folded hands resting on the planes of his stomach. Never far from his blade. "This fair keep you find yourself in is none other than Castle Sedgewic. And I . . . well, I am the lord of Sedgewic and your host." To his dismay, he swore her hand flinched at his name. Her skin paled as she worked to unhinge her jaw.

"You brought me here?" The simple question, spoken a little louder than a whisper, did something to him internally, awkwardly heating parts he chose to ignore.

"Yes." He bent forward, trapping her hand to engage her attention. "You can trust me." Fear flashed in her eyes, causing a guilty twinge to bite at his conscience. Briefly. "Where are your people? 'Tis dangerous for a young girl to travel alone." His thumb slid over the back of her hand. "Were you attacked? 'Twould pain me greatly to know my lands are not safe to cross. Is that how you came of your wound?"

She pulled her hand away, tucking it by her chest. The edges of binding peeked out from the coverlet and fur. The pink skin above it drew his attention. It looked painful to the touch.

"Why was the child tortured?" she whispered, disregarding his question.

"No one is tortured here. You heard a wayward lad crossing Mistress Erwina's path one too many times."

A frown tugged a line between her raven brows. "The watcher?"

He shrugged, doing his best not to convey his annoyance with her questions. "I've never thought of her in those terms, but I suppose you are right. She watches over all of us. Been here for years. Came with the castle."

The dismissive sniff that followed reminded him of a woman he once called his wife. The triangle of muscles between his shoulders bunched.

"She doesn't do a very good job," the girl said, her tone proving her displeasure.

"Ah, because she forgot to remove those hideous bindings? Pray forgive her. She has had a trying time with young Hamish's disappearance."

"Binding?" she squeaked.

He flicked his hand. "Slide over, child, and I'll help you with them. Wouldn't want you to harm yourself again." He nodded his approval as she wiggled to the far edge of the bed.

"I should wait for Mistress Erwina."

"'Twas an ingenious way to make yourself seem larger than you are. Indeed, it fooled young Hamish. The lad was terrified at first." He paused, searching her face. "I thank you for not using your little knife to cut him. Here," he motioned. "Turn and I will deliver you from the binding."

"Do not bother yourself. I'm fine, really! I do thank you for your offer, but I can tend to it myself."

"Takes a steady hand to wield a sharp blade."

She clutched the coverlet closer. "I would wait upon Mistress Erwina's help instead."

Bemused by her reaction, he held out his hands. "You have no need to fear me. Our castellan is busy keeping the workings of the castle running smoothly. In truth, your wait for her help will be long."

The simple explanation given, he waited for the bedcover to drop. Instead, for his patience, he watched it climb even closer to her chin. 'Twas as if he had barged unbidden into a lady's chamber. Her eyes were as large as the duck-egg sapphire 'twas rumored King Henry had given to one of his favorites.

His skin itched, recalling the feel of her curvaceous hips as he dropped her into the bed. Memories of hidden shapes, hips, and buttocks flashed before him. Ranulf squinted at the maiden. *Correction: make that woman, you fool.*

His blood sizzled with the memories of accidentally brushing against curves that should not be on one fresh from the nursery.

Thanks to the pressure in his breeches, he rose on unsteady legs. "I—ah—believe you will have to tend to the binding after all." He moved from the bed and brushed against a tattered piece of embroidery. Picking it up, he smoothed out the stiffened fabric, bloodied from the wound it had staunched earlier. The bits of thread formed a design he had seen before. What were they? Frowning, he tucked the discarded bit of satin under his belt and turned for the door. "I'll have Erwina return with a bite of food for you."

"Wait!" she pleaded. "You . . . you cannot mean to keep me here."

Ranulf stopped, his hand resting on the latch. Unwilling to let go of the door, he looked over his shoulder.

In her effort to sit up, the fur had slipped to reveal the gentle slope of creamy skin. 'Twas all he could do to keep from returning to her side and press a kiss to the nape of her neck. His resolve firmly in place, he looked closely at his captive. He could not ignore the truth. No longer was the patient a mere innocent. This woman, lying so invitingly in his bed, played a game of deception. And uncovering deception was what he did best.

He watched the color of her eyes shift to cobalt. Tears glittered beside the deep pools that pleaded with him to wait. *Wait? For what?*

For her to stick a blade in my heart? For her to open her mouth to my kisses?

"Please." A single tear streamed down her cheek, punctuating her plea. "Am I your prisoner?"

"Prisoners are kept in the tower dungeon." He tilted his head, sliding a fierce gaze over her face. "You are a guest and will dwell here until I deem it safe to release you. However, if I don't receive answers to my questions when next we speak, then that is where you'll reside until I do."

Her fingers dug into the bedding, bunching it under her hand. "Guests are not kept under lock and key."

"They are when they threaten my household and continue to keep their secrets."

"Please, don't lock me in. Anything but that."

"Anything? You value your worth so poorly?" Ranulf shook his head in dismay. "What a pity."

Stepping out of the bedchamber, he wearily shut the door. Drawing in a breath, he slowly inserted the key. The metal bolt turned in the lock and slid home.

His heavy steps down the stairway had carried him away, but he feared he had left his soul behind, torn apart by the plaintive cry for his return.

Chapter 10

"Enough," Ranulf roared over his two friends' voices. Darrick and Nathan stared at him as if he had lost his mind, and an uncomfortable silence settled over the great room. The people of Sedgewic kept their heads down as they scurried past to continue serving the evening meal.

He stood, knocking the chair over in his haste. Shoving his hair out of his face, Ranulf met Darrick's gaze with a scowl. "What would you have us do? We cannot chase over the countryside in the off chance that we cross the bastards' path."

"Agreed." Darrick rose slowly. The muscles in his jaws clenched and unclenched. "Unfortunately, your little foray over Margrave lands didn't flush out our prey. And I'll not bide my time here waiting for a notable bit of information to drop into my lap."

"One attempt has already been made on the king," Nathan added. "We need to move now—" His eyebrows arched high.

Ranulf looked up in time to see Hamish slide out from the corner hallway. He caught the boy by the back of the tunic and spun him to a stop. "Eavesdropping is a nasty habit. I suggest you find something else to do with your time."

Rewarded with a quick nod, Ranulf swallowed a chuckle. The boy never ceased to cause him consternation. "Go. Make haste before Mistress Erwina learns of your behavior."

He turned his back so the lad could scamper out of the room unheeded. Although Ranulf knew it futile, he prayed the child would stay out of trouble. Erwina might not leave Hamish's ears intact should she have to deal with him again so soon. And 'twas obvious the guest residing in his bedchamber already had caused the old woman great distress.

The mere thought of the maiden made his loins tighten. Before he left for France, he would have her whisper every secret she held dear. Then he would taste the curve of her neck and dip into the cleft of her breasts.

And yet there was something troubling about her that he could not quite put his finger on. He pulled out the scrap of embroidered banner he had found on the table in his bedchamber. Although severely damaged, there was enough embroidery left intact to make out the colors. He searched his memory. Where had he seen this design before?

He lifted the pitcher on the hearth and poured a generous portion of ale into his mug. The cool liquid slid down his throat.

With a placid smile in place, he turned, holding out the pitcher to Nathan and Darrick. After seeing their mugs filled, he lifted his own. "To truth, my friends."

Their mouths shifted into firm lines. Nathan lifted the pitcher, examining its contents as if he had never seen the like before.

The back of Ranulf's neck itched as they eyed him over their ale. Those two had another reason to bring them to Sedgewic. Watching them under furrowed brows, he waited.

Darrick set his cup down with slow deliberation and rose from the table. He knocked the dirt from his black leather boots. Dust motes floated in the air, threatening to make them all sneeze. The smell of decay blended with the musty scent that penetrated the old walls.

"Been two years since I last set eyes on Mary Dunley at court," Darrick said.

"Mary?" Ranulf bristled. He had a feeling this was not going to go well.

"And," Darrick added, laying a hand on Ranulf's shoulder, "it's been a year since last I saw you tearing off in a hurry to return to your new bride."

Ranulf forced his muscles to relax. "A fat lot of good it did me, yes? By the time I finished fulfilling Henry's orders, our chance for a good life together was gone."

"What goes on here, Ranulf?" The pitcher Nathan had been holding hit the trestle table. "Are the rumors true? Did you murder your young bride in a fit of jealousy? Or have you imprisoned her in this godforsaken castle? Is that who cries out for mercy?"

The outrage Ranulf kept in check seethed under the surface. "My wife and unborn child were laid to rest in the castle cemetery."

Nathan leaned back in the chair, folded his arms over his chest. "Then we'll insist on seeing who resides in the chambers overhead."

"You *insist*?" Ranulf glared over the trestle table. He clenched the cup in his hand, fearing if he let go, he would reach for his sword instead. "'Tis an injured maiden. Discovered by that boy, Hamish. And 'tis what brought me back to Sedgewic. Nothing more."

"Then we shall not keep you." Darrick propped his back against the hearth and showed no sign of leaving. "But first, give us the tale of how you came by her." He took a shallow sip from his cup. "And how well you've faired since your Mary's death."

Hours later, Ranulf leaned against the wall, his forehead pressed to the cool stone. It had taken more ale than he'd desired to quiet Nathan's questions. 'Twas now obvious to him that he had grown used to the quiet country life. His skill in drinking his friends into the wee hours required honing. But outlast Nathan he did.

Grimacing, Ranulf waited for the stairway to stop its incessant spinning. His head thundered its complaint of too much ale and not enough sleep. It rang from the continuous arguments beaten upon his ears. The rumors tossed about the room had nearly destroyed friendships built on admiration and mutual trust.

He could have ordered the maiden dragged from his chambers, stripped down, exposed for what she was. *What? A woman?*

That was all the information he had. But he wanted more. *So much more.* 'Twould have satisfied one of their questions. Who was held in the chamber? But their accusations cut him deep. Murder his wife and babe? *Never.* How could they consider such a thing? They had to know he would never do what they suggested. In truth, he had killed in the name of the king. Never for his own satisfaction.

Blood pulsed along the reddened scar with renewed vigor, threatening to disrupt his concentration. He probed the raised flesh with his fingers. This badge of pain was his to wear for the rest of his days. And every day he would wonder about the events of the dark hour that took his wife and child from his life. The scar was a reminder to leave his lofty dreams of family behind him. Wanting too much had tested the fates and he had lost everything.

Darrick and Nathan's challenges rebounded, echoing in his head. What events had taken place the night Mary and their child died? How had he come by the scar that ran its path into his hair? They were the same questions he himself had asked every night for almost a year.

The pain in his heart was clear. The rest remained hidden behind misted memories. *Surely I did not kill my wife and my unborn child. Impossible.*

He stumbled up the stairs and ran into solid planks of wood. Rattling the bedchamber door handle, he cursed when he found it locked. After fumbling in the dark, he withdrew the key tucked in his belt and unlocked the door.

Pushing aside the vexing notion that tonight his bed should be in the stable garrison, he paused in front of the hearth. The glowing embers in the fireplace confused him. He had stopped demanding the fire lit after Mary's death. Erwina had too much to contend with to see it done.

As he picked his way across the room, his balance tilted. He grabbed at the curtains enclosing the great bed and steadied his legs. The string holding his chausses in place fell away. They dropped and tangled on his boots. Toppling into the bed, he let the spinning room have its way.

Eyes closed, he inhaled and caught the perfumed scent. His eyes flashed open. He could not have planned the location of this interrogation any better. Smiling, he wrapped his arm around the woman in his bed. *To duty and truth.*

Clarice jolted awake to find an oversize male lying next to her. A heavy bare arm flung on top of her chest squeezed the air from her lungs. Damn him; the lord of Sedgewic thought to share the bed.

Her pulse raced as she tried to wiggle free from his arm. It slid down and wrapped around her waist, blocking her escape. Heat radiated wherever his body touched her. He pressed against her back and soft puffs of air caressed the sensitive skin along her neck. Each breath brought her bound breasts precariously close to his palm.

Fearing she would wake him, she edged one leg out from under the covers and then the next, until her toes touched the cold floor. Her skin pebbled from the chill. Scooting over, she lifted his wrist and peeled away his arm. He snorted a complaint and Clarice froze. Her feet planted on the floor and her hip half off the mattress, she waited until the soft rhythm of his breathing deepened and slowed. Then she catapulted off the bed and scrambled to the door.

She tried the handle and found it gave way under pressure. Cracking it enough to let the light from the wall sconce in, she peeked through the slit. Her heart leaped like a rabbit in her chest. Her mouth went dry. Two guards stood at the door with their pikestaffs at the ready. They shuffled and began to turn in her direction.

Clarice shut the door, allowing the faintest click as the bolt moved into place. Braced against the wall, she listened and prayed the guards would lose interest. The man in the bed tossed in his sleep before rolling to his side. Time stretched out, moving at a snail's pace.

Crouched in the shadows, she sorely missed the warmth of the bed. Her teeth clamped together to keep them from chattering. As the hours passed, her irritation grew with every cramping muscle. The man had no business coming into a chamber holding someone he thought a danger to the castle. Why he felt the need to dislodge her was inexcusable. But he was the lord of the castle. She supposed he could do whatever he pleased. It certainly worked that way in the Margrave household.

As the moon shifted, its light fell on an extra fur at the foot of the bed. If she moved quietly, she could snag it without waking him. Crawling closer, she tugged on the fur until it slid to the floor. Returned safely to the corner, she curled into the fur and watched the hulking man sleep like the dead.

Relentless curiosity nibbled at her good sense. Moonlight washed over the auburn hair falling across his cheek. Matching brows arched over a serene face. A puckered red scar, showing fresh signs of healing, marred his temple. Her heart tore in sympathy for his pain.

How odd. She blinked at the thought. She was certain he had been in charge of the men who had invaded her home. Even though he rode under King Henry's banner, he had entered her life intent on destroying her family, her home, her life. Her brows furrowed. She must be sure to remember that simple fact. Yet here she sat, feeling safe enough to examine him as he slept.

As she watched him, she let her thoughts drift to her father's parting words to Maud. How in the world would she find the wolf if the lord of Sedgewic intended to keep her restrained behind the castle walls? She bit her lip. Could she turn to the lord and beseech his help in locating its lair?

She shook her thoughts free of that consideration. 'Twas best to remember that he, too, was the enemy and could not be trusted. If he were to learn she was Nicholas of Margrave's daughter, she stood an excellent chance of losing her head. But how was she to reach the king for help if she could not reveal her lineage? Clarice of Margrave existed only to Maud and those who would see her dead. She was doomed if she did not claim her heritage and as sure as dead if she did.

Bone-weary, in the wee hours Ranulf slipped out of bed and, without waking her, lifted the petite woman off the floor. He cradled her, torn between doing what he knew was honorable or listening to his ever-tightening stones. The place where her small hand wrapped around his neck pulsed with heat.

Determined to leave her in peace, he placed her gently on the mattress. He recalled the relief that had rushed through him earlier when he had realized she was not a young maiden fresh from the nursery. Now all he had to do was gain her confidence. Then he would know the truth behind her wounded eyes.

Providence could not have provided a better situation for him in which to start his interrogation. He was willing to allow her the opportunity to tell him her secrets. Then he would decide what to do with her.

Careful to put enough distance between them, he laid down beside her. A satisfied sigh rumbled through his chest. He might have had a momentary lapse of judgment in choosing his place of rest for the night, but what a delightful lapse 'twas. He burrowed deeper into the furs, enjoying the fact that he was not alone.

Chapter 11

His loins tightened, throbbing with need. The woman wiggled her bottom into his cock. Stones drew, tightening in anticipation. His palms brushed over her nipples. They rose and pebbled. Her feminine scent penetrated his dreams. He growled, pulling her close to nuzzle her neck, lapping the skin that tasted of honey. Eyes of sapphire locked with his as they rolled together in a field of lavender. She spread her legs, both hands traveling up her thighs until she arrived at her apex. Her fingers swirled over her mound. She bit her lip as she dipped and stroked her core. Eyes, heavy lidded, full of pleasure, she watched his need grow. Her laughter rippled over his skin, enticing him to lose control. Nudging her hand aside, he took over, carrying her to the edge. There he entered, joining her in the pleasure that stole his ability to think, only feel. Heat building, a firestorm of passion crashed as wave after wave took over their souls.

Ranulf awoke with a start. His imagination had taken control and left his body rock-solid and alert. He blinked away the sleep, stunned that he felt more rested than he had in over a year. He looked down at his bed companion, caged in his embrace. However, those passionate blue eyes glittering above pale cheeks were not happy. They tipped the scales between outrage and murder.

"Unhand me!"

"Ah, 'twas a dream after all." He braced his arms, keeping his more tender anatomy out of harm's way. Their legs entwined, pressing into his already aroused loins. His dream came back to him, urging him to make it real.

"My lord." Mistress Erwina's high-pitched voice penetrated the chamber door. Insistent pounding from the other side beat against his brain.

"Go. Away!" he shouted.

Mistress Erwina rattled his back teeth. Had the dratted women forgotten he was the lord of Sedgewic? This was not the way he intended his day to begin. If that assault were not enough, his mood worsened as the human-size kitten nestled in his arms was rediscovering her claws.

A grunt hissed through his teeth as he caught the wench's wrists. Reminded of her wound, he lowered her hands, caressing the delicate flesh with his lips before holding them to his chest, where they could do no harm. Thoughts of her cuddling up to him in the middle of the night sung through his body, addling his brain. He leaned in, allowing himself to hope for a more welcoming morning with his guest.

The door bounced against the wall and the castellan of the castle pushed past the guards. Wide-eyed, she stood at the threshold, her ring of keys in hand. "My lord."

Ranulf looked over his shoulder and frowned. "For the love of God, Erwina," he said. "Unless the castle is on fire or under siege, there is no cause for tearing my brain out through my ears."

"But—" Erwina said.

"By whose permission do you enter my chamber?"

"Yours, my lord. You gave me orders to tend to the . . . uh, patient, come the new day."

Faint memories nibbled at his wits. Slowly, he recalled how he came to find his bed in error. He should have known the previous night would not be swept away. Annoyed with the intrusions into his life, he could not keep the impatience from his words. "Be quick about your duties, then."

Erwina cast a quick look about the chamber. "Do you wish to break your fast in the hall?"

Keeping the maiden's wrists trapped, he allowed her to dive under the bedcovers. Ranulf propped his back against the headboard and made no effort to cover the tent created by his very alert cock. "By all that is holy, I am lord of this castle. I refuse to rush about the room like a misbehaving boy."

He glanced at his bedmate and wondered if she had been aware of the way their thighs had brushed. Or if she had noticed the heat shared between them on each turn of her body. The caress of her soft breath as she sighed in her sleep was still fresh in his mind. His loins tightened again. He could still feel the warmth of her rounded bottom, cupped in the angle of his hips. Did she know how she had tortured him with her backside? Forced to wait until the wee small hours of the morning, he had nearly lost control of his need when she rolled over and snuggled deep within his arms.

He lifted the fur and continued to study her. She had silenced her complaints and lay huddled under the blankets. Each inhalation brought her bound breasts closer to his chest.

Their gazes met. The maiden's eyes were as blue and dark as the deepest pool. He had the uncanny feeling of having found something that until that moment had always been unattainable.

Her damp ebony lashes lowered. Defeated, her claws retracted and her arms went limp. Her fingers curled into defenseless balls.

Ranulf's gut twisted. He never could abide tears. He would rather she were spitting and clawing at his head than to give in so easily.

Her breath came in short pants, fighting against the binding around her chest. His gaze slid down until it rested on the tender skin rubbed raw by the coarse linen. "Bloody hell," he cursed. The damn thing would probably leave scars. "Not under my care," he muttered.

"You are right as always, Erwina," he said. "My attentions are needed elsewhere. I shall break my fast below. But not until I've corrected a great injustice."

He yanked the pelt off the bed and rose. His swift movement came near to dispatching his bedmate onto the floor. With one swoop, she caught the remaining blanket and pulled it over her head.

"Here now," he said, swatting the lump he assumed was the wench's rounded bottom. "'Tis a new day. Time to move your lovely arse out of my bed."

"My lord." Erwina's voice rose over the muffled curses that worked their way out from under the blanket. "I pray that I might speak with you. Immediately."

"We will," Ranulf said, "after I have tended the maiden's wound. I've noticed 'tis deep and requires close watch." He eyed what he believed must be the curve of the wench's thigh. Turning a wintry gaze upon the frazzled castellan, he added, "This fact does bring to mind that you have failed to follow an order of mine."

Erwina paled. "Sir?"

"The bindings."

Her voice shook as she asked, "Bindings, sir?"

"I am sure you noticed them when you tended to the wound on her arm."

Erwina nodded, wrapping her hands in her apron. She fidgeted as she kept her eyes on the protrusion in the master's bed. "If I might ask your indulgence—"

Ranulf feared Erwina was on the brink of having some form of fit before his eyes. If he were not certain the bindings were left intact, he could have sworn she already knew 'twas not a helpless waif lying in his bed but a wench of questionable background. That thought bothered him a great deal. 'Twould not serve to have his people hold secrets against him.

With the fur cinched close to his waist, he advanced toward Erwina and patted her thin shoulder. "Go. We shall talk once I'm finished here."

Finished here? Clarice's cheeks heated, threatening to engulf her in flames. Did Lord Whatshisname think she intended to allow him to come near her? She burrowed deeper under the blanket. The soft tick of the door closing made her flinch. To her ears it sounded like a thunderclap. The blanket was ripped from her grasp, torn from her fingers like a lightning strike.

She jumped from the bed as if struck by the power filling the bedchamber. Dragging the bedlinen behind her, she shivered in anticipation, alert to every possible place to escape the lord of Sedgewic's attention. Air caught in her throat. She gulped it down. The rise of her chest, fighting against the binding, bit at her flesh.

He walked toward her. Despite his height and broad shoulders, his steps were light, hesitant, as if he were cornering a wild animal. His gaze held hers, gray eyes warmed with a hint of green and brown, keeping her from the stupidity of running to a corner of the bedchamber. Trapped, she had nowhere to go.

He held out a hand, palm up, to show that it held no threat. But where was his other hand, and why did he keep it behind his back? A flash of sunlight sparkled on the wall. Clarice shifted, turning to look at the bedside table. The sheathed dagger he kept on the table was gone.

She took an involuntary step back, bumping her legs against the bed.

His brows arched, questioning her. "Come, Sweeting. Stay where you are. 'Tis all I ask of you." His stance shifted. Anticipating her next movement, he caught her as she leaped to the side.

Argh! The air squeezed past her lips. His mouth, close enough to kiss, twisted in a firm line, reminding her that she had disobeyed an order. Fearing he meant to press his mouth to hers, she ducked out of the way. Her palm bumped into something quite hard, silken, and very much awake.

The fur wrapped around his middle had fallen to the floor as he reached for her. The linen, still clutched at her breasts, opened up. A draft cascaded down her shoulder, slithered down the base of her back and across her rump. Heat traveled over her skin, penetrating the flesh where he wrapped his arm around her waist. She shivered despite the flames licking at her senses. Flashes, moments of warmth, caught in the stillness of the night, tugged at her, calling to her to trust him.

That thought dissipated just as quickly when he caged her in his embrace, moving her to stand against the wall. *Twist out of his hold, you fool.*

Without a word, he guided her, nudging her body. His thighs bumped into hers, leaving behind a trail of lightning to run through her blood. He allowed her to keep the bedlinen, still clutched in her fist, but it hid little more than her bound breasts and the space between her legs. The chill of the stone wall licked at her bare thighs. Lifting her arm, he placed her palm flat, fingers spread.

"My lord, I—" What she meant to say slipped away like wisps of smoke as he nuzzled the back of her neck, then bent to nip at the angle of her shoulder blade.

"Be still," he ordered. The two words glided over her as he released his hold around her waist. "I mean to cut this offensive thing off before it marks you for life. Don't turn until I say 'tis safe."

She followed the whisper of movement. It grew nearer. He touched her back, his callused fingers, rough from labor, tugging at the binding. A flash of cold grazed her spine.

"No." She turned as the blade glided over her skin and cut through the binding. Blood rushed to her breasts, screaming into flesh that had been crushed for days. Her nipples ached as they pebbled. Liquid warmth pooled between her legs, sending rivers of pleasure through her middle.

His hands shook as he shoved the hair from his dampened forehead. "Are you injured?"

Cool air nuzzled her bare hip, reminding her how little of her was covered. She clutched the linen to her chest, whipping the remainder around her body. "Christ's blood," Clarice muttered. She shook her head and took a deep, shuddering breath that made her nipples arch out, as if searching for him.

"I didn't mean..." He reached out, then withdrew his hand. Backing away, he put distance between them.

She squeezed her eyes shut. Her body warred with her mind. She was relieved. "Just go ... my lord." And mortified. How could she want him to hold her again?

"I'll send Mistress Erwina to tend to your..." Hitching the fur around his middle, his eyes took on another shade of color as they inched up, viewing her bare limbs. His attention slid over the marks made raw by the binding. "... wounds. 'Tis certain by now she has found something suitable for you to wear."

"Thank you," Clarice whispered.

A long, uncomfortable silence filled the room with unanswered questions, hanging between them. So much left unsaid and unexplored.

"Have her bring you to the solar when you are readied."

Clarice nodded and sank into the mattress as he closed the door.

Ranulf continued to pace the solar as he waited for Erwina to arrive. He must have the maiden's trust and her name before he left for France. For the king's safety, of course.

The patter of footsteps drew his attention toward the door. He stopped in front of the fireplace and rested a hand on the stone mantel. "Enter," he ordered at the light tapping.

Dressed in clothing that was much too large for her frame, the blue-eyed maiden looked like a ragpicker's wench on the streets of London. The gown, the color of congealed gruel, turned her complexion to the color of paste. The neck gaped and drooped from her chest. Noting the moth-eaten slippers, he could not help worrying her tender feet already bore signs of injury.

Despite his efforts, visions of delicate toes brushing the calves of his legs came to mind. Before shaking his attention free, he decided he would one day like to ease the pain from the arches of her feet, kissing each curling toe.

He lifted his eyes. She seemed to pore over every inch of his soul, divining truth from fiction. Pain from pleasure. Weighing his trustworthiness. She paused at the cursed scar. The damn thing would scare off a saint. He stiffened, prepared for the disgust to register in her gaze. But it did not come.

Despite her colorless attire and pale cheeks, he found solace in her countenance. Suddenly parched, he swallowed to clear his throat. "I see that Mistress Erwina has supplied you with clothing. The gown looks somewhat clean."

Bowing her head, she pretended to examine the dusty slippers. Her fingers stole over the sagging pockets of the apron and picked off a lump of congealed food. "Yes, there is that." Her hand slid over a grease stain. "As you say, if nothing more, the clothes are clean."

He stepped closer, noting she did not shy away. "Why do you lie?"

Her back snapped to attention. "What? I—"

Ranulf inhaled in her direction and frowned. "The clothing is neither clean nor well-fitting. I wonder what you've done to stir her ire so soon upon your arrival."

"I'm certain Mistress Erwina did the best with what she had to offer."

"I fear we are a rustic bunch at Castle Sedgewic. Constant repairs keep us busy. At times we are caught unprepared for sudden arrivals." He dipped a finger to the curl tucked against her cheek. "But my castellan should be punished for her lack of effort in providing you with a decent wardrobe."

Fisting her hands, she made herself taller, nearly pressing her nose toward the center of his chest. "I won't permit you to punish her."

He allowed one auburn brow to arch. "You won't permit it?"

Her cheeks flushed over lips flattened in a tight line. "Please, Lord Ranulf, I ask you not to punish her for my sake."

Ranulf itched to slide a finger over the pink flesh. Enthralled, he wondered what 'twould be like to be lost in their lushness. "And what would you give me for this favor? A story? A truth? Perchance a name of your own?" Lips, surely as soft as satin, trembled under his scrutiny. "I would know your name."

Her eyes narrowed. "M—my name?" she stammered.

The pounding of hooves and the clattering of wheels digging into the cobblestones rang through the castle window.

Panic washed over her face. "I must go. I cannot be here." She spun on her heel to leave the solar without his permission.

Ranulf caught her wrist, pulling her to his chest. "If I am to help you, I must at least know your given name," he said. He gave her a shake. "'Tis no time for lies."

"No. I—"

To prove his point, his mouth came crashing down, devouring all lies that threatened to form. He held her gently, one arm around her waist, the other cradling her shoulders. Wisps of raven hair tickled the back of his hand.

He lingered over her mouth until she pulled away. "Though you hide your passion well, no innocent maiden would kiss a man as you did just now."

She took a deep breath, eyeing the door. "'Tis Clarice." Her lips sealed against additional information. Her body trembled over the simple announcement.

Heavy boots clipped across the floor. Somewhere outside the solar, raised voices called for Lord Ranulf to come at once.

Ranulf's concentration did not waver. Whoever was on the other side of the door could damn well wait. "So, that is all you are willing to give me?"

"Please," she whispered. "'Tis all I have."

He stroked her jaw. "We're not finished, Clarice."

The door swung open, banging into the wall. Nathan filled the doorway, wearing his leather gambeson over the chain mail with ease. 'Twould be obvious to even the most feeble-minded he was accustomed to its weight and wore it like a second skin.

"Sir Nathan, what is the urgency?"

"A visitor has arrived," Nathan announced. "A merchant. Says he must speak with you."

Ranulf frowned at this declaration. "Mistress Erwina shall see to it until I am free."

"I fear not," Nathan said with a shake of his head. "Your Mistress Erwina is near falling into a fit. I fear she will take to her bed if she is not settled soon."

"I beg you." Clarice grabbed at Ranulf's tunic and clung to him like a kitten escaping a hound. Her voice rose in panic. "Grant me sanctuary. I promise not to be a burden. I will leave as soon as they are gone."

"Who do you fear arrives?" Ranulf placed a comforting hand

around her slim back and felt her shudder under his touch. Her eyes widened. Their centers darkened, the ring of blue thinned. "Come. If I don't know who you fear, how can I protect you?"

She pressed her fingertips against his mouth. "If-if someone were to ask for me, you would not hand me over to them?"

"No, not yet." He swept her knuckles to his lips. "I have no plans to grant your leave until you have satisfied my curiosity."

Clarice gasped and tried to pull away. "I've done nothing. I swear it."

"We shall see, won't we?" Ranulf yanked her close, plundering her mouth with his tongue before breaking free from her spell. He glanced up at Nathan. "Find Hamish to direct you to the back stairway and take her to my chambers."

Before releasing her, Ranulf lifted Clarice's chin with his knuckles. "Mayhap, in time, you will share more than your name with me."

Chapter 12

Weary after settling the castle's affairs, Ranulf made his way to the parapet. He stood on the stone walkway, surveying the wide expanse of bailey and outbuildings, and let the wind crash around him. Arms behind his back, he flexed his shoulders, loosening stiffening muscles. Rectifying the castle's immediate turmoil had taken up most of the day. Before he knew it, the sun had moved from a high position and now dipped low into the horizon. Only recently had he found the privacy to read Henry's latest missive.

He ran his thumb over the raised emblem on his ring. The swan's emerald eye twinkled in the twilight, reminding him of his vow to Henry. Ranulf tucked the flapping cloak more securely around his chest. He shook his head. With Clarice's toothsome distraction, he had almost missed the merchant's veiled signal.

In the pocket of his cloak, hidden in the many folds of wool, was a message rolled into a tiny ball, small enough to hide under the hood of his new falcon. It gave the details of Nicholas of Margrave's death. How long had it been since Ranulf last thought of the man and the mysterious maiden hiding behind the manor walls? A few hours at best.

Had it not been for the merchant's relentless shouts of his wares, he would have sent the traveler marching past his castle walls. *Swans.* What was he to do with the pair of swans he had purchased? He no longer had an urgent need of them. Lord Nicholas of Margrave's death had seen to that.

Ranulf crushed the missive in his hand. The news of Lord Margrave's death should have brought a reasonable amount of relief. Instead, it affirmed his suspicions. The traitor had not plotted alone.

He recalled the whisperings at court: The old lord had never recovered from the death of his first wife and her stillborn child. Soon after their deaths he had wed again, this time to his late wife's sister, Lady Annora, and she had borne him a son, Robert.

The death of a loved one was damaging to the mind and heart. Ranulf knew this. The death of his wife and unborn child had crushed him, too. His brain had frozen on the eve of their deaths. Yet that missing span of time had left him with a scar on his face to carry as a reminder of how life could change in an instant. It kept him wondering who had been there on that evil night. Had his soul become so dark that he could have taken the lives of those he cared most for? *Did I murder them?*

'Twas unfathomable.

Ranulf took a deep, steadying breath and did what he had done every day since their deaths. He searched his memory, trying to find the missing pieces.

King Henry had arranged their marriage in the name of the crown. Ranulf had no choice but to agree to wed Mary. Fate had allowed them only two nights to discover each other in their marriage bed before the king's business had taken him away. 'Twas a miracle their brief union had produced a child. *A glimmer of happiness. Before it faded.*

Ranulf refused to admit it to anyone, but he had begun to doubt whether his marriage had been real. Their time together had been too short. And their last night together had ended in heated words and accusations. He had returned home early to beg forgiveness for his distrust of his lady wife. He had found her in the stables. And then . . . ah, if only he could recall more than returning from the darkness, confused and bleeding.

He gripped the stone ledge. Those moments he could not recall had left his wife and child dead in their wake.

His mouth twisted. Death was for men. Soldiers trained to fight, witnessing destruction all around them. 'Twas not meant for little ones who had never experienced the first rays of sunlight or the many colors of the setting sun. Nor was it meant for good women . . . like his wife.

Bracing his hands against the parapet, he hung his head and leaned against the wall. He did not deserve happiness and peace. His life of secrets had become too dark for a wife or children of his own. Loneliness was for the best.

* * *

Clarice turned over on her stomach and rested her cheek on her hands. Had she any good sense, she would have refused to lie in his bed another night.

Exhaustion won out in the war of wills, forcing her to nestle within the pile of furs. She punched the thick mattress one more time and squinted at the window. Lord Ranulf's veiled threats kept her worried, wondering if he meant to take his interrogation into the evening hours, when no one would witness his cruel treatment.

She pulled the ribbon from under her pillow and slid the satin across her lips. When she had heard a peddler requesting entrance to sell his wares, she had hoped 'twas *her* peddler standing at Sedgewic's gate.

Clarice let her imagination bring the dark stranger back to Sedgewic. Determined to succeed in his quest, having searched the lands, he had at last found his lady fair. He would scoop her up, cradling her in his strong arms, promising never to let her go.

She snorted. Instead of a rescuer, her enemy had become her jailer. Instead of freedom outside the walls of Margrave Manor, she had found another prison.

They were an uncivilized bunch here. That child, Hamish, was as unruly as the rest of them. He must have thought his dark tales would frighten her. However, Robert's behavior had served her well, teaching her that not everything said could be trusted.

She fingered the rough edges where the binding had gouged a ridge along her skin. Tender to the touch, her breasts ached after the release. Sensitive from the coarse linen, her nipples crested as the soft linen slid over their peaks. The ache increased.

Heat rushed to her cheeks. Eyes the color of mist rising from the glen surrounding Margrave Manor danced in front of her face. Arms, strong as any steel lock, banded around her waist. She placed a tentative finger against her lips. A wave of warmth spread across her breasts, down through her belly, centering between her thighs.

Restless, she listened to the guards outside the door speaking of their desire to ride with the king. She, too, prayed they would get on with it. Striding to the high window with the fur wrapped around her shoulders, she searched the bailey and the parapet, outlined by the moon, rising from the shadows. More guards remained on the wall.

Her father's death weighed heavy on her heart. Walls within walls were closing in.

Shivering, Clarice worried about Maud. The chores might prove too much for her frail bones. She knew Annora and Robert would never lift a finger to help themselves, let alone each other. Pulling the fur closer, she drew the soft down to her cheek.

Maud's words echoed in her heart. *Find the wolf. Discover who forced the noose around your father's neck.* Once armed with the evidence of her father's murderer, she would carry it to King Henry. 'Twas certain the king would then proclaim Nicholas of Margrave's innocence and forgive all charges against her family.

With or without the lord's approval, she had to find a way out of Sedgewic.

Clarice paced the floor, the tail of the fur sweeping across the wooden planks with each step. No one brought up a load of logs and the fire in the hearth had long since died. Her stomach complained of its emptiness. Hungry, shivering, and exhausted, she was certain this was some type of torture.

Determined to greet anyone who stuck his head through the doorway with honeyed words and a pasted-on smile, she nearly jumped out of her skin when the door was thrown open. All thoughts of graciousness disappeared as she turned on the unwelcome company.

"Oh, 'tis you."

Despite wanting to disregard Hamish's presence, she felt her shoulders relax under his quizzical gaze.

"Who'd you think 'twas? Lord Ranulf?"

She lifted her empty hands. "Have no fear. I am unarmed."

He stayed near the doorway, proving he did not believe her. "I'm not afraid of you." He responded to the rise in her brow. "You'd already be dead if you were to harm me again."

"I see." She wrapped her arms around her middle, warding off the child's chilling declaration.

Clarice watched as he pulled out a chunk of bread from his pocket. The scent from the warm feast swirled in the chilled room. Its heat curled in little coils of steam. Staunchly pretending not to notice when he smacked his lips over the crusty treat, her stomach betrayed her and growled.

"What consumes your lord's attention for half a day and into the night?"

Hamish peered over his next mouthful, licking the flaky crust off his upper lip. Shrugging, he bit down before answering. His mouth stuffed, he pushed the wad to the side. "'Tis a secret meeting. Something 'bout traitor swans."

"Trumpet swans," she corrected him.

Cocking his head to one side, he squinted, feeling the words. He shrugged and ripped off another bite.

She focused somewhere past his ear to avoid seeing the half-chewed mess in his mouth. "How would you know what they speak of if they meet in secret?"

"I can show you," he said. "If you'd like to see."

"Leave this chamber without permission? The guards may have something to say about that."

"Already told them the lord sent me to fetch you. They'll never know I lied." He watched her, weighing his decision, then motioned for her to follow. "I might even show you the hidden tunnel."

"Why?" Clarice eyed his palm. 'Twas greasy from the spread of butter and creased with black lines of dirt. "Why would you do that for me?"

"Never mind." Hamish withdrew his hand and rubbed it on his backside. "If you like being locked in here, don't bother coming with me."

She knelt in front of him, gently touching his shoulder. "I don't want to see you punished."

Hamish glanced at her hand resting on his tunic. He pulled out another chunk of bread from his pocket. "Aren't you in trouble, too?"

Clarice rocked back on her heels. "You heard this in their meeting?"

He shook his head and handed the bread to her as a peace offering. "No. I heard you tell him in the solar."

Ignoring the dirt and grease, she snatched the bread from his fingers before he took it away. Savoring every flaky morsel, she took her time as she pondered the boy. 'Twas possible he told the truth. Sedgewic's household had forgotten her. The lack of food and fuel for the hearth was proof of that. If she were to go with Hamish, she might just slip away without notice.

She licked her lips of the crumbs. "Show me your secret, my dear Hamish."

He eyed her, looking as if reconsidering his offer. "Do you promise not to tell?"

"I promise. We'll be as quiet as fairies in the forest."

His face lit with excitement and he held out his cap. "You'll want this. There are spiders and such. I don't want you screaming when they get in your hair."

An involuntary shudder suppressed, she nodded and tucked in her curls.

Hamish opened the door and led her out. His chest puffed out, he lied with perfection, telling the guard his lordship had requested the prisoner be brought to the solar. Before the guard thought to detain them, they scurried down the hallway and around the corner.

They skittered to a stop in front of a threadbare tapestry portraying a stern-faced rider sitting astride a rearing destrier. The castle's white spires stood proudly behind his shoulder. Hamish lifted a corner of the dusty wall hanging. He crooked a finger and pointed to the shadows.

"This way," he said and slipped behind the tapestry. The maw of the stairway led them into darkness.

Stifling a sneeze, Clarice pondered which step would not crumble under their weight. There had to be another way. "Hamish, I don't think—"

The boy was gone.

Chapter 13

Ranulf stood at the hearth, gripping the back of his neck. With a great sigh, he spun on his heel and headed straight for the pitcher. He lifted it to his lips, draining it dry before dropping it to the table.

The wooden bench groaned as Nathan shifted his long legs. He cast a questioning look toward Ranulf, who chased the drip of moisture formed on the side of the pitcher with his finger. "Problems?" he asked.

Ranulf grunted and threw himself into the chair by the fireplace. He brooded over the tips of his boots. Annoyed beyond explanation, he chewed over the words before spitting them out. "I won't be joining you on your journey to France."

"What?" Nathan leaned forward. "Surely you jest. By Christ, we need your sword."

Ranulf shook his head. He looked up, struggling to contain the anger boiling his innards. "He needs me here. Those who plot against the throne are still running loose."

"But you said Margrave was dead."

"Yes, Nathan, but nothing was proven before his death."

Darrick wandered over to the hearth to warm his hands against the heat of the flames. Frowning, he turned to include both men in his news. "I've word that Henry's departure from Southampton has been delayed. He still gathers his men and has yet to leave port."

Ranulf rubbed the aching spot at his temple "Leaving him vulnerable."

"More vulnerable than at any other time," Nathan agreed.

"That is why you must leave at once. You'll—" A crumbling of stone rattled inside the wall. Bounding to his feet, the conversation forgotten, Ranulf searched the corners of the old solar.

Once again he noticed the shabbiness of the old tapestries. It appeared no one had cleaned them for some time. He peered closer. A breeze from some unnoticed hole rustled the edges. Eyes narrowed, his hand rested on the sword's hilt. Ranulf tightened his grip and attempted to regain his focus. "—take your men. See to our king's safety."

Nathan nodded and rose to take his leave. "Darrick?"

"A moment." Darrick paced the short steps to Ranulf, seeking his attention. "We never finished our talk the other night. About your Mary's death. Have you still no memory of that night?"

"None that makes sense. Bits and pieces. Fragments."

Darrick rubbed his chin and looked up to where Ranulf was still gazing. "I spoke with your stableboy."

"Micah?"

"Good lad with the horses but likes to talk. Given enough encouragement, that is. Says you had a visitor that night."

"Not that I can recall." Ranulf pinned him with a glance. "What else did he say?"

"Said he came to visit while you were away." Darrick cleared his throat. "Many times."

"Did Micah give a name? A description?"

"No. The visitor kept to the lady's chambers. Came and went without anyone the wiser. Appears no one except Micah ever laid eyes on him." Darrick tapped his ear. "But they can hear."

Ranulf's muscles bunched when Darrick placed a hand on his forearm. He shook himself free. Turning his focus to the wall again, he worked to regain control over his rage. He fisted the hilt of his sword until his bones ached. *Fool. Fool. Fool.* The word pounded in his blood, impaling his heart.

Nathan joined them to stare up at the spot and nodded. "Rodents." He angled toward Darrick. "Leave it be. We've our king to protect. Have you any message for Henry, Ranulf?"

"Tell him that his wolf will watch his prey from here."

The walls trembled, drawing Ranulf's attention.

Darrick stepped back a pace as he spoke. "Henry knows of Mary's death?"

Nathan lifted the talisman he wore at his neck, kissing it as he moved away as well.

Ranulf shot a look at his retreating friends. It did not surprise him that Nathan was given to superstition, but the wary look in Darrick's eyes gave him pause. "Of course."

Nathan's brows rose, and he raised his palms to the decrepit surroundings. "This is his idea of punishment?"

Ranulf ignored him, but Darrick could not. "Idiot. Mary lived here for almost a year by herself. His young bride waited for him while he was on a mission for Henry."

"What was so urgent that made you leave your new wife in your matrimonial bed?" Nathan poked Ranulf in the ribs. "Still say you did nothing to gain Henry's ire?"

Ranulf lunged for Nathan but found his right arm held in an iron-fisted grip.

"Let it go," Darrick said. "'Tis jealousy that makes his lips flap."

Ranulf nodded, ready to convince them he did not wish Nathan harm. Laughing good-naturedly, he shrugged off Darrick's hand and led them to the door.

Nathan spun on his heel and bowed low. "Sir Ranulf, lord of Sedgewic, we go to do your bidding." He lifted his head and grinned. "So that our king will not serve us up a like punishment."

Nathan stumbled back as Ranulf's fist connected, knocking him into Darrick's arms. Ranulf rubbed his hand, checking for broken bones. A year of frustration and grief, unanswered questions, and regrets had fueled that blow. Good Christ but 'twas satisfying.

He returned to the solar and listened to the quiet rustling buried somewhere in the wall. Time passed at a snail's pace while he moved about the room, pressing his ear to the stone every few paces.

Saint's bones. He hated to admit Nathan was correct. Vermin overran his home.

The king's wolf? Clarice wanted to scream until her throat bled. Instead, the words tore through her head.

Thanks to the loose stones on the hidden stairway. At one point, she feared they would both go over the cavernous edge. They could not return the way they came. 'Twas now impassable. She and Hamish were trapped behind the wall. Neither one had any idea how to extricate themselves.

She glanced over at the dirty little boy and wondered if he was ever out of trouble. How had he managed to involve her in his adventure in the first place? She must be deranged.

"The wolf," Hamish whispered with awe dripping from his words. "He is the one the stable lads whisper about. The other night they said that the lord was not really a man but an enchanted beast." He leaned toward the spy hole and peered through the wall. "Suppose 'tis true?"

"Get away from there," she hissed. "He might hear you!"

"No, his ear is pressed against the stone by the chimney."

The hole in the wall tapestry offered her enough light to see the tired shadows under Hamish's eyes. Upon entering the tunnel, she had been terrified of finding him at the bottom of the stone passageway. Had she been quick thinking she could have kept him from climbing down into the dark abyss. She should have been surer of foot, lighter of body—the list was endless. However she looked at it, she was to blame for finding herself caught inside the castle walls. She would save his scolding for later.

Seeing that he was going to dine on yet another dirty fingernail, Clarice dug in her apron and found the small bite of bread she had tucked inside her belt.

Hamish looked at the offering, his stomach grumbling before he reached out to take the tiny morsel.

She pushed back a ringlet of his soft cap of hair. "Have you thought of another way out?"

His head dropped, his chin trembling against his chest. With a violent shake of his head, he confirmed what she had dreaded. Her stomach threatened to do a dizzying dance.

"Mayhap there's another tunnel? There has to be a way for sound to travel to the other side of the room."

Hamish considered that possibility and nodded in agreement. He pressed his ear to the hole. "Wait! 'Tis someone else in the solar." He rolled a shoulder to look up at her. "Lord Ranulf doesn't sound very pleased neither."

Erwina stood in the solar, looking more frazzled than Ranulf had ever seen her. "My lord, if you please. If I may have a word."

"Hmm?" His brows furrowed. He had no desire to hear any more complaints regarding the leaking ceilings, crumbling walls, or sagging floors. It seemed the endless list of repairs grew with every day. He was tempted to turn over the responsibilities to someone more deserving and request—no, beg—for a mission that sent him far away from the daily concerns surrounding his broken-down castle.

He waved her in, hoping her complaints would not take long. A scratching sound came from within the walls, drawing his attention. "Wait. Did you hear that?"

Shaking her head, she hurried to his side. She eyed him closely, her hands fidgeting with her apron.

Incredulous, he leaned in. "You cannot possibly say you don't hear anything."

Erwina rocked on her toes. "'My lord, 'tis urgent that I tell you about the young . . . guest in your bedchamber."

Ranulf grabbed her arm, drawing her closer. The attempt to shut out what he was convinced was the impossibility of pounding coming from within the walls and outside the door was in vain. "There. You had to have heard that thumping sound. Clearly, it sounds as if it's coming from inside the walls."

"My lord," her voice rose. "If you please—"

Startled by her tone, he released his hold. Mistress Erwina looked at him as if he had grown three eyes and a tail. His gaze leveled upon the poor woman and shut out the sounds that surely everyone in Christendom heard. "Speak."

"The maiden, Clarice." Her trembling fingers pressed against her lips before she spoke again. "She is not a child," she whispered. "She is a young woman."

Keeping his face hidden behind a mask, cool and calm, he bent over and whispered in her ear, "I know."

He turned as a round-cheeked maiden popped her head into the solar. "What is it . . . ?"

"Faith," Erwina said, interjecting the servant's name.

The cherub bobbed her head once. "Sir Nathan sent me to tell you that a stranger rides this way."

"Christ's blood on the cross." Ranulf gripped the back of his neck, kneading the tense muscles there. The siren's call of the battle-field grew stronger. He needed to leave this all to someone more deserving. Perhaps Sir Nathan Staves . . .

"Please." Erwina grabbed Ranulf's sleeve, blocking his path. "Before they arrive." Her eyes darted to the door. "Until a few days ago I believed her dead, but now I have to believe otherwise. She is—" Mouth gaping, she stumbled back.

A man dressed in homespun leggings and a plain tunic barged

past Erwina. His rat-faced mouth pinched tight. Beneath a woodsman's cap, his eyes glittered with excitement as he stopped in front of Ranulf. He swept back his cloak and bent his knee. "I come to you, my lord, with a message."

Ranulf's gut tightened. "Leave us, Mistress Erwina."

Erwina cleared her throat and cast the messenger a withering glance. "Of all the damnable interruptions. My lord, I really must . . ."

"Now."

While he waited until the tormenting woman was out of earshot, he searched the man for markings to reveal his identity. "And who might you be?"

"Name's Harald." Waving aside additional questions, the stranger removed his cap in a flourish. "There has been an attempted murder."

"Here? On Sedgewic lands?" Ranulf's hands fisted at his waist. "By whose order do you deliver such a rumor?"

The man bobbed his head like a duck diving for its meal in a pond. "No, my lord. I've been sent by one of your neighbors to the west. To warn you."

"Margrave?" Ranulf folded his arms over his chest. "This is not news. The man hanged himself."

"Not the old lord. The new one. A serving wench attacked Robert of Margrave. I witnessed it."

Something about this man made Ranulf search his narrow face. Perhaps 'twas the man's nervous fidgeting or his inability to meet his gaze. The man told half truths; he was certain of it. But why be linked to someone wanted for treason? "You saw the woman attack the Margrave's only son and you could not stop her?"

"No! I arrived after the murderous bitch ran off. 'Twas easy enough to see she stabbed him in the leg and left him to die."

"I suppose leg wounds can be a dirty business if left untended." Ranulf shook his head.

Harald crushed the woodsman's cap in his hand. "'Twas his noggin that took the brunt of it. The way he was bound to the table, he looked like a bleedin' hog readied for the spit." His throat bobbed as he held out a parchment. "This here is her."

Ranulf took the rough sketch of a nondescript woman with long dark hair. It could have been half the population. Strangers came across his lands on a regular basis but always in groups. Women never traveled alone. Except for one.

"'Tis suggested that she is dangerous and will strike again." Harald shoved his straw-colored hair from his sweating brow.

The walls seemed to breathe with every renewed thump and bang. Ranulf focused his gaze, peering into the messenger's pale face. "How do you come by this?"

"I . . . uh, was hired." His eyes shifted to the nearest door. "To bring this message. As a friendly gesture."

"And you would do this for someone who is wanted by the king for treason? This family is said to have plotted against the king of England. Your king and mine. I should hold you here for questioning."

"Oh, my lord," the man cried. "But I know nothing! I'm just a messenger."

Confusion erupted as the hole in the wall spewed out its contents onto the solar floor with a blast of thunder. Harald danced out of the way, protecting his feet from coming in contact with the whirling bundle of limbs. He lifted his cloak away from the debris and bent to peer under Clarice's oversize cap. "And what of the murderess?"

"Murderess?" Ranulf firmly moved Harald out of the way but kept a solid grip on his shoulder. "I assure you that we'll send word if we see someone who fits the woman's description." He gave him a quick shake, drawing him away from casting frightened glances to the nearest escape. "Where did you say Lady Annora and her son were hiding?"

"I didn't . . ." Harald's mouth gaped like a landed fish. "I don't know."

"I see." The lord of Sedgewic pointed to the spot beside the rubble. "Stay here until Sir Nathan can see you on your way." An awkward pause settled between them before he added, "He'll want to ride with you. For your safety, of course."

Clarice kept her face hidden underneath the hat. Without a word, she rose from the pile of rubble and dusted off her skirt.

Ranulf strode toward the beasties wreaking havoc to his albeit crumbling, home. His jaw muscles leaped in irritation. "What? No apologizes for demolishing my solar? Unsettling my home? Injuring one of the children?"

Lips pressed together in a firm line, Clarice jerked away from his hand when he reached out to steady her balance. "Really, my lord, I don't think any of these can be considered my fault. Perhaps you should hire additional masons. Your castle appears to be in disrepair."

After locating the slipper that had fallen off in the flight through the wall, she limped over to fetch it.

Hamish's plaintive moan drew their attention. He lay in a ball, covering his head with his hands.

Ranulf tugged her cap down low and nudged her toward the boy. "See to Hamish. Take him to his room."

She opened her mouth and snapped it closed. Her eyes narrowed as she stumbled over to the boy.

Freed from his prison inside the wall, Hamish grinned up at them. There were scratches on his face and hands. Dust and chunks of crumbling stone matted his hair. Two almond-shaped holes peeped out from under gray lashes coated with dirt. "I told you we'd be just fine."

"Expect me to deal with both of you later," Ranulf said. He cast a glance over his shoulder. "Damn."

Harald, the rat-faced messenger, was gone.

Chapter 14

While Sir Nathan and the soldiers gave chase after Harald, Clarice hid on the parapet, high above the bailey. There had to be a way for her to escape the castle. She watched the men as they carried out their orders, hauling planks of wood to shore up the outer wall. Their backs were bent, strong muscles stretching and straining under the weight of stone.

One broad back in particular caught her eye. Lord Ranulf labored far into the morning, rarely stopping for a break.

In a rare moment of rest, he poured a pitcher of water over his head. She gasped as rivulets cascaded over his shoulders, racing to the narrow band at his waist. The clothing plastered to his body allowed her a full view of the form beneath.

She leaned against the stone to get a closer look and flinched as the laborer turned. Her fingers dug into the wall, knuckles whitening under her grip. *The king's wolf. Father's red wolf. Was he friend or foe? Had she been sent to the wolf's den? Very possibly to her death?*

He stretched his arms overhead. The wet linen clung to his chest, molding around the planes. Bands of lean flesh pressed against the seams of his breeches. He arched his back, bringing the juncture between his legs to full view.

Clarice frowned, chewing on the inside of her lip. *What kind of a fool am I?* A score of men worked in the yard and she followed the enemy as if he carried her last meal. Tearing her gaze from the man, she forced her attention to the children in the courtyard.

Mistress Erwina had found Hamish. He squirmed under her hold, dragging his feet as if being led to the devil himself. Pulling him along by the ear, she led the boy to the lord's side.

Clarice regretted that Hamish had showed her the secret passage. She was the reason the lad was in trouble. Her knees wobbled as shrieks filled the bailey. She stood on tiptoe to lean over the parapet, searching for the fastest way down to the ground.

"What's this?" Her head cocked to one side as she listened in disbelief.

The shrieks had turned to laughter. Lord Ranulf now stood under the shade tree, holding Hamish upside down and tickling his ribs. After Hamish's tepid plea for release, he set the boy back on his feet and nudged him toward the workers. She sighed, her back pressed against the castle wall. The lad did not need rescuing after all.

Clarice rubbed her lip and searched the bailey yard. If she planned well, she could escape Sedgewic while everyone was busy attending to the repair of the solar. There were horses aplenty tied at the posts, awaiting their riders. However, they stood in plain sight and offered no chance of escape. Her attention caught a tall black horse, saddled and standing by itself near the edge of the stables. It looked similar to Robert's stallion. Hidden in the shadows as it was, had she not been searching, she never would have noticed it.

She wasted no time in finding the stairway leading to the kitchen garden. She kept to the shadows, recalling the layout of the outer buildings, which she had seen from the window of the bedchamber. Angling away from the corner of the garrison, she made her way to the bailey yard. Smoke swelled from the smithy's hut, creating a cloud of haze to help her slip past the fire pit and anvil. Once across the bailey, she headed to the stables and ran to the side where she had seen the beautiful black horse.

Clarice skidded to a stop. "Shite," she whispered.

The horse looked much larger now than it had from the parapet. She swallowed the dust lodged in her throat.

The stallion towered over her. Noting a stranger's scent, it tossed its head. Nostrils flaring, its fiery gaze cut into her resolve. The powerful hooves stamped the earth, threatening to shatter her hope of escape.

She had to hurry. The racket seemed to be louder than her heart attacking her rib cage. Someone was certain to come to see what agitated the beast.

Frantic, Clarice glanced around. A mounting block was nowhere in sight. There was no possible way she would be able to get into the saddle, let alone manage that demon. There had to be another way. Another horse. *Buttercup.*

After checking to see if anyone came, she ran to the stable's large double doors and slipped through. Darkness enveloped her. Without light from the lanterns, the shadows consumed everything. Her nose itched from the musky scent of horses and hay. But the stables were empty of groomsmen. Even the stableboy was absent. *Why? Where was everyone?*

Clarice's skin prickled under her chemise. Someone was there, stumbling in the shadows. A curse and a clang of metal rang out in the stable. *Hurry! Hurry!*

Forcing her legs to move, one by one she searched the stalls. Buttercup, her father's gray palfrey, nickered. The old war-horse leaned its neck over the door and nudged her cheek.

Relief flooded through her veins, weakening the dam that kept her tears at bay. Someone had tied bits of ribbon in the long strands of white hair. "Oh, Buttercup, you are a treasure," she whispered against the horse's neck. "Who has treated you so well? Micah? The one Hamish chatters about?"

Buttercup's velvet ears twitched, then flattened back. She began backing up, fidgeting anxiously, shaking her full mane.

With everyone distracted, she opened Buttercup's stall and led her out of the stable.

She turned to soothe the agitated horse. "Come, girl, 'tis a short walk to the gate and then—"

Their escape came to an abrupt halt when she backed into a solid wall of muscle.

Ranulf stood in her path. Fine white lines bloomed from his thinned lips. Silently, he held out his hand and waited for her to surrender the reins.

Clarice measured the distance from stable to main gate and knew she would never make it. Buttercup had only known her father's seat and had had little time to adjust to her own. If she were to ride without a saddle, 'twould end disastrously.

She bit her lip and winced. Nodding in surrender, she handed Ranulf the reins and turned to walk away.

His arm, corded with muscle, wrapped around her waist. "I think not," Ranulf said softly.

Clarice closed her eyes. The knot in her stomach grew. She refused to give him the satisfaction of knowing he terrified her at that moment. "Lord Ranul—"

"Enough."

Before she could attempt an argument, he flipped her over his shoulder and had her hanging upside down. Gasping for air, she bounced upon his shoulder as he took the stairs two steps at a time.

Her head pounded with her heart. She glared at his backside as it came perilously close to her nose. The waistband she had noted earlier was close enough that she could touch it with her lips. Eyes squeezed tight shut, she hoped at least one of her prayers would be heard. *Dear Lord, let me survive his punishment. Then let vengeance be mine!*

She kicked out and bit his back. Although rewarded with a yelp, her joy was short-lived as she earned a resounding smack on her backside.

"Try that again," Ranulf said, "and I swear by all that is holy, you'll get more of the same."

Clarice peeked out from the veil of her hair. Her humiliation mounted as giggling children followed behind them like a flock of ducks. They had paused, watching wide-eyed as he carried her up the flight of stairs. When she heard the door kicked shut she realized they had reached their destination.

Chapter 15

What am I to do with this wench?
'Twas unclear why he had brought Clarice to the privacy of his bedchamber. 'Twould have been a better idea to question her in the remains of the solar, his friends at his side to add their opinions. Instead, Darrick and Nathan were out chasing their own prey.

In times past, he had been too softhearted with the gentler sex. And what had it gained him?

Grimacing, he scanned the bedchamber. Until recently, it had been devoid of Mary's memory. Now there were signs of a lady's presence. A woman's cloak hung on a peg. A brush lay on the table by the fire, ready to bring shine to her hair. Blankets, tossed about, showed signs of a restless sleep. His blood stirred at the thought of Clarice in his bed.

Her skirt rode up her leg, revealing tender flesh and a well-turned ankle. She had stopped flailing long enough for him to rest his hands on delicately shaped calves. No longer dodging a well-planted foot to his chest, he enjoyed the satiny feel of her skin. His thoughts danced out of control. *Is the back of her knee as soft as her calves? Does she sigh when a lover places a kiss upon that tender crease?*

"God's nails! Take your hands off me, you whoreson dog." Her muffled voice reverberated against his spine.

Ranulf hesitated. As much as the thought of letting her drop to the floor was compelling, he could not bring himself to do it. Instead, the bed beckoned him, standing as a refuge in a desolate land. It promised him a brief paradise in a lonely, barren life.

"If you don't, I swear I will give you the same as I gave Robert," she warned.

Ranulf froze. *Robert of Margrave? She knew his given name?* Her barb struck him solidly. *What did they mean to each other?*

He ran his hand up her backside and jerked her forward. Freeing her waist from his shoulder, he let her slide down the front of his chest. Without a word, he whipped her around, pointed her to the bed. He gave her a little shove between the shoulder blades with the palm of his hand. She landed on the mattress with a thump.

Her lips curled in a snarl as she pushed the wayward strands of hair out of her wide eyes. "Touch me again my lord," she said, struggling to rise, "and I promise you will get what you deserve."

Was she one of Robert's whores? Willing to spy for her master? Ranulf stepped closer, shrinking the space until the air between them felt as if it snapped with lightning. He squashed the urge to touch her, jerking his hands away and clasping them behind his back. "You will not ply your trade in Sedgewic."

Her outraged gasp twisted his gut. Clarice came within an inch of his chest. "Exactly who . . . what do you think I am?"

Ranulf lifted her chin. "You're Robert's play—"

She jerked her face away. "I would rather stick a blade into his putrid flesh than have him look in my direction." She stepped out of his reach, clutching her skirt as if to run. "I've done it before. I'll do it again."

"You are his serving wench?" Ranulf advanced, stalking her as she attempted to evade his questions.

"You're wrong."

He jammed a hand through his hair and refused to hear her denials. She was crying now, and he hated it when women shed false tears. Had it been a lovers' quarrel? Had she wanted too much from the Margraves? This should have encouraged him. Her allegiance was attainable for a price. But whose? His jaw tightened. *I have to know.*

He grabbed her arms. "Did you tire of a defeated old man to pursue his stepson instead? 'Tis the truth, is it not?" He pushed his point. "What's the matter, my sweet? Did you learn what a snake Robert really is?"

"No! I—"

"Was there poison in his bite? His fangs a bit too sharp?" He stopped, suddenly aware of the difference in their strength, and released her.

"Please. I beg you to hear me out."

Ranulf snapped his head in agreement, regretting it as soon as he did. He searched her face, looking for the lies.

"Robert came to my bedchamber and tried to . . ." Fear hid behind the shadows in her eyes. She shook her head, the cap of raven glistening in the light. ". . . I protected myself. I didn't try to kill him." Her legs sagged and she dropped to the floor. "I didn't mean to hurt him. Just scare him away. Fa . . . Lord Margrave was no longer there to see that Robert kept his distance."

Another abused servant? But how did they miss her in their raid on Margrave Manor? Clarice trembled, her teeth clicking together. Ranulf sighed and knelt where she sat huddled on the floor. Perhaps she knew of the maiden with the long raven hair. Pressing her might break her, but he did not need a broken soul. He needed answers. He tipped her chin so that she met his gaze and found himself lost in the azure chips wet with tears.

"There was another who needed my protection from the snakes of life. And I failed." He stroked the pad of his finger across her cheek and caught a crystal tear before it followed the others. "I was young and foolish to believe that here in this dilapidated castle we were safe enough, even without walls to protect us. But I forgot that sometimes we must be protected from ourselves." He let his hand settle on her shoulder. "My offer of protection stands. The Margraves will no longer harm you."

"I . . . uh, thank you." She withdrew, leaning away from him. Her mouth wobbled in an attempt to smile. Her hands never ceased plucking at the folds of her skirt.

Ranulf caught her fidgeting fingers, urging her to trust him. "And now, thanks to two adventurers, I am forced to examine the inner walls sooner than I planned."

Grimacing, she ducked her head. "I'm sorry about the damage to your castle, Lord Ranulf."

Ranulf smoothed back her hair. "Not to worry. You and Hamish have done me a favor."

Her eyes wide, she tilted her head as she waited for an explanation.

"I have finally found a task that will keep Hamish out of the way, and Erwina will get her wish. For some time now she has been begging me to work on the inner rooms."

"All the same, my lord, I know I should have stopped Hamish."

"Agreed. But it's over and done with. We have much bigger things to discuss."

The wary look returned to her eyes. "Such as?"

"Such as what you overheard in the solar."

"Nothing, my . . . my lord." Her lips trembled. "What shall you do with me?"

Ranulf felt as if he was questioning one of the children about the theft of a pastry. She lied like no other. He drummed his fingers against his thigh. She told a tale as well as any child. Something tied Robert to her skirt, and that thought tasted like a piece of foul meat.

"I think, for now, we shall keep you to ourselves. I believe Robert will be busy enough hiding from the king's men. He should have no trouble forgetting a pretty maiden. Even one as succulent as yourself. Until all the Margraves are run to ground, you may consider this your sanctuary." He rose and dusted off his breeches. "Well?" he said, holding out his hand. "Do you prefer sitting on the cold stone or would you rather a chair?"

A tenuous peace hung in the air with his outstretched hand.

Nodding, she put her hands in his. Although he led her to a more comfortable seat by the hearth, he could feel the fear radiating through her shaking fingers. *Jesus on the cross, I'm not taking her to the gallows.*

After seeing her settled, he helped himself to the contents from the pitcher on the table. Keeping his distance, he watched Clarice continue to fidget. The fire illuminated hints of scarlet in her dark hair. Dust and dirt sprinkled over her bodice and skirt. Clarice tapped her fingers on the arm of the chair. Her delicate mouth formed a firm line. She leaned forward, perched on the edge. A pretty peregrine falcon. "Why do they call you the wolf?"

Ranulf flinched, tipping the cup he had raised to his lips. Regaining his composure, he shook his head. "I know not what you mean."

"No use denying it. I know what I heard. You are close to the king, are you not?"

"You must have misunderstood. My given name is Ranulf." He sounded the last slowly, pronouncing each syllable. "A minor lord with a decaying castle."

"Lord Ranulf—"

"Just Ranulf will do."

Clarice squinted at him as if she had images of wolves dancing in her head. Releasing a defeated sigh, she conceded, "Ranulf . . . what can you tell me about a red wolf that is said to dwell on these lands?"

"Only grays live in the hills to the north."

"'Tis the red wolf I am interested in." Holding up her finger, she indicated the solitary figure. "One red wolf."

"'Tis an odd curiosity you have." He moved to the door before she probed further. "I must go now."

"Wait." She rose from the chair. "Please don't lock me in."

Everything he had learned in the last few minutes rang in his mind. Clarice was close to a man accused of treason and Nicholas's loathsome stepson, Robert. Her questions about the red wolf bothered him even more. And she had lied about not hearing any of the discussion in the solar. He hated to think of her pretty neck stretched for the executioner. Although Margrave was dead, the plot continued. She might have knowledge he could use to save the king. He had to keep her close. Very, very close. On second thought, perhaps he should allow just enough rope to snare his little rabbit.

"You will come with me." He held out his hand, wrapping his fingers around her wrist. "'Tis said that idle hands are the source of mischief."

She let out a breath and followed him obediently to the door. With a commanding nod, the guards moved their speared staffs so they might pass. Her steps dragged as they walked through the hall and beyond the sweating soldiers practicing in the yard.

"This way." Ranulf looked back when she did not move. He gave another tug. "Come."

"What is that?" Clarice pointed to the lone tower standing in the corner of the bailey. She dug her heels into the ground and clawed at his hand. "Please, I pray you, don't take me there."

Ranulf scratched his jaw. The woman was daft. Mayhap Erwina would have a draught of something to calm her. "Come," he said again.

Ignoring her objections, he unlocked the heavy gate. He turned to draw her in, noting her ashen face, her eyes wide with fear. He paused and waited until her struggles dissipated. Her lips parted, she gasped for air. Her bodice rose and fell. He fought the urge to close her open mouth with a kiss. Drawn into her web, his body leaned in of its own accord. *A spider's web of lies,* his head argued, *or an innocent pawn in a deadly game of power?*

He jerked back with a start. Instead of tasting her lips, he touched her jaw with the pad of his thumb. The heat raced to his heart. Riveted by the rapid beat of the delicate vein in the vulnerable hollow of her slender neck, he could not tear his gaze away.

"Draw the water, my sweet. 'Tis time to bathe."

Ranulf smiled wickedly when her mouth snapped shut in disbelief. "And do not attempt to leave." He nodded to the parapet, where guards stood watch. "I will know as soon as you set foot outside these walls."

Chapter 16

Clarice set her jaw in disbelief. He had walked away. If the man's bones were available, she would have ground them into meal for her bread. Draw the water for his bath indeed. Fortunately for him, he had left before she'd found her tongue. And her teeth. Her lips pressed together, she bit back the words she wanted to fling at his head.

Hands on her hips, she edged toward the garden gate to test its lock. Movement on the wall caught her attention. She froze as the man standing guard lifted a gloved hand in salute. "Save me from idiotic brutes," she muttered and spun on her heel.

Steaming with anger, she followed a path that led away from the garden gate. She kicked at patches of emerald green lawn. Thoughts of devising a way to sabotage her . . . host's . . . bath flitted through her mind. One by one, she regarded and discarded each idea.

Disappointed with her lack of creative ideas for retribution, she had to admit that she had no solid proof that he was responsible for her father's death. Yes, he had led the king's soldiers to Margrave Manor. But try as she might, she could not imagine Ranulf returning to force her father to hang himself from the broad beam in his chamber. He himself had dealt with her without raising a hand in anger. 'Twas more than she could say for her own family. However, the day was young. She dared not think what he would do once he discovered she was Nicholas of Margrave's daughter.

She so wanted to discount Maud's whispered words of her father's final message. The similarity of Ranulf's name was nothing more than a coincidence. But she was certain the other knight had called him the king's red wolf. And if the Lord of Sedgewic was not the red wolf, she had to keep searching.

She ruffled the purple tufts of lavender growing along the path. She had to leave Sedgewic. Find her answers elsewhere.

Lost in thought, she paused, the purple buds in her palm forgotten. Knowing her family as she did, they carried themselves far from king and creditors. Certainly they would not return to Margrave.

Her pulse raced. She must go back to Maud and question her once more. There had to be a missing piece of information. Her dear friend might recall the remainder of the message. With another clue in hand, she might find the right direction and finally be free.

Her gaze cut to the watchtower. First she would have to learn how to scale these fortified walls. Grudgingly she gave Lord Ranulf his due. While setting out to create an impenetrable wall, he had made one that kept them in as well. Young Hamish would know a way to conquer the castle's barrier, though she hated the thought of involving the lad in her next escape. The knot of purple flowers along the path received a swat of frustration. There had to be another way.

She stumbled to a stop and stared at the odd sight before her.

Erected in the garden was a tent spreading over the lush garden. 'Twas a ridiculous collage of colored silks. Caught by the gentle breeze, the vibrant silk threads danced and shimmered under the sun. 'Twas reminiscent of the harem tents her father had spoken of on his rare visits. A tent of which any Saracen worth his salt would be envious. Visions of dancing girls, glittering jewels, and kohl-lined eyes drew her closer.

Was the lord of Sedgewic forming a harem? Unable to stop her imagination, she added a man to her vision. She slipped her hand into her pocket and touched the ribbon. The peddler.

Flipping open the tent flap, she peered inside. Shadows wavered as the rose-filled breeze wafted through the silken structure. An oval brass tub stood under the canopy. 'Twas big enough to accommodate the handsome lord's muscled body, with room for one more. Heat bloomed in her cheeks.

On shaking legs, she stepped inside the doorway to closer examine the container. She groaned. 'Twould take forever to fill.

Lord Ranulf had made an effort to point out that he found it necessary that everyone in the castle bathed on a regular basis. Not that she had any aversion to being clean. But this monstrosity was just too big.

The self-centeredness it took to expect a servant to fill the copper tub was unfathomable. Even if he bathed on a monthly basis, let alone once a week, the task to fill it 'twould be great.

She flicked the edge, creating a hollow ringing. Never would she expect Maud or the other servants to carry enough water to fill that thing. At Margrave all she had bathed in was a washbowl. Unless one counted the quick dash to the spring, she had always found the water in her chambers sufficient.

Her nose twitched when she caught her own scent and realized the smell of dirt and sweat had penetrated her clothing. The pungent odor threatened to cover the perfumed soap lying on the worktable.

Lifting the pot of soap, she inhaled deeply. Ranulf did have a few redeeming qualities after all. Sage, rosemary, and mint made for a heady perfume. It reminded her of the night he had come to the bed-chamber. Her curiosity grew. Not wishing to examine her next thoughts too closely, she searched for a bucket in which to fill the great tub.

After exploring that area of the gardens, Clarice finally found the well. She cranked the rope up until the end surfaced and discovered the bucket was missing.

Frustrated, she settled herself on a bench outside the tent. What would the lord say when he discovered his bathwater did not await his pleasure? A slow smile began to form. No bath would be drawn for him. She would refuse to bathe as well, letting her stench fill his chambers until he relented. A man so keen on cleanliness would be forced to provide her other accommodations. Then she would work on breaking free from the castle walls.

A sundial nestled in the middle of the lawn. Clarice watched the shadow move gradually to the right. Too soon, the stone bench poked the bruises she had tried to forget. She would rather bite her tongue than admit she was sore from her tumble with Hamish. But the ache was almost beyond ignoring.

Her plan to greet Lord Ranulf with defiance and an empty tub dissolved as the sun bore down upon her head. She was certain that in a matter of minutes 'twould cook her brain. Unable to wait any longer, she had barely taken a step before the garden gate opened. Ready to pounce, she swung around on her captor.

"Saints," a blond cherub yelped. Her eyes were round as saucers as she balanced a tray on one arm and a large bucket hooked on the crook of the other.

Blood rushed to Clarice's cheeks, enflaming her face. In an instant it dawned on her. The child had a key. How else did she enter the garden? "Wait." She put her hand out to stop the child from running away. "Forgive me. No need to be afraid."

Clarice gripped the rim of the bucket, tugging the thing out of the child's clawlike grasp. "Not to worry. Lord Ranulf isn't here."

The child yelped again and took a step back. She turned, tossing the bucket to the ground. Clarice dodged it, avoiding the wooden missile so it didn't strike her shins and grabbed at the serving girl's shoulder.

Air whooped out when the corner of the tray caught Clarice's stomach. Fighting to regain her breath, she almost dumped the tray, laden with a great crust of bread and one large chunk of cheese. The cloth covering the remainder of the tray's contents slipped, revealing two golden apples and a pitcher of something cool and wet to quench her thirst.

Her patience lost, she glared at the food. "For Mercy's sake, will you desist? You needn't fear me!"

The cherub's lips trembled as tears pooled in her eyes. Her cap of blond ringlets bounced as she shook her head. "I'm not Mercy."

With a firm grip on the tray and the girl's attention, Clarice stated her question directly. "Who are you?"

The cherub ducked her head and refused to answer.

Clarice sniffed dramatically at the aromatic cheese. "There is a great deal here. Would you care to partake with me?" Hoping for the best, she tossed her request over her shoulder as she located a place to sit. "Grab the bucket, won't you?"

Warmth settled over her as she heard the obedient clank of the bucket. Her new friend followed, albeit at a safe distance. Clarice sat under a shade tree and held out a large chunk of the bread.

"My thanks," the child murmured around the mouthful. "I'm called Faith."

Clarice smiled back at the rosy-cheeked angel. "And who is Mercy?"

"She is my twin." Faith bobbed her head. "Erwina says we are blessed to have each other, but there are some who believe we are a curse instead."

Clarice held a cup of watered mead to Faith. Gracefully, the little one took it from her hands and waited for her to pour her own.

Although Clarice had been kept from outsiders, Maud had made a point to ensure that when the time came she would have grace and manners so that she would not embarrass herself. She saw that Faith had been taught the same.

"How do you and your sister come to be here? Where are your mother and father?"

"Erwina says we all come from heaven." Her blond curls bounced as she shrugged her shoulders. "Erwina says since our father went to help the king's men, the king's men can help our father."

"Mistress Erwina knows your father? What of your mother? Does she not have a say where you and your sister are fostered? Surely there are more . . ." Clarice searched for the right words as the child's lips begin to tremble. "More exciting places to live. Filled with fairs and laughter."

Faith shook her head. "Our mother and father are gone now. Father died fighting the Welshmen. Erwina says Mama died of a broken heart."

"But why here?"

"Erwina says since the orphanage burned down long ago, Castle Sedgewic has been a place for orphans. Sedgewic can better serve King Henry by allowing us to stay here."

Clarice drew a finger through the green lawn, separating the blades of grass. She dreaded the answer but had to ask. "How did the orphanage burn down?"

Faith's eyes rounded. "You don't know?"

"No. I fear not."

"You have never heard the tale?" Puffed with pride to have a willing listener, Faith launched into her story. "Erwina says—"

Clarice groaned. "Does anyone besides Erwina say anything?"

Faith's brows furrowed as she pondered the question. "Mercy. But Erwina told us both, so it doesn't matter what Mercy says, does it? And Micah tells us stories, although I wish he wouldn't tell them so soon before bed. Mercy says I behave like an infant, but Micah's tale of intruders in the night frighten me. Erwina says he makes them up to hear us squeal. And of course, Lord Ranulf tells us things." Faith leaned over. "But he doesn't raise his voice like he does with the soldiers. Erwina says—"

Clarice waved her hand in surrender. "Pray tell, what did Erwina say?"

Faith paused, cocking her head to one side like a curious little bird. "About what?"

Clarice stifled a groan and rubbed her pounding temples. "I forget."

Faith swung her feet and tapped the rim of the bucket. "Are you ever going to heat the water?"

"I don't think I shall."

Faith's round face registered shock. "Why not?"

The child's delicate sniff told Clarice more than she wanted to know.

"Don't you care to be clean?"

When Faith added that question, Clarice realized she'd heard enough. Without another word, she snatched up the dreaded bucket and marched toward the tent. She stopped. She had no idea how she was to draw the blasted water.

Faith continued, oblivious to the fact that what she was saying barely registered in Clarice's mind. "No one has ever been allowed to bathe in the lord's tub before now. Nor have we ever been allowed in his bathing tent."

"Wha . . . what?" Clarice sputtered. She was the one to take a bath, not Lord Ranulf?

Faith pointed to the corner of the garden. "Over there is the well for fresh water. Beside it is the stone hearth Lord Ranulf built to warm the water. It's kept burning all the time. Hamish says in case of attack it will already be lit." Sensing Clarice's dismay, she tugged on her sleeve. "Don't worry; 'tis only a few paces. I would help, but Lord Ranulf has declared me too young to carry a heavy bucket."

Faith eyed Clarice's dirty gown, ignoring the bandage wrapped around her forearm. "I don't think you are much stronger than I, but I shan't ignore his orders." She plopped her bottom on the nearby bench and sat with regal bearing to watch Clarice haul the water up from the well.

Clarice bit her tongue. 'Twas all she could do to keep from throwing the bucket down the well and walking away. However, she had no idea where to go. Setting out without a plan had not worked well for her so far. Instead, she kept hauling up the bucket and pouring it into the various kettles on the fire.

She was relieved Faith had decided to watch in silence. It gave her ears some rest. Her breath came faster and faster as she worked. The sun's glare beat down, amplifying the fire's heat.

"Would you like me to tell you the tale?" Faith asked.

Startled, Clarice caught the bucket before it hit the ground. Water sloshed out over the edge, drenching her legs. She smiled through gritted teeth. "What tale would that be?"

"How the orphanage was set on fire, silly." Faith squinted up at her. "Are you always this forgetful?"

Resigned, Clarice choked back a snort. "Go ahead. Tell me your tale."

Faith pursed her lips. Clarice had begun to think the child had changed her mind, but she could not be so lucky; Faith launched into her tale.

"Erwina says—" She stopped and eyed Clarice. "You really must have Erwina look at your bandage."

Clarice waved her on. "The tale, if you please."

"There once was an orphanage that was run by the Brothers of God."

"Monks?"

"Yes." Faith cocked her head. Gaining Clarice's silence, she began again. "One terrible night a fierce knight came to the orphanage demanding a baby. 'Twas many years ago. Nearly a score. 'Tis said that the babe was his own. Yet there was no mother. 'Twas an enchanted baby, for how else would it come to be there? He yelled for his angel, but the angel did not appear. There was a battle and he stole the babe from the nursery and carried it away. In a fit of rage, he torched the orphanage, razing it to the ground. Not once did he stop to consider the other children sheltered there."

"Were they not under a lord's protection?"

Faith nodded. "The king was so displeased, he ordered the old lord of Sedgewic to find a home for every child. All but one boy was fostered out."

Clarice forgot the bucket hanging in her hands until the handle cut into her flesh. "What became of the child who was left behind? Why did no one take him?"

"Erwina says sometimes there is no accounting for taste. Soon after, the boy was called into service for the Prince of Wales."

Visions of a small redheaded boy, homeless, crying for his mother, threatened to bring her to her knees. "Lord Ranulf was that boy?"

A frown tugged at Faith's brow. She shook her head. "'Twas so long ago. No one recalls the lad's name."

Clarice sighed as she poured the last of the water into the large kettle and sat down to watch it heat. Still pondering Faith's tale, she spoke her thoughts aloud. "What knight would do such awful things?"

"Erwina says he was once a brave knight, but his broken heart never healed."

A deep sadness welled up from deep inside Clarice's soul. She wanted to weep for the lost love. "Was there a name for this knight?"

An identical blond head popped up between them, interrupting Faith's answer with her own mimicking singsong reply. "Erwina says . . . Erwina says."

Faith's twin, Mercy, stood with her hands on her hips, her blue eyes sparkling with mischief. "I'll tell you what Erwina says. She says Faith talks too much and should have been back long ago, and if she is not, 'tis I who gets her meat pie."

"Oh!" Faith jumped up from her perch, and ran past Mercy. Clarice knew at once that Erwina had said no such thing. She recalled the other time she'd observed Mercy baiting her twin. One day that minx would find she needed her precious sister.

Mercy cringed under Clarice's gaze and mumbled, "Faith does talk too much."

"A little, but she means well."

Mercy snorted and turned to go.

Frustrated, Clarice shoved her own sweaty cap of curls out of her face and stomped her foot at the insolent girl's back. "Now I shall never know that evil knight's name."

Mercy paused. "Everyone knows the knight's name was Margrave."

Chapter 17

Clarice raced after Mercy, missing her as the girl slipped through the gate.

Furious, she kicked at a raised tree root. Regretting her foolishness, she limped back to the well. Her body ached with each miserable step. Her bandaged arm throbbed. She refused to believe her father could ever do something so vile.

She scooped up the empty bucket and returned to the stone where Faith had perched earlier. She gritted her teeth, refusing to cry out. A few moments ago she had been bemoaning the darkness of her life. Had God forgotten she existed? Just as her own father had abandoned her? She could not push back the persistent question quickly enough. It dug into her mind with sharpened talons. Why did Father leave her for months at a time? What other secrets did he hide?

Lost in the past, Clarice propped her back against the stone. She ran a hand over her eyes and tried to imagine her father as the mythical evil knight. 'Twas unfathomable.

Though absent for most of her life, the man she knew was loyal to the king. Quiet and gentle. Maud swore he had demanded the right to care for Clarice when she was an infant. But Father's sweet nature had been too easy for Annora to conquer. Her stepmother had chipped at his soul until 'twas nothing more than an empty shell.

Now she found she questioned everything about her life. If Father had loved her so much, why had he chosen to hide her? Wouldn't he have wanted to present his daughter to the world?

She glanced up at the stove. Steam rose and danced above the kettle. Soon, buckets of hot water would have to be carried and heaved high enough to fill the tub. Heavy work before the reward of soothing bliss yawned ahead of her. She groaned at the thought of lifting her arms one more time. When she stood to begin the chore she was blinded by the sun's reflection, snaking through the lawn.

A spigot she had missed with all Faith's distracting chatter extended from the kettle. Hinged to the spigot was a steel trough. It ran all the way into the tent. Eager to learn why the steel contraption was wasted here instead of utilized for armor, she followed it until she stood in front of Lord Ranulf's giant bathing tub.

The end of the trough, tied by a satin rope, hung overhead and out of the way. It stopped just above the tub. She climbed up on a stool and yanked the rope. The trough dropped, angling into the tub.

No more straining backs or burning arms for castle maidens. Poor old Maud and her ailing joints would bless the soul who had thought out this invention. If this contraption carried water all the way from the fire, she would kiss the feet of the creator herself.

She skipped out of the bathing tent and hurried to the kettle. Visions of perfumed bath oils caressing her aching muscles danced in her head.

She turned the spigot. Her eyes widened as the water rushed out and through the metal flume. She raced into the tent and knelt beside the tub. A stream of water cascaded into the bath. Filled to the rim, heat rising, the steam swirled in the air.

Clarice stuck her head out of the flap. Squinting against the sun's glare, she studied the sundial. The time it should have taken Sedgewic to return was well past. He must have forgotten his orders for her to prepare his bath.

She plucked at her soiled bodice. 'Twas certain if he meant to return, he would have by now. It had been a dreadful day. Robert's messenger, the tumble from the tunnel, all the spiders and dust held within now scattered on the solar floor, the grueling work it had taken to carry so many buckets to fill the blasted tub.

'Twas not as if she had never worked a day in her life. She had always been eager to do more than most who were her size and age. Many times she had tried to earn her family's acceptance by working twice as hard. Instead, all her futile efforts ever brought her was chapped hands, Father's pat on the head before locking the door, and Annora's threat to sell her for a price.

Hesitant to use the bath despite what Faith had said, Clarice counted until she ran out of all the numbers Maud knew to teach her. Then she started all over again. Impatient, she tapped her toe. After all, she was a patient person and had done everything she was told. Well, almost everything. Lord Ranulf was not returning to claim his bath. She could not let the water cool off without someone enjoying the benefit. Not after all the effort she had put to the task. Could she?

She caught her lower lip with her teeth. Her arm aching, her pinched-feet burning, the call of comfort was too much to ignore. She scratched at the dried mud sticking to her legs and scurried to claim her enjoyment before anyone else could. Including the lord of Sedgewic.

With one quick check, she tossed back the tent flap. Not a sign that anyone approached. Snapping the flap shut, she dashed from the doorway and proceeded before she changed her mind.

After prying off her slippers, Clarice nearly toppled over for the sheer joy of freedom and the cool grass between her toes. She yanked the gown over her head, tossing the filthy garment in the corner. Withdrawing the peddler's ribbon from her skirt pocket, she caught the wisps and chunks of what was left of her hair and tied them back.

A row of small bottles filled with perfumed oils stood near the tub. She lifted the glass stopper and sniffed at the different scents. One was of sage and mint. The other was an aromatic blend of lavender and roses. Not sure how much to pour in a tub so large, she tipped the bottle over the water and poured out most of the contents.

The flowery fragrance filled the tent, wafting through the air. "Mayhap it will give our Lord Ranulf hives."

Clarice dipped her finger into the tub, swirled the water, and watched the oil disappear into the depths. She climbed in, sighing as the soothing water blanketed her from toe to chin.

All too soon, her thoughts returned to her troubles, and she flinched every time she thought someone was coming.

The relentless questions still came. The answers rebounded without proof. 'Twas not in her father's nature to kill himself. Nor would he ever betray Henry. The years under Annora's thumb had done their damage. And that fact made the tale of him burning down an orphanage even more confusing. She was his daughter. It made sense that she was that babe. But if so, why had she been left at an orphanage?

Her father's message to look for the red wolf echoed in her heart. Had he meant for her to seek him out or had he intended it as a warning? Ranulf might have been eight years of age at the time. She would have been a babe. 'Twould give him reason enough for revenge. Although she had trouble thinking of him in that light, she decided it best to distance herself.

Memories drifted in and out, casting their shadows on her thoughts. There were fanciful conversations between father and daughter of an angel bringing another into the world. And there was Annora, spewing angry, hate-riddled venom.

Visions of red wolves and swans skimmed along as she let her mind drift. Peering into the mists, she forced the meaning to surface from behind her father's cryptic message.

The memories were unrelenting and brought flashes of the peddler who had graced Margrave's gate on the night of her father's death.

She would have liked to see his face. Instead, the cloak's cowl had kept him well hidden. She liked his hands, and the way they settled Fat Thomas's old nag. His long fingers had stroked the horse's mane, soothing the beast with his gentle touch. What would it be like to be stroked in that way? Stifling a naughty sigh, she sank a little deeper into the water, her hands roaming over the flat of her stomach.

His kindness toward Maud and her father had warmed her soul. Her heart filled with joy when he bestowed a ribbon upon her. So kind was he. Maud had received a ribbon as well. The dear woman had near been in a fit when she had entered the tower, her bony fists clutching the ribbons. She was nigh to bursting with news of extra food in the pantry and his imminent return. But he never came back. And Father was forever gone.

Warmed by the bath, Clarice yawned and rested her head on the back of the tub.

A pair of graceful swans floated into her dreams, wearing a red satin ribbon draped around their bent necks. They sliced through the water, reaching the bank where she stood. She reached out to lift the ribbon from their necks and her hand was stilled by yet another.

Focusing through the swirling mists, she stared at the sun-bronzed hand resting upon hers. Scarred from battle, there was strength within this masculine hand. Lightened by the sun, the coils of hair shimmered as it brought the gift closer. Gently, she was turned, her hair lifted as the ribbon wove into her hair. Nimble fingers danced through her mane, stroked her neck, caressed her shoulders.

She turned to see the face belonging to those gentle hands. But it was hidden behind the shadows of a peddler's coarse woven cloak. His identity whispered *the peddler*. She leaned into his embrace, trusting that no harm would come from this one. His lips touched her fevered brow, traveled to her temple. Cool fingers traced her cheek before plunging again into her hair. His breath danced beside her ear, down her neck, caressing her shoulder. She sought to find his mouth, in search of his lips so she might match them with her own.

The mists shifted and separated, like prisms in a looking glass, catching the peddler's visage as he bent for another kiss. She recoiled in horror as her darling gentle peddler's nose grew into a snout. His ears began to point, his coat of fur shimmering streaks of red.

Clarice awoke with a start and ran a trembling hand over her lips. Her stomach dropped, turning liquid at her spine. She had an odd, empty feeling she was not alone. Her skin tingled. Someone was close behind her.

Searching outside the tub for the bathing cloth to cover her nakedness, her hand touched something warm and strong. She felt along muscular planes, the mass too large to wrap her fingers around.

Gradually moving her hand away from the leather-encased leg, she inched her fingers toward the boar-bristled brush resting on the stool. Her pulse racing, she gripped the long wooden handle and thanked the saints above that she had had the foresight to lay it within reach of the tub.

Exploding out of the water, she swung. The impact jarred the wound on her arm as the brush landed against her target. Her feet, perfumed with oils, slid on the tub's polished surface and she went down. Her head dunked below the soapy water.

The club fisted in one hand, she pushed up with the other. The water splashed over the sides as she spun around, striking out in another arc of spraying water and boar-bristle club.

A roar of pain shook the tent.

Clarice shoved the hair from her face. Her eyes widened.

Upon seeing her victim clutching his head, she sank down to cover everything below her mouth with water and wished to disappear.

Chapter 18

Ranulf covered the growing welt on his temple and sucked the air between his teeth. "Woman, what runs through your mind!"

"I think I should ask you the same."

He straightened his shoulders and frowned. "And why should I have to be wary of entering where I please?"

"You shouldn't go skulking about," Clarice snapped. Her flushed cheeks flamed higher. "M-m-my lord."

"Skulking!" Ranulf arched his brows. The motion made his temple throb. "I was responding to your request."

"I asked nothing of you . . . my lord."

He edged closer. "Beautiful lady, just moments ago you requested assistance in washing your hair. In truth, you mewed and moaned at my touch."

The air hissed between her teeth as she sputtered, "I did nothing of the sort."

Ranulf bit his cheek to keep from commenting on her flaring temper. He pointed to the crown of her head. "How do you explain the lather?"

She raised a tentative hand, snatching it back when she made contact with the residue of creamy suds.

He stepped closer and flicked a glob of soap from her cheek. "I believe this is the point at which, were one so inclined, an apology would be in order."

Clarice snorted and locked eyes with his. Unwilling to be the first to turn away, he made himself comfortable and waited on the stool.

"You may apologize when ready, my lord," she said with a dismissive nod.

His jaw clenched. 'Twas unfortunate the maiden had to open her mouth. Their war of wills had just begun. "I meant you, wench."

"A chivalrous knight would apologize to the lady first and take his leave."

"If she were behaving as a gently bred lady, I would." He leaned back with his leg crossed over the top of his thigh. Eyes closed, his fingers locked, he rested his hands upon his knee and prepared for a long siege. "You are not that lady." Ignoring her outraged gasp, he listed her offenses. "My private bath has been invaded. The bath in which I planned to wash away the sweat and grime of the day has been spoiled by a selfish guest who doesn't have the decency to see more water is waiting for another." Sighing ridiculously loud, he added, "And now I must listen to your complaints when you are the one at fault."

Clarice sank deeper into the water. "You wish for me to apologize for falling asleep?"

Exasperated with her hardheadedness, Ranulf opened his eyes and could not help noting the faint coating of soapy lather had dissipated. Despite the steam that curled over her raven head, the bath would cool in moments. He trusted her slight shiver was from the cooling water and not from memories of her passionate dreams. For whatever reason, he did not find pleasure in thinking her soft sigh was meant for another. "Of course I don't mean for you to apologize for sleeping." Ranulf leaned forward, his elbows resting on his thighs. He pointed to the bath brush she still gripped in her fist. "You struck me. With my own damn back scrubber."

"But—" Clarice started to sit up taller; then, realizing her predicament, she slid deeper in the water. She glared up at him. "You startled me."

"You called out."

"I thought your plans for bathing had been dismissed."

His lips twitched. "I assumed you needed help."

"Not likely," Clarice muttered.

"I'll wait here while you form your apology." Ranulf leaned back and pretended to drift off to sleep.

"Oh, all right. I'm sorry I thought you were someone intent on mauling my person. But, as you can see, I am quite fine." Her point made, she dipped her chin.

He nodded. "Fine indeed."

Clarice sank until her lips were just above the crest of the water. One hand frantically searched for the washing cloth and more soap suds to block his view. "Lord Ranulf, if 'tis not too much trouble, please remove yourself from this tent."

His frown deepened as he paused to ponder her request. "'Tis impossible."

Clarice smacked the water with the brush and looked as if she wanted another good blow to his head. "I did as you bid me and offered my apology."

"And an insincere one at that." Ranulf shifted on the stool. "I doubt 'tis safe to let you out of my sight. You are a stubborn, dangerous woman with a tendency for finding trouble." He stopped to reconsider. "Or 'tis trouble that finds you. I haven't decided."

Clarice gripped the edge of the tub and pointed at the exit. "Lord Ranulf, get out."

Ranulf leaned forward. He wiped the drop of water from her pert nose and extracted the brush from her fingers. Certain she had no more weapons at her disposal, he leaned toward her. His lips moved against the delicate outer shell of her ear as he spoke. "My name is Ranulf. 'Tis how you will direct all conversation to me from now on." He found her mouth with his, plying a kiss to her lips. He lingered on her lower lip, tasting the full flesh with his tongue. Satisfied with his work, he finished by giving her a chaste peck on the forehead. "'Tis my demand as lord."

Clarice blinked before answering. Pink whirls bloomed on her cheeks. "Yes, Lord Ranulf."

He found it hard to believe she gave in for any other reason than her precarious situation. Frankly, he did not care how he attained her cooperation. At the moment, the sound of his given name was satisfying. "Ranulf will do."

He stood, the need to put distance between himself and her soft, ripe lips was imperative. 'Twas perilous for him to remain. She was intoxicatingly dangerous.

"Ranulf?"

"Yes?"

"The water grows cold." Her gaze lifted to meet his. "If you would give me a moment, I'll heat fresh water to fill your tub."

He sniffed the aromatic steam rising from her flesh. "'Tis nothing that cannot be remedied. I saw to it before I found you here." With a sure, swift tug, he pulled on the rope, and a spout of steaming water rained down on her head. He picked up the soggy clothing on the floor as he left. "I've always found fresh water is best."

Clarice's curses rang through the garden and into the bailey, threatening to unman the next person who set foot in the tent.

Ranulf dropped the bath linens into the laundress's basket as he made his way toward the outer wall and through the gate. Tonight no bucket held enough cold water to wash away the vision teasing his mind. The breasts he had unbound earlier were more beautiful than he'd imagined. He did not rest until he stopped at the small pond. Shucking his tunic and leggings, he dove into the chilled water.

The rest of the day he spent washing away the unwanted need rising in his blood. Even as he rose out of the pond, his body refused to settle. The sight of Clarice's pert breasts filled his mind. Gilded with a glossy sheen of oil and water, her skin had danced with light and passion. The perfumed oils had enhanced her scent. His need for her was all-consuming.

Every time he searched for answers to his questions, a path led him straight to Clarice. Every thought that led him to Clarice also led him to another dunking in the frigid water. After diving in for the tenth time, he stopped keeping count.

At one point he found himself yearning for winter. At least then he could plow his befuddled brain in a snowbank and be done with it.

Cursing the heavens for depositing her into his life, he gave up trying to wash her out of his head. He rammed his fingers through his wet hair. What was he doing? He was a man who had fought at the king's side. A Knight of the Swan. Lord of Sedgewic. And he knew how to seduce a woman. Even a treacherous one.

She had played her game well. She had to know her effect on him. No woman was oblivious to the power she held or was unwilling to wield her supremacy.

Ranulf grinned. He might even allow her to think her game of seduction was successful. At least until he learned all her secrets.

As time passed, Clarice banished all thoughts of Ranulf and his kiss to hell, where they belonged. Then the tent's flap snapped open. Water splashed over the sides of the bathing tub as she dived to cover herself.

Erwina strode in, her arms full of bathing linens. "Why do you still soak?"

Clarice pretended to fish the washing linen from the bottom of the tub. She prayed Erwina brought something clean for her to wear. However, one never knew what to expect at Castle Sedgewic. After all, Ranulf had left her without a stitch to replace her filthy clothes.

Erwina bent to pick up the boar-bristle brush and laid it on the side table. "If 'tis your death you are wishing, I should warn you, no one at Sedgewic has ever succumbed to death when bathing while they were under my care."

Unable to unlock her teeth, Clarice allowed her body to shake, hoping her head would eventually follow.

Erwina laid the bundle on the stool and turned to straighten the vials of scented oils. "Don't know how you managed to stay in a tub all afternoon. If you are not half dead, you must be half melted."

"Cannot get-t-t-t out! M-m-m-might come back. N-n-no clothes."

Erwina eyed the pile laying on the floor next to the bundle she had carried into the room. She held up the skirt of a woolen dress. "What's wrong with this? I know 'tis old, but I am certain it will fit."

"Wh-wh-where did that come from?"

"Lord Ranulf sent it earlier. He thought you might enjoy this gown more than the other." Erwina let the material drop and tucked a straggling gray hair behind her ear. "'Course if it were up to me, you would not be allowed any extra comfort until you helped clean up the solar."

"I was ordered to come here."

"And bathe all day?"

"No, but—"

"'Tis your choice, Clarice. But I will not have the children harmed by your actions."

"Mistress Erwina, short of taking too much time to bathe, I have done nothing wrong."

"You lingered in a tub with a man all afternoon. There are children about."

"N-n-not true!"

Erwina sniffed and lifted her shoulder. "They report what they see."

"Then they shouldn't tattle."

"They shouldn't have reason to have tales to tell—"

Clarice looked up. "But they do," she finished.

Erwina clasped her hands together. Lines of concern etched her face. "The lord of Sedgewic was seen entering this tent and you within."

"As you can see, he isn't here."

"No one has seen him since he left on foot through the castle gate. I thought it possible you might know his intended direction."

Clarice rose to get out of the watery prison. Smiling weakly, she thanked Erwina for the warm toweling sheet. She tugged on the chemise and woolen hose, followed by the brown skirt and green overgrown.

Erwina waited, urging her with stony silence.

Clarice glanced over her shoulder as she tied the satin ribbon under her breasts. "I suppose you want the full explanation for my tardiness."

"No."

Clarice knew better than that. Maud used the same technique when she was disagreeable.

Out of sorts was what she called it. She continued as if Erwina had begged her to tell all. "I feared his lordship would return and find me naked as the day my mother bore me. I was unaware fresh clothing lay on the stool. I don't know when they arrived."

"As I said, Lord Ranulf sent them long before he left."

"How's a body to know that?" Clarice muttered.

She could not explain it, but her heart lifted at the thought that she had been wrong. He had not even touched her; well, almost not at all. Her scalp still tingled where his fingers had scrubbed her head. And that single kiss, his playful lips on hers. She knew it was wrong, and even if it meant nothing to him, when he kissed her, a buzzing sensation had rushed clear to her toes.

Erwina scooped up the drying cloths and threw them into the basket. "Did his lordship mention where he intended to go? There is much that needs his attention."

Guilt leaped through Clarice. Had she hit Ranulf hard enough to muddle his brain? What if he was lost somewhere outside the wall? 'Twas dangerous to travel at night; she knew that first hand. But to travel in the dark without a clear mind? She shuddered to think what would become of him.

Fear hit her twofold when she stepped out of the tent. The last rays of light colored the sky a deep purple. A bank of clouds moved over the horizon, blanketing the moon and stars with its heavy haze. Clarice stumbled to a stop, unsure where to start her search.

"Erwina, we have to find him," she whispered. "I think I may have injured him greatly."

Sickened by her violence, she grabbed the small kitchen blade from Erwina's belt. She lifted the knife and pressed it to her heart. "Kill me," she cried. "Avenge your lord."

Erwina struck the knife from her fingers. "Don't be a fool. I'm certain he can withstand any assault you might deliver. We'll send a message to the garrison and inform Sir Nathan and Sir Darrick that the lord of Sedgewic cannot be found. We'll search for him until we have run out of places to look."

"How can you trust me to help?"

"I don't necessarily." Erwina patted Clarice's cheek and smiled. "But I think there is potential."

"'Tis all my fault."

"Oh, piffle." Erwina waved her hands. "His lordship has fought more battles and seen more pain than any of us will ever know in our nightmares. And yet he has retained goodness and strength. If he brought you to his castle, he isn't finished with you until he says 'tis so. Besides," she shrugged, "if he didn't trust you, you would have found yourself locked in one of the dungeon cells."

She laid her hand on Clarice's shoulder. "You need a cloak. Come, child. We'll head to the hall before daylight is gone."

Ranulf stood inside the garrison. After abandoning the pond's icy water, the need to thaw his aching limbs had become heavier than the need to be alone with his thoughts. He hunched his back, pressing his palms into the hearth. Warmth seeped through the stone and into his body. He shook his head. Water sprayed into the flames, sizzling as it dissipated.

His friends watched him. He could feel their stares burrowing into his shoulder blades.

"Your horse threw you?" Nathan called out.

Angling his head in Nathan's direction, Ranulf snarled, "Swiving bastard."

Nathan dropped the leather tack and cleaning rag on the floor. Grasping his chest, he pretended to have been struck by the slur. "You cut me deep, my friend." He leaned in. "Really, 'tis nothing to be ashamed of. A great number of gentlemen are thrown by their horses. 'Tis possible you've been taking life too easy and have lost your manly stones."

Darrick touched Nathan on his broad shoulder. "Not tonight," he warned.

The heat rose up Ranulf's jerkin, searing a path to the cords in his neck. "'Twould be best if you heeded his advice."

Ignoring both of them, Nathan sat up and rubbed the whiskers on his chin. "I don't think 'tis horse problems at all. Something else sours our friend this eve." Tapping his nose, he shot up from the bench. "Ah-ha! 'Tis a woman." He stopped, dejected, and dropped back down. "No, the women residing in this wretched castle are either spoken for or too old to catch a desperate eye. Unless, of course, you're an old sod like Sergeant Krell. 'Course there are sweet little maidens. But they are too young to notice unless you are a desperate mongrel." He held a hand up to stay Ranulf where he stood and rushed on. "While I know your character is not in question here. So, if 'tis not romantic pestilence that darkens your soul, then pray tell us, what ails—"

Ranulf flew through the air and landed on top of Nathan's back. The chant in his head to destroy the grin echoed in his blood. He drew back. His own grin stretched wider and he chose to cuff the knight on the side of his head.

Nathan took advantage of his leniency, tagging Ranulf's mouth with his knuckles. Ranulf stumbled and fell to the ground.

"Sweet Lord," Nathan crowed. He dropped to his knees, pinning Ranulf to the floor. "It feels good to be doing something besides waiting for the signal to push on."

In the midst of pausing to gulp in the air and enjoy the release of a good brawl, they turned to see a pair of small slippers standing at their heads.

Ranulf winced when he heard the smack of a stool against Nathan's shoulder. Nathan shoved Ranulf back and threw his attacker to the ground.

"No." Ranulf spun Nathan by the shoulder, planting his fist into his face.

"What the bloody hell?" Nathan glared at him before sagging against the wall.

Bending down, Ranulf yanked the harpy off the floor and flipped back the hood. He looked over his shoulder. "Nathan, I believe you two have met. This is my pestilence, otherwise known as Clarice."

Nathan wiped his nose with the back of his hand. His face blanched when she held out her hand and offered him her handkerchief.

An impressive streak of pink crawled up her neck. "My apologies . . . I thought you were hurting him."

"Looked like it, didn't it?" Nathan dabbed at the blood and grinned at her. "My apologies as well. I thought you a young maiden earlier." His brows rose higher. "I see now by the way you fill out your gown that I was wrong. Quite a beautiful wench, aren't you? Didn't know Sedgewic boasted tasty morsels such as yourself. If you've a mind and are through with his lordship, I'm willing to have you warm my bed."

"Not a word." Ranulf covered her mouth with his hand before she shredded her fragile apology. "By the gods, not a word."

Chapter 19

Ranulf tightened his grip around Clarice's waist, squeezing the breath and nasty comments from her mouth and dragging her through the doorway of his bedchamber. Where the devil had she learned to string a set of curses together? "Have you lost your wits?"

He snarled an oath as her teeth came uncomfortably close to his rib cage. "Bite me again," he warned, "and you'll regret it for the rest of your nights."

Ignoring the fresh wound, he spun her off his hip and wrestled the wench into the crook of his arm. He took a few steps toward a high-backed chair before lurching to a stop. He spun on his heel and landed on the wooden seat. The chair rocked back, threatening to dump them both onto the floor.

"Release me at once," she said.

"When you have learned to control yourself."

"I am not a whore to be passed around," she shouted, making his ears ring with her outrage.

"All right. All right," he soothed.

Dodging the elbow aimed at his chin, he trapped her arms at her sides. Their chests rose and fell as one. Her rigid back softened as she contained her emotions.

Heat radiated through layers of tunic and leggings. It slid across his thighs, pouring fire into his veins.

Ranulf closed his eyes, allowing a brief moment to let it seep into his soul. His mind argued against the foolishness of bringing the handful of trouble to his private chambers. Again. God, but the feel of her in his arms brought him back to life. She was light in a dark room. Her soft curves pressed into his lap, causing his breath to stick somewhere in his chest. "I'm sorry. I should have defended you."

"Agreed."

He dipped his head and the sharp edge of her shoulder caught him between the eyes. The brief pleasure that had disturbed his sound reasoning disintegrated into a thousand stars.

"Christ's bones." He squinted down at her through watering eyes.

She hitched a hip, turning to blink at him with false innocence, lashes fluttering. "Did I injure you? Mayhap you should see Mistress Erwina for a poultice. I'm happy to fetch her." She moved as if free to rise. Her hands grazed against thighs, narrowly missing his groin. "Oh . . ." She froze, hands trapped, her hips in midrise.

"I do not require Erwina's services," he snapped.

Thoughts of throttling the wench flashed through his mind. He quickly discarded it. The task would require releasing her arms. Instead, he tightened his hold, squeezing once to gain her full attention. "Peace."

Although he knew he should not dump her on the floor as he wished, he was tempted to do it all the same. She was the most irritating woman he had ever had the misfortune of meeting. However, his front parts were finding her posterior a fortunate situation.

Her stomach rumbled, reminding him that he had missed two meals that day. He doubted she'd had more than the bread and cheese he'd sent out to her. He hated to admit it, but he hungered for something more than warmed ale and a hearty joint of beef.

"Be still," he growled against the base of her neck. Her scent, blending with the perfumed oils, brought back visions of her body, shimmering just out of reach.

Nudging her with his chin, he tilted back her head until he found those blasted bottomless sapphire pools. Like a siren, they drew him to the edge, prepared to leap into their depths. The rapid rhythm of her heart vibrated against his body. The crests of her breasts shuddered with every breath. He shook off her gaze, fixing his eyes on the silky flesh escaping the soft woolen bodice of her gown.

His hands itched to skim across her curves. Duty won out and he kept her elbows pinned at her side. But his knuckles could not escape the trap. They brushed against the sides of her straining rib cage, fractions away from her luscious skin, taunting and teasing his restraint.

He let his gaze sweep across the top of her glossy mane, to the curving rise and fall of her breasts, to her pale kneecap peeking out from under a soft fold of skirt.

His visual expedition stalled at the edge of her battered slippers. The curious desire to know if her calves were as softly curved as the rest of her limbs tormented his good sense. Desperate, he sought to distract the awakening dragon coiled deep within his loins. Why did it matter to him if the ill-fitting slippers pinched her feet? He could just as easily explain his concern that the bodice might be scratching her delicate skin.

I'm a fool. There it was. The glaring truth. *I am a fool. She has misdirected my intentions for the last time.*

" 'Tis best for both of us if you cease your wiggling and listen."

"You are not my lord, nor my father." She ducked her head and snorted. "Am I to quake at the mere whisper of your name? Because you are the mighty lord of Sedgewic? Oh," she ground out. "I'm all atremble from your greatness."

Ranulf ignored the heated words spewing from that dainty mouth. He let the scent of lavender and roses fill his head. This interest in the maiden shook him to his core. Giving in to temptation, he breathed in her essence and almost did not hear her. His attention returned to her enraged tirade as she finished her reasons for not having to obey his demands.

". . . you could never be like Nicholas of Margrave. He was a loving, noble man."

"Of course. Very noble. 'Tis why King Henry wanted his head." His arms tensed. "Who is he to you?"

Anger flushed her cheeks to a rosy pink. She stiffened before responding with a tight whisper. "Someone who cared for me."

His gut twisted. Visions of the pasty-white, frail, gray-haired man pawed through his head. "Your lover."

"You're a disgusting pig," she sneered.

His hands tightened. "How do you know him?"

Blue orbs narrowed as she glared. "He is . . . was my father," she hissed out between thin lips.

"Liar." Ranulf's muscles twitched.

Clarice bucked in his lap. "I'm not a liar! I'm not!"

He trapped her jaw with his hand. "No, my sweet pretender. You are not his daughter. I knew Nicholas of Margrave well enough. He never mentioned any living daughters. The one born to him died when she was an infant. Believe me, if she had lived, his wretched lady would have paraded her in front of every eligible man with money in his purse."

She broke free of his hold. "I speak the truth. You cannot take that away. No one can. He loved me."

Ranulf's arms locked around her, hindering her freedom. "If what you say is true, why did he keep you hidden all these years, lying about your death? How can you call that love?"

"I don't know, but 'tis all I have," she said. "All I've ever had."

"Robert and Lady Annora—"

"She is not my mother," she whispered.

Ranulf rejected what she said against the facts he already knew. He hated to admit 'twas possible she was indeed connected to the plot that he had vowed to quash. And if what she said were true, she was the devoted daughter of a man accused of treason. She was a passionate woman. He had no doubt she would do anything for those she cared for. Even lie.

Henry depended on him, on the Brotherhood, to discover all who threatened his throne. Ranulf had vowed to annihilate any who would stand in the way of Henry's purchase of his birthright. France would be Henry's, but not without a fight and sacrifice. There were those who had their own agendas and awaited Henry's early demise, be it by pestilence or during a hard-fought battle. Against those threats, Ranulf was helpless. But protect his friend and king from the plots of evil? That he could and would do without fail.

His stomach soured. 'Twas not fate that had brought Clarice to Sedgewic. She had her reasons for being here. He would make it his purpose to know every secret she held close to her heart. His thoughts twisted. Who would she sacrifice her life for?

Clarice tipped her head to stare. His rigid body shuddered, fighting a silent battle. Although his arms still wrapped her in his embrace, she was certain he had all but forgotten she remained on his lap. As her concern grew, the outrage melted.

Hesitant, she touched the forearm that encased her waist and instantly pulled back. He pulsated with tension, straining against something that held him in its grasp.

"Ranulf," she said quietly. Gaining no response, she noted the taut line of his mouth. The sensual smile, reduced to a thin line, now twisted in pain.

Grazing his cheek with the back of her hand, she cupped the angle of his jaw, directing his head to hers. Mindful of the cut where Nathan had hit him earlier, she pressed a finger to his lips, caressing them until they relaxed under her touch.

"What ails you?"

Shaking his broad shoulders, he pulled away. His mouth twisted and thinned. Pain laced his eyes with a fierce, brittle cold that caused her to gasp.

"You," he snarled.

Afraid of his icy stare, she snatched back her hands, folding them in her lap. His predatory glare reminded her of a hungry wolf, guarding its recent kill.

Her breath hissed out as he suddenly chose to stand. Catching her moments before impact with the floor, he scooped her up and tossed her into the abandoned chair. His hands braced, imprisoning her with iron bars of chest and arms.

"Why are you here?"

Clarice met his question with silence. She should never have cared so much for his safety. He did not deserve her worry. Still trying to regain her own sense of balance, she turned her head and pretended interest in the dying flames.

Strong fingers curled around her jaw, directing her to meet his gaze. "I ask you again." The pad of his thumb traced her mouth. "What brings you to Sedgewic?"

Her heart beat against her ribs. The buzzing in her ears grew louder as he brought his lips down to her mouth, though not quite touching. He was so close. So very, very close. His breath caressed her cheek. He whispered something, but she could not understand it for the confounded buzzing. Her vision blurred as her stomach fluttered and rolled. Licking her lips, she struggled to focus on the man standing in front of her. When he bent at his narrow waist, she noticed tiny golden coils nestled on his broad chest. She itched to reach out and feel the silken mat under the weight of her hand. Instead, she curled her fingers around the chair's arms, digging her nails into the wood.

How could she want his touch? She should fear him. He was the king's wolf. Had led the attack on Margrave. Lord Ranulf might even be her father's murderer. He had to be. Why else would Father have sent her in search of the red wolf? The red wolf. Ranulf. Poor Maud had confused his last request. A red wolf indeed.

Frustrated laughter welled up and spilled out past her lips. Her elation deflated, sinking into a dark hole filled with forgotten hopes and dreams. Those dreams she guarded carefully, keeping them hidden from prying eyes.

All but one dream had been dashed. One dream remained. And rarely did she examine that dream. To be loved and accepted for herself. Hope had kept it alive. Desperation may have forced her to face the emptiness in her life. But a flicker of hope had been all she needed to flee her old life for a new one and to find her father's murderer.

Yet, now that she had found the man, she could not help wondering if she was mistaken. Her promise to a tarnished memory stood in the way of her new life away from Margrave Manor. She hated to admit that Ranulf's questioning her father's love echoed her own questions. A lone tear slid down her face, dropping silently into her lap.

"What's this?" He held out a finger that captured another tear escaping down her cheek. Sighing, he knelt down on one knee. "What brings tears to a face that deserves kisses instead?"

"You," she whispered.

"Me?"

"You bring me to tears."

He traced her cheek, trailing down to her jaw. His touch danced up to her mouth. All the while she watched his eyes grow deeper in color. He continued to weave dreams on her lips with his thumb, awakening passions she had never known existed.

"I also bring kisses to wash away your tears," he said.

Clarice leaned back, digging her nails into the arms of the high-backed chair, fighting the urge to wrap her arms around his shoulders and let him carry her away. "'Tis as I said. I am not a whore."

"Understood." His breath ruffled the loose strands of hair. They danced seductively against her neck.

She shook her head. "And I don't need kisses. Not from you."

"I'll have you know, my kisses are renowned in King Henry's court. They have been known to melt the coldest of hearts, to render the fiercest of shrews into quivering masses of passion."

"Hmph" she snorted. "As I am neither coldhearted nor of a shrewish nature, I have no need."

"That, my sweet, is debatable." His brows arched. "Ah, I see you doubt my word," he said, drawing her into his arms. "Allow me to demonstrate."

He rose, guiding her to stand in the circle of his arms. Ignoring her protests, he nibbled at the corner of her mouth. When she sighed against his lips, he tested the welcome presence of his tongue. She bade him enter, returning his kiss. His palm slid down the small of her back. Deft fingers glided around her hips and down her outer thigh. Flames shot through her veins, placing fire in her lungs. His hands, trembling against her skin as they danced along her skirts, testing the folds, became her undoing. She moaned and grabbed his shoulders, pressing her breasts against his chest.

Their kisses deepened until Clarice knew what she must do. She wriggled and mewed, clawing at his clothes. Her tongue danced with his, meeting his every move. "Yes," she whispered.

She advanced toward the proud specimen of male confidence and sexual prowess. With his tented leggings proving his distraction, she grabbed his tunic, drawing it over his head. The material caught on his broad shoulders. Just as she had hoped. In his passionate hurry, he forgot the all-important need of loosening the ties at the neck.

"Clarice?"

"Yes, my lord?" She quickly tied the ends of his sleeves together in a tight knot. Growing more confident as her plan unfolded, she trussed him up as well as a fine fat goose.

'Twould take some time before he loosened himself from their hold. She would be off Sedgewic lands before a cry was raised. Riding Buttercup would not be easy without a saddle, but her only hope to put enough distance between herself and Sedgewic was on horseback.

"Clarice," his muffled voice growled. "Untie the knot before you force me to make you regret your actions."

"I think not, Lord Ranulf. I dare not overstay my welcome." Remaining for a moment to wonder what might have been if he were the man of her dreams, she turned to make her escape.

Ranulf split the tunic from neck to hem before she reached the door. Air rushed from her lungs as a wall of muscle smacked against her back. Her stomach dropped. She had miscalculated his strength and the time that would be needed to free his arms. Her plan dissolved before her eyes.

"You shatter me, my lady." The arm around her waist stiffened, tightening with each word he spoke. "I don't recall giving you my leave."

Clarice shivered. Tears blurred her vision. She dared not turn to look at him.

He released her with a flip of his hand. Their separation splashed over her like a bucket of spring runoff.

"I told you . . . I am no one's whore." Clinging to the newel post for support, she shoved the hair out of her eyes before spinning on him. "If you dare come near me again, I'll—"

Ranulf paused at the door. Rage crackled in the air. "Remember, do not leave this chamber." A veiled threat of his own dripped from his tongue. "The guards are posted with orders to stop you."

Chapter 20

The cold, stony ledge bit into her legs. Clarice shifted on the uncomfortable seat. Earlier in the night she deliberately had selected it over the lure of the overstuffed chair by the hearth. Though, recalling Maud's wise words, that regret served only the master of the past, she clung to her decision and stayed by the drafty window.

She scrubbed her mouth with her knuckles. The angered promise he had left between them swirled in her head. Her insides knotted. The misbegotten plan to truss him up like a goose served at Michaelmas had certainly put her in dire straits.

The sun crept over the trees. Castle life unfolded with the dawning of the day. And she sat on her perch, ignoring the siren's call coming from the warm fire. The memory of that intimate moment with Ranulf was still too fresh. She took a deep breath. His irresistible scent still filled the air. It coursed through her traitorous mind and body with passionate speed.

Her hand dropped to her waist, settling on the band resting just above her hips. She trailed her fingers along the same scorched path he had skillfully traveled. Heat inflamed her cheeks as she recalled the bold manner in which he had stared, the way his gaze had slid over her breasts and down to her knees.

"Plaguey hell," she muttered, swiping at her unkempt hair. Embarrassment replayed again in her head. Of course, Ranulf had to notice the way her breasts were escaping the confines of her bodice.

"'Tis a blessing the man isn't in the room." Defying her commands, her skin prickled in anticipation of his caress.

The press of his engorged flesh had nearly distracted her from her purpose. She shuddered, desperate to erase the memory of the way he had cradled her in his lap, nestling her in the crook of his arm, offering comfort she had never known before. *How can I desire the stroke of his hand? 'Tis madness.*

Clarice turned as Hamish entered and dropped a bundle on the floor.

After a breath of silence, he nudged the pile of clothing with the toe of his boot. " 'Twas told to bring these."

He stood with his short legs braced, his hands on his hips, mimicking the lord of Sedgewic's arrogant stance.

Clarice arched a brow, allowing the slightest sign of surprise. Her lips twitched just once. Determined not to let the little urchin see how stiff she had become, each movement an effort of concentration, she casually slid from the window ledge. Every step brought a silent vow never to sit in an open window all night.

"Are you always in the habit of entering a chamber without knocking?" she asked primly.

" 'Twas ordered. So I did."

She lifted one of the garments from the pile. Her hand froze, held in place by Hamish's knowing stare. He stood proudly over the offering, daring her to say anything with which he might disagree.

Confused by his attitude, she pulled her hand back. She had no idea how to go about settling a child. Sheltered from the world outside Margrave, she rarely had dealt with children. Most servants were sent to Margrave House in London. Resolved to regain his trust, she would try to speak with the boy one more time. After all, she had survived Annora and Robert. Could one sour, pinch-faced little boy be that difficult to manage? She cleared her throat. "Thank Mistress Erwina, won't you?"

Hamish shoved his hat back and peered up thought rough-cut bangs. "Don't think this changes things."

"Changes things?"

"Just 'cause he sent you clothing doesn't mean you get to travel with him. You aren't wanted. Heard him say so."

Thumbing his puffed-up chest, he added, " 'Tis me that he wants to bring. Not you. I'm to begin training as squire of the body." Poking the air, he pointed, striking it with his finger. "Heard him say that, too."

"Is Lord Ranulf leaving?" Clarice's breath caught. With his mighty lordship away, she would find a way to slip off without anyone noticing. "Will he be gone long?"

Hamish's eyes narrowed. "'Tis obvious enough. Open your eyes. There are soldiers everywhere." He continued to shake his head, the floppy cap moving dangerously close to covering both eyes. "Those other soldiers are wrong. You are too slow in the head and don't have the strength for what they have planned."

"Excuse me?" she squeaked. "Strength for what?"

"Said," Hamish pointed to the pile, "don't see how these clothes will make a difference." He peered at the fabric she held in her hand and shrugged. "Just 'cause you're going to wear her favorite day dress, it won't make a difference. 'Tis not like you'll be murdered, too."

The soft woolen material slipped from her fingers. "Whose dress?"

Something the size of a goose egg lodged in her throat. Her thoughts flicked through the various facts already accumulated. Were the accusations they had overheard in the solar true? Had Ranulf murdered his wife and then her father?

She braced her palms against the back of the chair. *What if I'm next?* She looked wildly around the room. If provoked beyond reason, would he harm the children, too? She reached out, meaning to place a protective hand on Hamish's head. Nevertheless, he dodged it.

"Lady Mary wouldn't care. Even if she were still alive." Pausing for a breath, he added, "You feel all right? You look like the fish Erwina cooks after she rolls them in flour." Nodding to his own question, he patted her shoulder. "You look a bit gooey-like."

He led her to the chair she had been avoiding all night. She shook her head and tried to pull away. Hearing nothing of it, he managed to push her down.

"Don't worry," he said, "least ways you don't smell like a dead fish."

Closing her eyes, she tried to concentrate. Hamish moved with dizzying speed, scurrying to pick up the fallen pieces of clothing. She dropped her head in her hands and prayed he would go before she embarrassed herself.

"What was that, Hamish?" Clarice cocked her head. "I believe 'tis Erwina calling you."

He stopped to listen and grinned. "No, 'tis them new swans just delivered. You should see them. They are an angry bunch. But no angrier than his lordship. Says they're too late to do him any good." He paused to scratch his shoulder blade. "Although why he's mad at them I don't know. Everybody knows birds cannot mark time."

"Swans," she said. "What did he want with swans?"

"Erwina asked that very thing. She is fierce upset. Said she had enough to worry about without having to watch that they don't peck the children."

Clarice nodded. "She is right. Be sure to keep out of their way."

"I said *the children*," Hamish said. "She wasn't talking about me."

There was no doubt the lad was more resourceful than to be caught between a cob and his lady swan. All the same, he did have a knack for getting into the thick of things. "Of course, how silly of me," Clarice said.

Hamish let his disgust ooze all over her. "Micah calls me a child, too. He told Faith and Mercy that I'm a babe. He says Lord Ranulf doesn't want me and I'll never leave Sedgewic. Do you think 'tis true?"

Clarice squirmed under his pitiful gaze, unsure how to reassure him when she herself was the one always left behind. Besides, she had enough troubles of her own.

The appearance of new swans lifted her spirits. As she had discovered, the distance between Sedgewic and Margrave lands was not that great. 'Twas possible the peddler—*her* peddler—had returned to Margrave and found the manor deserted. In his need to dispose of the expensive swans, he'd carried them to Sedgewic. The peddler might be her means of escape. Together they would find the proof of her father's innocence and search out the king's protection. She required an ally inside the castle walls. Otherwise they were impenetrable from all sides.

"Hamish." Erwina marched into the chamber. Her gray head bobbed as she searched for her prey. "You were to deliver the clothing and the invitation. Why do you still stand here?"

Certain she heard his chubby knees knocking together, Clarice rushed to his aid. "Mistress Erwina, I was going to have Hamish thank you for the clothing," she announced. "But as you are here, I'm pleased to thank you in person."

Erwina blinked away from Hamish, then turned to pin him with a look that spoke loudly that he should run while she had her back turned. "'Tis the lord of Sedgewic's orders. Said 'twas important that you had a change of clothing."

"Oh. I'll have to thank R-Ranulf—" Clarice's tongue stumbled over his name as Erwina's eyes widened. "I mean his . . . lordship."

The woman's gnarled fingers twisted and untwisted the limp

apron tied around her waist. She cast a furtive glance toward the large bed in the chamber. "'Tis not my place, but . . ." Weighing her words carefully, she trudged on. "Your mother would be greatly saddened by your behavior."

"Annora? I assure you, Mistress Erwina," Clarice patted her stooped shoulder, "my stepmother has never been pleased with anything I have done."

Erwina shifted, continuously twisting the defenseless apron. "Oh, of certes, your sainted mother would have always had your best interests at heart."

"I fear you have her confused with someone else. Annora's heart doesn't have room for me."

Erwina nodded. "One day, child, you'll understand." She nudged her toward the fresh pile of clothing. "Hurry now. You had best make haste if you plan to ride with the lord of Sedgewic and his men."

"What?"

Chapter 21

Before Clarice could press Erwina for the meaning of her veiled comment, Ranulf stood in the doorway. His raw strength filled the chamber. "What must the lord of this domain do for a lady to attend his wishes?"

He eyed the abandoned pile of clothing lying on the floor. "Mistress Erwina, my time is short and my patience thin. If the wench dislikes the clothing, show her the trunk."

Clarice took several steps toward the irritating man. "Lord Ranulf, I'm right here. There's no need to speak of me as if I'm not standing in the same room."

He scowled, dismissing her comment with a flip of his hand. "Erwina, find something of my wife's that will fit her. See that she is prepared to ride before the hour is out."

Murderer. The word circled Clarice's thoughts like a vulture. Was it possible? She could not believe he would murder his wife. But at the will of his king? The ache in her lungs squeezed tighter. He would indeed.

Clarice stilled the pounding in her heart. She folded her arms, matching his attitude and glare. "Where exactly do you intend to take me?"

His gaze roamed over her person, lingering for a moment upon the valley between her breasts.

Her cheeks flushed with temper. The devilish man had heard her but refused to answer. Shoulders straightened, back lengthened, she tried stretching her height. "'Tis a simple enough question and I refuse to leave this room until you have answered me."

Ranulf turned. "Erwina, I require her presence at the bailey yard before the horses are brought around. Don't make me wait."

"Please." Clarice touched his sleeve, failing to still the trembling in her fingers. "Do you mean to send me away?"

"Mayhap one day, little one." He placed his palm on her fingers, cupping her hand. "But not today. Today I have a great deal of work to do before we leave for France."

"Then you intend to take me with you." Hope leaped through her veins. Plans raced through her head. If she could not escape the devil, she would outsmart him and meet with the king himself. "Then I'll have the opportunity to speak with King Henry."

Ranulf's misty gray orbs narrowed. "What of great importance would you share with our king? Have you spent time with royalty? Does he even know your name? No, of course he does not." He continued to examine her as if she were an insect. "Ah, 'tis as I thought. Your silence speaks for itself."

Clarice waved the air as if it were of no great importance. "Once I meet with him, he will want me to attend him and his court."

"You outstep your boundaries. Our king doesn't have time for a frivolous court romance."

"'Tis you who oversteps propriety." Hands on hips, she looked him up and down as if seeing him for the first time.

"Many a bitter word laced with syrup has brought foolish men to their knees."

Seeing her window of escape begin to close, Clarice licked her lips and tried a different tack. "Pray, hear me out. You are a man in favor with the king."

"My sweet, you are not riding past Sedgewic lands. You'll remain here until my return. Besides, Henry is too busy to give you audience."

Clarice's plans evaporated like the mists in the morning sun. Determined to change her situation, she pressed on. "But you said—"

"Silence! My concern is for today. Our numbers are limited and I don't have enough men to allow even one to guard your every step." He rubbed the back of his neck, ruffling his hair. "As I see it, I'll have to undertake the task of keeping you out of trouble. 'Tis the reason I request you ride with me." He held his hand up in warning. "Only for today."

Her thoughts swirled. Christ's blood! Joined at his hip at every turn, she might never escape. Nor did she care to explore the growing discomfort she felt whenever Ranulf was near. Desperate to leave the confines of Sedgewic and the truth of her feelings, she grasped at an alternative to his plans.

"As you've said, Mistress Erwina is overtaxed with the duties of the household. I should stay here and help her. 'Tis certain you can see the poor thing is nigh on to wasting away."

He tilted his head as if sniffing out his prey. "'Tis a tempting thought and much easier to obtain than gaining audience with the king, but I think not, sweeting. Although I'm certain you meant it to the marrow of your tender bones, I cannot expect Erwina to waste her day guarding you from yourself." He pressed his hand over her mouth. "As you said, she carries a great load and we wouldn't want to add to its weight. Would we?"

Clarice nipped his fingers. 'Twas small satisfaction when he winced before he jerked out of reach of her sharp teeth, but 'twas worth the pleasure just the same.

"I see you prove my point without effort, wench. My decision stands."

"Oh, piss and bother." She stamped her foot. "What if I swear an oath and promise not to venture from this room?"

"You expect me to believe one word you say? Oath or not, it holds no value."

"Horse's ass," she muttered. "May a plague find its way to your codpiece."

Her breath caught when he dragged her to his chest and planted a kiss on her parted lips. He buried his hands in her hair and drew her closer, assaulting her senses. His tongue danced lightly, luring her lips to offer sanctuary to his own. He stopped as suddenly as he had started and dragged his mouth away.

Wide-eyed, Clarice ran a hand across her throat. "Do not attempt that again," she whispered.

"Do you threaten me?"

"No," she said. "But there are ways to hurt that leave no visible scar."

She took a step back, sensing she had gone too far. As his hand drew back, a moment of something akin to disappointment pierced her heart as she braced for the punishment. Disgust with her inability to see through his lies roiled in her stomach. Physical pain she would have expected from someone like Robert. Not this man standing before her.

Continuing to surprise her, Ranulf's hand rammed through his hair, unaware that as he did so, he revealed the edge of the jagged scar running from his temple. Her heart tugged at the sight.

"Yes," he said. "And there are ways that leave their mark, no matter what you do." His thumb slid over her sensitive lips. "I wonder which you intend. Either way, I fear there will be damage to both of us before we are through."

Clarice glanced at Erwina, who looked as if she wished a hole would open up and deliver her from this house of madmen.

"Begging your pardon, my lord," Erwina said, bobbing a curtsy on her spry old legs, "but what are your wishes?"

"My wishes?" Ranulf paused. "I fear my good nature has taken a turn. I'd be hard-pressed to conjure it up for the king himself." Once again, his mouth formed a stern line. "I don't give a bloody good damn. Do with her what you will."

The door slammed in Erwina's face and she whirled on Clarice. "If she hadn't already passed on, your mother would be dying of shame. I am beginning to think you deserve the life you have been given."

Clarice attempted to pull her shoulders back, but they refused to go. She slumped to the floor in rejection.

Erwina drew close and rested a hesitant hand on her head. "There, there, lass. Don't give in to the trouble that surrounds us. All will be well."

"How can you say that, Erwina?"

"Well, he did say I could use you as I willed."

Clarice looked up, wary of the punishment to be meted out. It should not have mattered, really, as she was accustomed to labor. The servants at Margrave were too few to work the fields, so she did her best to help. Many a night she fell into bed out of sheer exhaustion, surrounded by her dreams.

"'Tis a great castle, teeming with hungry mouths," she whispered meekly. "I shan't dare try to figure out how you managed for so long. I imagine 'twas a little easier when Lady Mary was alive to help."

Erwina grunted. "That one? She had no desire to learn the ways of running a household."

"'Tis certain she had been taught by her fostering family."

"That one preferred the servants learned their places. She was most offended when Lord Ranulf brought her to her new home. Castle Sedgewic was in worse shape when she arrived than 'tis now."

Clarice lifted a disbelieving brow. "'Tis unimaginable this castle is for the better."

"Lord Ranulf has made great strides in putting it in order. Not one chamber was fit for use when they first arrived. If the roof was safe, then the floors threatened to fall down. If the floors were sturdy, then the roof had holes in it. Lady Mary demanded to go back to the court, but all her tantrums were ignored. There were rumors the king did not wish for her immediate return. It wasn't long before his lordship had to leave to tend to the king's needs."

Clarice thought of the times she had been left to molder while her family traveled to London. On one recent occasion, Robert had bragged to her that he would soon earn the king's favor and have all the women begging at his feet. He had said one in particular came to mind. Then he scampered off to lift the skirts of Annora's latest maids. Poor thing. 'Twas a blessing Annora had removed the young chamber maids from Margrave Manor and sent them to the house in London. However, 'twas whispered Robert abused his position in Margrave House, too.

"Whatever did Lady Mary do to occupy her day?" Clarice asked.

"She managed to find her mischief—" Erwina cleared her throat. "'Tis wrong to speak unkindly of the dead."

"Hamish spoke of the lady's death. That she was murdered."

"Ack! That child needs more than a beating, but it would do us no good anyway."

"Mistress Erwina—"

The cap shook as the old woman crossed herself. "And there'll be no more talk of Lady Mary. If you wish to know more, speak to Lord Ranulf."

Clarice suppressed her curiosity and returned to Erwina's earlier words. They buzzed around her, confusing her with things she did not understand.

"What did you mean about my mother?"

Erwina stopped bustling around the chamber. Her back to Clarice, she stiffened before answering. "Oh, I think you misheard me, dear."

"You said she would be disappointed. Did you know my mother?"

"Hush now! We haven't time for a game of questions."

"I never knew her . . . my mother."

Tight-lipped, Erwina moved about with precision, gathering items from chest and pile. "Hurry, child," she called. "You must make haste." Erwina propelled Clarice toward the pile of garments. "No time for chatter."

Before Clarice could question the woman's frantic pace, the gown she wore was replaced by a dress of fine green wool. She traced the intricate geometric patterns embroidered on the sleeve. *A bit much for daily tasks, is it not?*

Erwina looked up from her rummaging through the pile and frowned. "'Tis a pity, but men do not always think of the simple details required for a lady's dress. It appears they forgot the head covering. Should it be necessary, you'll have to use the hood on your cloak to cover your head. The headband will hold your hair in place. The pins should do the rest."

"'Tis lovely work." Clarice peered at her reflection in the bowl of water, unsure how she was to manage the skirts while she labored at household chores. "I am most amazed by your efficiency. One day you'll have to tell me how you came to be so handy."

Flushed with pleasure, Erwina hastened her charge to the door. "'Tis a tale left for a day when we aren't in a hurry to be off."

"Where are we going? Erwina, you heard the lord's orders. I am to help you."

"He also said to do with you what I will, and I will it that you ride with him."

Clarice gaped. "'Tis unwise. He was sorely vexed when he left. I cannot just go to him."

"True. Let me think." Erwina tapped her lips.

Her smile left Clarice feeling like a sacrificial virgin. As she thought about it some more, she decided she felt more like the chicken with its neck stretched on the chopping block.

"Ah!" Without another word, the woman ushered her down the stairs, leading the way to the buttery, where she went to work loading baskets. Their baskets full, Erwina guided them across the castle yard until they reached the empty bailey without mishap. After patting Clarice on the cheek, she left her standing, arms loaded with baskets laden with food, balancing a wineskin on one hip, waiting for the lord of Sedgewic.

Feeling like that doomed chicken, Clarice's heart pounded in her chest. As the master of Sedgewic marched up with his two large friends, she imagined the butcher block under her neck and the bite of the steel cleaver.

Sir Darrick and Sir Nathan walked purposefully beside Ranulf. The occasional slap on Ranulf's broad shoulder punctuated their quiet conversation. Hamish skipped behind their every step, attempting to keep up with the three. Their long strides covered a span that required him to half-run and skip to keep up. The chubby colt fighting to keep up with the virulent stallions.

Despite all the reasons she should not enjoy the sight, Clarice admired the way Ranulf poured a certain determination into the carriage of his person. His bearing told of his comfort with leadership. His size spoke of the strength and power contained within the man.

As they drew closer, she swallowed, prepared to feel the sharp edge of his tongue. "You are late, my lord." Tipping her head, she struggled to lower into a curtsy without dropping the bundles of food.

Sir Darrick took her elbow as she rose and removed the weighty load from her arms.

"My thanks, Sir Darrick," she said.

"What are you about, Clarice?" Ranulf asked.

"I do believe you said to meet you here within the hour." She made a show of shading her eyes as she cast a gaze about the empty bailey. "And I see the horses have yet to be brought 'round."

Ranulf's gray eyes glittered with an emotion she could not determine. He braced his arms across his chest before making a final decision.

Clarice jumped when he grabbed the wineskin from Darrick and shoved it into her hands. Without another word, he balanced the remaining baskets in his arms. "Come," he snapped.

Heat flooded her cheeks as he walked away, leaving her to juggle the wine and fight her heavy skirts all the while trying to keep pace. Pausing to catch her breath, she glanced over her shoulder at the two men behind her.

Darrick laid a hand upon Nathan's shoulder as the taller knight made to go after them. "I would not become involved. Let them deal with it."

Nathan shrugged off his friend's hand. "The devil, you say. Ranulf is behaving like an ass."

Mischief reflected in Sir Nathan's green eyes as he strode up to Clarice. Her skin pebbled a warning under his scrutiny. Dread seeped into her bones. Whatever he planned would get her into more trouble with the virile lord. She yelped when he lifted her into his arms with ease. Nathan's chuckle reverberated against her ribs. His auburn brows rose before dropping a wink her way. She caught the sight of Ranulf's rigid stance before he methodically placed the baskets on the ground.

"Nathan," Darrick called, "be a knight of honor and hand over the lady to the lord before he claps you in irons."

Nathan met the advice with defiance. "No matter. The walls are weak and the irons are probably rusted. I would be free within the hour."

The lord of Sedgewic marched toward them. His wolf eyes glittered over a deadly grin. "Do you care to make a wager?" he snarled.

Chapter 22

After a wordless scowl from Ranulf, Nathan surrendered Clarice into his waiting arms. Shrugging sheepishly, the redheaded giant grinned and stepped out of Ranulf's reach.

"Coward." Clarice shouted at Nathan's retreat. "Go. Quiver and shake. Run away." She shook her fist. "Ignore the maiden who needs your help."

"Cease before you awaken his wrath," Ranulf said, depositing her on Buttercup.

His back straight as a pikestaff, he motioned her to follow. Without a backward glance, he mounted his horse and rode away.

As Clarice nudged Buttercup forward, she caught the sight of Nathan and Darrick, holding their sides as if their ribs would break. Heat surged to her already flushed cheeks. Angry oaths bubbled to her lips. She bit down hard to keep them from spewing outside her head. Snapping on the reins, she sent her mount trotting.

She matched the pace he set and stifled her questions regarding the castle. They rode past the walls in silence. In time, her boiling temper slowly reduced to a low simmer and she examined the possibility of escape.

Gently nudging Buttercup, Clarice coaxed the horse away from the rider in front of her. She pressed to the left and Aldwyn's rump cut them off. When she pressed to angle to the right, Aldwyn blew softly through his velvet nose and planted his hooves in her path. Hope plummeted as she realized that even though Ranulf appeared busy with the affairs of the castle, he was aware of her every move. Resigned to wait for another time to make her break from Sedgewic, she settled into the soothing rhythm of Buttercup's gait.

With the voice of caution ringing in her ears, she strived to keep her thoughts away from the fascinating play of muscles that made up Ranulf's distracting backside and stared at the back of his head. However, to her frustration, the ripple of movement across his broad shoulders brought fresh memories of a potent strength hidden under his leather jerkin.

The palfrey did a sudden step to the side and had Clarice clinging to her seat. With one leg draped over Buttercup's neck and the other wrapped under its belly, she strained with limbs and arms, pulling her bottom back onto the hard saddle. The reins slipped from her hand.

Ranulf brought his mount to stand beside hers. He held the bridle while she righted herself. "Haven't spent much time in the saddle, have you?"

"No." Heat rose from her neck as she fiddled with the reins and mumbled a halfhearted thanks.

He returned the reins, concern reflected in his tone. "Best ride close and keep those sapphires open."

"So my father had often warned me," Clarice muttered. "'Tis a dangerous world outside the walls and one must ignore the desire to leave their safety."

Ranulf leaned in and brushed her cheek. "Do not spend all your energies fearing the unknown. Although our enemies dare not breach Sedgewic lands, we won't venture far today."

A shiver trailed down her spine. "'Tis not always the unknown that casts the shadows on the day. Danger can be found in the faces of friends as well as enemies." She searched his face. Which one was he?

Ranulf raised a brow and motioning her to ride beside him. Squaring his shoulders, he turned to speak. "Allies or foes. Caution is yet a wise warning for all of us to follow."

Signaling to raise the portcullis, Ranulf directed their horses under the iron gate and past the thick castle walls. He inspected the repairs of the old stone structure while Clarice observed the work already accomplished, and the daunting amount awaiting his attention. Before she could voice her appreciation, he swung his mount around and led them away from the castle's protection.

They rode down to the valley, weaving through the fields of lush meadow grass to the ribbon of dirt road below. Dust swirled through the air as they stopped at the next rise.

Noting Ranulf's knitted brow, she followed his gaze to the decaying outer wall. "You should be commended for your efforts. How do you manage when you and your men are away?"

"'Tis not my efforts as much as my coin. The people of Sedgewic desire to see their homes thriving with health and prosperity. The castle walls and all that dwell within their protection fight for the same reasons. They wish to remain strong and safe."

"Don't you worry for the lives you leave behind when you go off on your adventures with the king?"

"'Tis something we must do."

She sniffed at his comment. "I believe 'tis nothing more than to feed one's self-importance."

Scowling, Ranulf shifted in the saddle. "There are also times when we are not given a choice. What would our king think if I told him to fight without me? These walls may well have cracks on their surface, but they do not run deep. The walls will stand against an attack. But the protection I can offer in my absence is much greater when I have the king's pleasure. Would you have me deny my king and put that protection in jeopardy?"

Thoughts of her father's desperate last days raced to the forefront. "Having Henry's favor is vital and serves your people as yourself. This I understand more than you might think. But don't you miss your home?"

"Often. Some nights I wonder. If I were never to return, would life go on, my absence unnoticed?"

"Your absence is apparent before you cross the gate. I am sure a celebration of your return is already in the midst of preparation." She cast a glance, veiled under her lashes. "Your lordship is not easy to forget."

"You would never be forgotten," he said.

Clarice's heart warmed at his assurance. She turned to cover the heat creeping into her cheeks and looked back at the fresh stone blending into the ancient wall. How would it continue without the lord's guiding hand? After her father and Annora had quit coming to Margrave the work became harder to see through to the finish. Would it happen here, too? "Does Mistress Erwina manage the men as well as the children?"

"Ol' Scoggins directs most of the work that needs to be done outside. However, Erwina would tell you she requires no help. Her obstinate strength became apparent after my wife's death."

"I'm sure a great loss was endured when she passed."

Clarice winced as soon as the words were out of her mouth. Silence stretched between them. She scrambled for sturdier ground.

"Will the masons continue with their work? 'Tis a great deal to be done. Not that I don't already see where you have left your mark, but how will you afford the materials to keep your castle in repair?"

"The lord of a land is also its steward. I have an advantage over those born with privilege. I understand 'tis important to protect what is mine, but 'tis also important to make a profit."

The hills and valleys stretched out before her. "Does the land reach so far? Have you enough men to keep it patrolled? My father chose to keep the guards stationed in the manor." Sighing, Clarice spoke her thoughts aloud. "Although why Margrave would need guards at every corner inside the walls instead of working the fields to provide most of our supplies, I will never understand. But soon even those were removed."

She shifted in her seat and prayed he had not noticed the mention of her father. "I haven't seen the soldiers carrying your banner. Don't you have one?" Peering closely, she raised an eyebrow. "In fact, now that I look at you, I fear I am unable to discern a design of your own."

Ranulf jerked as if struck. "Mary meant to design one for me, but there were so many things for her to take to task that she didn't have the time to see it done."

"Oh," Clarice said. "But I understood your wife was bored by the country life and found time here stood still. I would have thought she would grasp at anything to keep herself occupied."

When he did not respond, Clarice feared she had struck a nerve. In fact, with his brows drawn together and his mouth pursed, he looked as if he had an aching tooth. He nudged his mount forward, stretching the distance between them so that 'twas impossible for him to hear her questions.

Forced to accept his silence as an answer, she studied the man sitting astride his horse. The weight of so much labor and the cost incurred would be enough to make any brave man race to the battlefield for peace. The king's plans to claim France would drain more funds than Ranulf could afford.

She tilted her face to the sun and let the breeze ruffle her hair. A gust of wind caught the edge of her billowing skirt. Warmth radiated through her body. She closed her eyes and breathed in the heavy pine scent.

Fear seemed so small when faced in the sunlight. A joy she had never known before lifted her spirits as easily as the breeze. Gone were the imprisoning walls. Margrave Manor and Castle Sedgewic did not hold her anymore. She was free to race the clouds. Free to follow the birds as they flew by. *Freedom.*

Ranulf reached out and tickled her nose with a long blade of grass. "Remember my warning, little one. Always keep your eyes open."

She swatted at the offending weed. "I cannot imagine anyone foolish enough to come across your lands without your permission."

"In truth? Then please explain how we found you here. Did a fairy drop you?"

Clarice thought of her father's palfrey and smoothed her hand over the horse's shoulder. "Buttercup is definitely not a fairy. And if you recall, I was injured." The leather saddle creaked in response to her fidgeting. "Otherwise I would not have stopped on your land, but would have finished my journey."

"How could I forget?"

She shivered, heat gathering as he perused her body.

"I've meant to ask you. Where were you headed?" Ranulf squinted into the sun "A copse of trees stands over yon hill. We'll rest there."

Flooded with relief that he let his questions drop, she nearly wept as they rode up the hill.

Ranulf brought his mount to an abrupt halt. Clarice jerked the reins, almost losing her seat again when the horse stepped to keep from running into the back of the stallion. He twisted in the saddle. A single brow arched as if waiting for a response.

After settling Aldwyn, he cast Clarice a scathing look from under his too-long lashes. He moved his mount closer and leaned in to run a finger over her arm. "I said, 'tis time to confess."

"Confess?" She searched his face for answers. "What might you need to confess?"

"No, 'tis not I who needs to lighten the weight on my heart. I would have it that you found me friend enough to tell how you arrived wounded and on my lands." He paused. "The truth this time."

The truth. How much could she tell? Clarice tilted her head and watched the clouds drift overhead before answering. "My father foolishly sent me on a hunt for a mythical red wolf. Sedgewic happened to be on the way. With lands as vast as Sedgewic, I was bound to run into them at some point."

"Mayhap that was your father's intention all along."

Feeling the first hint of chill in the air, Clarice shivered and moved restlessly. "Possibly."

Chapter 23

"'Tis time we turned back," Clarice gritted through her teeth. "The weather—"

He could not help noticing that his probing had deepened the pinched corners around her mouth. "What makes you as skittish as a cat in a stable full of horses?"

Her shoulders hunched, she looped the reins around the pommel and turned her gaze toward him. "In truth. . . ." The wind lifted her hair, tugging it free from her braid to dance around her flushed cheeks

Ranulf leaned in. "Yes?"

Thunder rolled from the storm forming in the distance. A crack of lightning shook the earth.

"The truth is—" She bit her lip as if to lock in a confession.

The palfrey stamped its hooves. Its ears pressed against its skull. A gust of wind caught her skirt, flapping it against Buttercup's rump. The reins slithered out of Clarice's hands as the horse squealed and raced off with her rider to the valley below.

"Clarice!" Kicking Aldwyn with his heels, they galloped after her. Muscles in his jaw clicked as he watched her bound over the grassy knoll.

Never in his life had he seen a horse ridden in such a manner. He hoped she would manage to stop the palfrey on her own. If she kept flailing her arms as she was, her ride would come to a quick and painful halt.

Leaning forward in the saddle, he and Aldwyn flew to the valley and then up the hill. Clarice was too far ahead of him. His gut twisted as she rode out of sight.

Where is she? Ranulf cut his eyes to the sky. The storm overhead continued to roll in and would soon be upon them.

Sweat trickled down his neck. Finally, near the trees, he spotted the pale mare wandering among the flowers, her head buried in clover. Clarice was nowhere in sight. He rode closer, angling Aldwyn so as not to force the mare to bolt.

A flash of green waved against the meadow grass. Clarice lay on her side, her skirt bunched high around her thighs.

"Are you hurt?"

"No . . ." Clarice pushed herself upright. Her hand trembled as she worked to right her hair. ". . . my lord.

Ranulf worked to control the fear that threatened to cut off his ability to think as he slid from his horse. He held out his hand and had it waved away.

"See to Buttercup instead."

His hand wavered in the space between them before he let it drop to his side. Giving her a nod, he turned away as he was bid. With a soft, murmured word in Aldwyn's ear, he set the destrier loose to nuzzle the meadow grass.

Buttercup's coat shivered under Ranulf's gentling hand. He ran his other hand across her shoulders, down her foreleg. He lifted her leg, examining each hoof before letting it drop to the ground. Although relieved that she did not seem to be injured, he shook his head. Micah would be distraught when he saw the mare's condition. Lather coated her pale hide. Weeds and brambles stuck out from her tail. Bits of meadow grass clung to her mane. He led her beside Aldwyn to munch on the greens. "Go on with you," he said with a pat on the rump.

Her ears flicked back and forward. Sensing distress, she moved out of harm's way.

Ranulf took notice of Clarice, her arms wrapped around her ribs. As if the simple act would hold her together.

Ranulf grabbed her sleeve. "Clarice—"

"Is . . . is Buttercup all right?"

Envisioning the scene before, he clasped her to his chest as if to ward off the wave of fear that threatened to come crashing down.

"'Twas the thunder and lightning." Clarice jerked free and bent to gather her horse's reins.

"You'll ride with me," he said, holding out his hand. "Buttercup needs her rest and I've no desire to fetch you over the next green knoll."

She straightened, eyes flashing. With reluctance, she placed her hand in his. "I did not intend for any of this . . ."

"I know." Softly, he brushed her lips with his. She leaned into him. Her heartbeat reverberated through their clothing. A gasp of awareness told him she felt the same heat. *God, what am I thinking?*

Despite the yearning, he swept her up as if she weighed no more than a goose feather and placed her on Aldwyn's back. Hooking the stirrup, he swung his leg over the saddle. When her bottom pressed into his groin, he nearly groaned. Stifling the desire to pull her closer, he urged the horses toward the castle. If he pushed their pace, they would soon be free of each other.

She rode in front of him, silent and stiff. Each breath caught the scent of rosemary in her hair and teased his senses. His grip on the reins tightened. The distance to the castle seemed to stretch farther than he could recall.

He hated to admit it. His concern for her bothered him.

He had hoped after Mary's death that he was beyond caring. It was less painful that way. That dark and empty night remained in the foggy parts of his brain, making it impossible for him to know peace. The secret life she had led while he was away on the king's business would forever tear at his heart. Happiness was a myth, buried in the shadows of her betrayal.

He rubbed the puckered scar along his brow. It mattered little to him if 'twas Mary or her lover who had inflicted the injury to his head. That was the least of his worries. What he feared most was that he might have been the one who had delivered the deathblow to Mary. He would never forgive himself. Deep down, he could not fathom doing such a deed. He had hoped that despite their arranged marriage, they eventually would have found happiness with each other.

But that had not been the case. Unable to hide her revulsion at their union, Mary had fortified her nerves with wine until he had to carry her to their marriage bed. On their wedding night their joining had been brief.

In the days and weeks that followed, he had hardened his heart to her weeping and deafened his ears to her outbursts of rage against him and the crown. He could ill afford to pay off all listening ears pressed to the door of their chambers and took his young bride to the country. Every day thereafter, the people of Sedgewic had heard their mistress's rage at him for damaging her for another. In his cowardice, he had returned to traveling far-reaching lands for his king. When he had received word that Mary was with child, he had hastened home with visions of a loving family greeting him with open arms. Instead, that first night back, he had regained consciousness only to discover Mary was dead. *By whose hand? Mine?*

There was a time when he had thought he could sacrifice no more than he already had. One never realized the value of peace of mind until 'twas no longer there. He would forever be haunted with the knowledge that he had failed to protect what was his.

Although his thoughts held him, at one point Ranulf stopped to rearrange Clarice's seat and strove to ignore their close proximity. She, with her thighs and rounded bottom nestled by his lap, and he with his legs spread astride the great horse, his need became more apparent with each step of the stallion's undulating gait.

Soon his discomfort became more pleasant as he felt her ramrod back relax against his chest. Wary of her submissive silence, he rode toward the castle walls.

Aldwyn's muscles bunched under Ranulf's legs. Buttercup struggled against the lead rope. The smell of damp earth rose up and filled Ranulf's nose. A jagged lightning bolt lit the premature nightfall, leaving the hair on his arms tingling from the vibration.

Wind came on its heels, whipping through the branches. Leaves on the trees had flipped in the blowing wind. Their silver underbelly waited for the first splash of rain. The sky opened up, releasing the brewing storm.

Jarred from her silence, Clarice shouted over the punishing wind. "Ranulf."

He adjusted his hold on the reins and leaned over to speak into her ear. "I know of a place not far from here. We shall have to ride hard. Hold tight."

Fat raindrops soon became rivulets in a steady stream. 'Twas as if the gods had decided to pour great buckets of water upon their heads. The faster Aldwyn flew, the harder Buttercup ran, the heavier the rain fell. A tree limb cracked from the wind and the weight of the falling rain. They raced out from under the branches without a moment to spare.

A rain-induced river cut into the bank of rounded earth, slicing past stones, washing away the months of winter decay. Aldwyn's footing slid in the mire.

"We're almost there," Ranulf said.

A burned-out building stood against the storm. Its skeletal remains offered little more than a shell for protection. No light shone from the jagged holes in the wall, nor did the smell of a fire in the hearth fill the air.

"What is this place?" she croaked.

Ranulf hunched further into his cloak. "Just bricks and mortar."

Chapter 24

The rain showed little sign of letting up. A streak of lightning raced above their heads. Thunder rolled, shaking the ground beneath Aldwyn's steady hooves. The air was thick with the pungent smell of wet horse and leather.

Clarice tilted back the hood of her cloak. The pooling water caught in the folds of the fabric trickling down her shoulders, splashing bare skin. She scrubbed her cold fingers against her legs for warmth and squinted through the dull gray light. "What happened here?"

Ranulf leaned over her back. "Devastation by man and time."

"Will it be safe?" she asked, her voice rising to keep the wind from carrying away her question.

"I promise 'tis safer than where we are now."

As if to punctuate his words, a crack of lightning sliced through the ever-darkening sky. The limbs of the trees creaked and moaned, whipping in the wind.

Ranulf threaded the horses through moss-covered tree stumps and fallen branches. They stopped behind a fragrant juniper.

Clarice turned to speak but stopped when his arm tightened around her waist. He squeezed once to gain her attention, twice to have her silence. Wary of any unexplained movement from the shadows, he spoke quietly to the horses and moved them toward the burned-out building.

Blackened timbers looked like grasping fingers sticking out of the crumbling walls. Despite its charred outer shell, the tallest timber stood strong against the prevailing winds. Beams stretched out, crossing and overlapping, forming the building's crippled backbone. The roof was gone, exposing the remnant to the elements.

"Are you certain 'twould be best to stop?" She lifted her face to speak above the whistling wind. "I assure you, I will come to no harm if we should ride on."

"No, this is where we'll remain."

"Just until the storm subsides?" Clarice asked, wary that the people of Sedgewic would take note of their extended time alone.

"Yes, just until. See here." He pointed to a wide path of smooth stone, covered in layers of dirt and moss. It drew them to the cavernous opening that once had had the makings of a doorway.

Ranulf brought Aldwyn to a halt and touched Clarice's shoulder. "Stay where you are. Should we need to leave quickly, you'll be where I need you."

Clarice nodded and held her seat while he dismounted. She bit her tongue to keep from asking why they could not enter.

He looped the reins over a blackened timber sticking out from the slanted doorway. "Remember to stay alert."

Ranulf picked his way past the main entrance. It appeared the rear of the building had received less fire damage than the front. What had not been felled by fire showed signs of imminent collapse. The remains of the swaybacked roof hung low, sagging under the weight of time and abandonment.

Clarice remained on Aldwyn's back. Although reluctant to leave the horse, the thought of waiting to stretch her limbs was almost unbearable. She felt a rush of relief when Ranulf returned. He held his arms up and motioned her to trust in his strength to lift her from the saddle. "We'll stay here until the storm passes."

She nearly fell into his chest. Her hands braced, her palms pressed into his upper arms. His muscles contracted and bunched when he lifted her off her perch. Her breath caught. Their mouths were so close. Near enough for her to nibble his lip.

"Many thanks." Her eyes widened. If she were to lean in, she might brush his lips with her own. She cleared her throat. "You can let me down now."

"True. I could." His large hands encompassed her waist as he drew her close, suspending her in his embrace. Ranulf smiled, then gently, slowly, lowered his arms.

Clarice touched the solid ground with the tips of her toes. His fingers heated the flesh covering her ribs, inches away from her breasts.

She held her breath, hoping he would not be aware of his dangerous hold.

Their chests touching, his heart throbbed through the layers of leather jerkin and linen shirt. The steady beat burrowed under her skin. It was as if the raging storm had discovered an entrance into her body and raced through her blood.

Her breath escaped as she slid against his manhood. Her skin heated. Her legs trembling, she leaned into his solid wall of muscle and absorbed enough strength to release his arms and push away. She rushed to ask the first question that came into her head. "Did you bring the food Erwina sent with us?"

Ranulf tucked an ebony strand of hair behind her ear. His finger grazed over a drop of rain clinging to her cheek. "Yes. Mayhap while we eat you will entertain me with tales of your life before our paths crossed."

Clarice looked away, hoping to avoid his prodding comments. "Maud did always say a full stomach made for a better companion."

He gave a long-suffering sigh, feigning acceptance of her game of avoidance. "She'd make a lucky soldier well and happy."

Warm memories flooded Clarice's mind. Maud's skinny legs flashing under a work-worn hem, her grizzled hair and failed hearing were all sweet visions of her dear friend. However, the idea of Maud giving a man pleasure was enough to make her snort.

"You might laugh," Ranulf observed, "but a soldier's life is connected to the plentitude of food." He held up the linen-wrapped food and grinned. "Have you failed to note the generous portions Erwina sent for two people?"

"'Tis a wonder the horses carried both rider and parcels."

"This?" He glanced down at the wads of cloth nestled in the leather satchel and shook his head. "This is nothing compared to the preparations she'll make for my men before we leave."

"My Maud could feed an army if she had need," Clarice said. "But I cannot imagine her devotion turned anywhere but toward Margrave Manor. As she tells it, she hasn't set one foot off the land since I was placed in her arms."

Ranulf peered into her eyes. "Loyalty is priceless. Henry desires to find it in all the people of England."

Clarice refused to turn away and met his gaze. "My father knew this fealty to his king. He has always said one's honor is tied to family and throne."

"Your father sounds like a good man." Ranulf smiled and played with a damp tendril clinging to her neck. "I would share my bench and break bread with him one day."

Her hunger fled with his comment. "I'm afraid that would be impossible. As you are well aware, Nicholas of Margrave is dead."

"You wish to claim a man accused of treason as your father?" He reached out, erasing the distance she had tried to place between them. He stroked the tension along her jaw. Cupping her cheek in his hand, he applied enough pressure with his thumb to tilt her face up to look into his.

Clarice allowed her heart to indulge in the tenderness of his touch. She smiled up at his concern. "I will take consolation that you have accepted my claim. For now, that will have to do."

She stepped out of his reach and untied the leather thongs that held the blanket rolled behind Buttercup's saddle. Pausing, she waited for Ranulf to lead the way.

He took her by the elbow and led her to a corner of the barren room. Large fallen beams angled close together to form a partial roof over their heads. Ranulf stretched his cloak over it, creating a barrier to slow the drenching rain.

Clarice eyed the makeshift shelter. While the winds continued to whistle, the worst of the storm was held at bay. "Stay here. I'll move the horses closer," he said.

She turned to offer her help and found the space where he had been standing empty. All she could see of him was the shadow of his back weaving through the fallen timbers. After draping her wet cloak out to dry, she unfurled the blanket and wrapped it about her shoulders. Then she peeled back the linen from the food.

Her task completed, Clarice stepped back to admire the victuals and waited for Ranulf's return. Shivering, she dreamed of a small fire to warm her toes and dry her clothing. After a while, she considered whether Ranulf would mind if she went through his satchel in search of flint and steel for a fire.

She dipped her fingers into the leather pouch and pulled out a wad of stiff material. Slowly, she smoothed it out across her knee. With shaking hands, she held the satin strip closer. 'Twas from her father's banner; the scrap of material used to staunch the flow of blood from the wound on her arm.

Ranulf searched the corner of the building, looking for anything to aid in their comfort. Clarice's determination to lay claim to a man disavowed by the king made little sense. She would be a fool to want to be connected to a traitor. She had spoken of someone named Maud. A common enough name. Being Margrave's daughter would not protect her. In truth, she should deny ever knowing the man. It went against what he knew as his duty, but he had to convince her to stop telling the foolish story. The lies might take her head.

As he moved about the remnants of the orphanage, memories of another life flashed and swirled in his mind. He walked past areas of his life he had thought he'd placed well behind him. He found that in ignoring the rebuilding of this lord's house, he had ignored the beginning of his life.

Mayhap, if I had tried harder, been there to protect Mary from her unhappiness, I might have earned her love. In time.

Lost in regret, he wove his way past the fallen beams. Upon entering the alcove, he found Clarice as she knelt beside the food. Displayed upon the woven blanket was a glistening wedge of yellow cheese, hunks of fresh brown bread, a mound of smooth, diamond-shaped almonds, and two red apples. His stomach rumbled as he took a step toward the banquet.

The hunger gnawing at his stomach vanished when she turned toward him. In her hand she clutched the material, stiff with dried blood. He knew she would question his motives for carrying it with him.

"Was this once a monastery?" Clarice asked, her voice faint and without strength.

"Not here. This portion was used as an orphanage."

Clarice glanced around, her fingers moving blindly across the stiff scrap of banner. "Whoever lit the fire didn't start it near the children? 'Twas not meant to harm them?"

"Who said 'twas set by man and not by an act of God?"

"The tale of the avenging knight. 'Tis true, is it not?"

Ranulf swallowed and took a deep breath. "Yes. Although at the time, in a child's mind, 'twas a demon."

"You were here? Did you see that child's monster?"

" 'Twas a long time ago."

"But 'twas your home."

"A place to rest my head." Ranulf held out a hand to help her rise. "Never my home."

Clarice touched a tentative finger against his tunic sleeve. "Were you lonely?"

"There are times when one is never alone but constantly lonely."

She looked at where his wide hand covered her own. "I am familiar with a constant loneliness. It penetrates the soul."

Ranulf could not ignore the pain in her voice. His heart ached for her. "A beauty such as yourself? I cannot believe you have been kept from companionship."

Her smile lifted the corners of her mouth. The sadness never left her eyes. "Oh, Maud is a dear, right enough. She has been my constant companion. Until of late, that is."

His fingers tightened over hers and gave a gentle, reassuring squeeze. "And you have your family."

Clarice tugged against his hold. "I have no one until my return to Margrave."

"Your family still resides at Margrave? Were they not removed by the king's men?"

"Didn't you hear my words, my lord?" Frustrated anger glittered back at him. "My family is *of* Margrave Manor."

Ranulf traced the crease between her brows with the pad of his finger. "I had hoped you would turn from this tale once you realized I don't believe it."

Her face paled. Clarice stepped back, drawing out of his embrace. "Must you cling to your disbelief? Why are you unable to accept that I am Nicholas of Margrave's daughter?"

Ranulf reached out and pulled her closer. She let out a feral growl. He wrapped his arms around her shoulders and spoke as he rested his chin on her head. "You forget. I've met the Margraves."

Her fingers dug into his chest, pushing him away. "Then you should understand that I wouldn't make this up on a whim. You must know I speak the truth."

"Clarice, you bear no resemblance to them. Besides, how could you be a Margrave without the king knowing of your existence?"

His heart twisted as she struggled to find the words to explain the contempt in which her family held her. "Annora is my stepmother. Robert is my stepbrother. I was never allowed to leave Margrave lands."

"What reason would keep them from introducing you at court, let alone to the rest of the world?" Ranulf argued.

"My father always spoke of protecting me." She gripped her elbows, a wary look in her eyes.

"Protect you from whom?"

She blew out a breath of frustration and threw up her hands. "I don't know."

Ranulf stepped closer, pressing her to tell the truth. "You still maintain your father is Lord Margrave?"

"Yes," she said through gritted teeth, poking him in the chest with her finger. "And I'll remain steadfast on this fact. Listen well, Lord Ranulf of Sedgewic, for I'll not repeat myself again. Believe me or not, I know who I am. Can you say the same?"

As soon as the words leaped from her lips, she realized the hurt they caused. Her eyes widening, she clapped a hand over her mouth.

"'Tis true, there was a time when I couldn't say the same. That life is done. I am King Henry's man and he has named me lord of Sedgewic." He peeled her fingers from her mouth and tipped up her chin so that he might look into her eyes as he spoke. "Truce. Tell me of your life and how you came to be so lonely."

"Before I do, would you grant me one boon?"

Ranulf lifted an eyebrow. "Only one?" Seeing her hesitation, he offered his encouragement. "Speak and I shall do my best to grant your boon."

She nodded and rushed forward. "Do you deny that you despised my father?"

Ranulf took a deep breath of the damp air. Clarice stood before him, braced for his response. His glance skimmed the structure that stood around him. He noted the charred remains that clung to the life that once was. Memories flooded back, forcing their way to the forefront of his thoughts. He gathered them to him and then held them out to ponder.

"There was a time when I both despised and thanked Nicholas of Margrave. The demon who came to the monastery, demanding his angel, caused many a night filled with nightmares." He held his hand up for silence. "Eventually all the children found new lives and I remained. The oldest of the children, I was the least likely to find a new mother or father. My lot was to go to the next farmer who required another hand to wield a hoe. 'Tis that uncertainty that held me in torment. Then came the day they sent me away."

Ranulf paused when he heard her gasp. Glancing down, he noted the tears shimmering in her eyes. The realization caught at his heart. Never had anyone shed a tear for him. Not even his wife had shed a tear when he left for battle.

He stroked Clarice's silken cap of ringlets, inhaling her scent as he once again rested his chin on her head. He reveled in the need to hold her there so that he might feel the warmth of her form nestled next to his. The chill of the rain and wind vanished with the knowledge that in this he was not alone.

Clarice wrapped her arms around his waist. She lifted her gaze to his. "Was it far?"

"To a lad it seemed to take an eternity to travel. However, once I got over the fear of the changes in my life, I learned there was a grand world to explore. When we stopped at the camp I soon discovered what my new role would be."

"Were you mistreated?"

He chuckled. "Not to worry. My lot had improved. I was to be Prince Henry's friend and companion. To this day, I remain his friend and sometimes unwilling confidant."

"King Henry's childhood friend and confidant? You lived in Wales?"

"Unless we were embroiled in battle. Henry learned at a young age to become a man. Taught the ways of battle almost before he left the nursery. It shapes a man to choose his friends with caution."

"And my father? Did you know him when he was at court?"

"Distantly. However, the man of whom you speak, at one time, was both friend and confidant to Henry. Many years earlier, I forgave the man who burned the home around me. Had he not done so, I would more than likely be digging the soil and wondering where my next bread might come from."

"And now?"

"You know of the accusations before his death. The man of whom you speak . . ." He shook his head. "One who hides a daughter from all sight and doesn't claim her as his own. He, I would not recognize. The man accused of treason. That man I don't know either.

His secret life confounds me." Ranulf pulled her closer, snuggling her into the crook of his arm. "I would have liked to speak with him one last time before he took his life."

Clarice turned and spoke with clear confidence. "Regardless of the rumors, my father remained a loyal friend and servant of King Henry. He did not take his life. My father was murdered."

Chapter 25

Ranulf extracted his arm from Clarice's shoulder to retrieve a small wooden barrel hidden in the corner. He set it down on the blanket with a quiet thump. Her accusations of murder echoed through his mind. Before he spoke, he searched her face. "What proof have you that Nicholas was murdered?"

"I know my father."

He rubbed his jaw. "This is the same man who didn't claim you as his daughter. And yet you feel you owe him your faith?"

Clarice looked up, bristling at his question. She tossed away the damp kindling beside the fire. "Yes."

Ranulf towered over her, bracing his arms across his chest. "And you still maintain you don't know why he kept his silence."

"I told you," she said, her voice clipped in forced patience, "To. Protect. Me."

"From what?" The pain in her eyes made him want to sweep her into his arms. Instead, Ranulf gripped his biceps and dug for more answers. "For what reason?"

"I don't know," she whispered. Defeated, her shoulders melted under the weight of his doubt.

"Your father was accused of treason. Of plotting to kill our king. Is he worth the price it may cost you?"

"Any price."

He pushed her to understand. "There may be consequences beyond my control."

She tilted her head to study his face. Hope shimmered in her eyes. "You would do that for me?"

Clearing his throat, he wondered what made him offer his help to a woman he did not trust. "If what you say is true, I cannot ignore the murder of a man who once was one of Henry's favorites. 'Tis not that I disbelieve," he cautioned. "But I must have proof to take to the king."

"I'm well aware of the accusations that have damaged my father's name." She gripped the folds of his jerkin, gaining his attention. "Whoever spilled this venom over his character is his murderer. I'm convinced of it."

Ranulf caught her cold fingers and led her to the blanket. He motioned for her to sit and dropped down beside her. He drew a small blade from the sheath tucked under his belt and sliced a hunk of cheese. "How can you be certain?"

"That is a question that has no clear answer." She rubbed her knuckles over her skirt. "The eve of his return has puzzled me until I can think of nothing else."

Ranulf held out the yellow cheese and noted her caution. "Things are usually clearer if more than one head is used to polish the thoughts. If you are willing, my ears are ready to listen."

She nibbled on the corner of the pungent cheese. "News of my family's trouble arrived when King Henry's men were at the gate." She looked up, her eyes boring into his. "You were there. You led them."

He swallowed, nodding in agreement as he recalled that day.

"Nearly a week passed before Father, Annora, and Robert arrived."

Realization slammed into Ranulf. Could it really be? Clarice was the maiden from Margrave Manor? Had the shadows been so deep that he had not recognized her? He swore he would have known her voice anywhere. Guilt boiled under his skin.

"They were arguing," Clarice continued. "Annora encouraged him to give himself up. Father refused to admit that he had a hand in anything so heinous. Robert added his taunts, accusing him of weakness and lack of spine."

Puzzled, Ranulf stroked his chin. "Why would your father allow it?"

"Annora had found a means in which to hold him under her thumb. What, I do not know." Clarice's chin lifted, defiant at his criticism of her father. "He did manage to challenge Robert, but not before my stepbrother had crossed the bridge of no retreat."

"How so?"

"'Twas during the argument that Robert physically attacked Father." Clarice watched him, willing him to hear the truth.

"Robert never did understand the meaning of honor," he said.

A raven brow lifted in amusement. "Truer words have never been said. Thankfully, providence did quickly smile and gave Father courage to seek another day."

Ranulf leaned in. "He didn't desire to take his life?"

"On the contrary. 'Twas after the peddler came to call that hope returned to my father's eyes."

"Peddler?" The confrontation played out in his memories.

"Yes." Shards of sapphire glittered over the firelight. Her fingers dug into the folds of her gown. "Without him, we would have spent many hungry days."

Uncomfortable with her praise for the peddler, Ranulf cleared his throat. "Lord Margrave—how did he change?"

"The last night he came to visit me, he told me that soon—in a week or two—we would be free of the rumors. I was certain he had an ally at Henry's court. Someone to help clear his name. He promised to introduce me at court once his troubles were over."

Ranulf held out the loaf of bread for her to tear off a portion. "Tell me of that night. What happened in the hours before and after?"

She shook her head and answered around the moist cheese and soft bread she had stuffed in her mouth. "I cannot help you there. I was locked in my chamber."

Taken aback by her quiet acceptance, Ranulf's gut twisted. His thoughts dashed to the time he became her jailer. He had ignored her terrified pleas and turned the bolt. Was it any wonder she had pleaded and pounded until her knuckles bled?

They sat in quiet silence, each focused on the food in front of them. Without her notice, Ranulf moved the meal closer to Clarice. Serenity surrounded them as they ate. How his world would have changed had he known her before Mary. Would their king have arranged a marriage between Sedgewic and Margrave instead? No! Henry would have taken advantage of her attributes and created a marriage bond with a noble of greater holdings. That thought thoroughly vexed him.

* * *

Eating as if she would never eat again, Clarice tucked another bite of cheese and bread into her mouth. After filling her stomach, she ended her meal with a few handfuls of almonds.

She itched at the silence that had grown between them. Was he angry at her appetite? She hated to admit that she would have devoured every morsel had she been by herself. As it was, Ranulf ate too little to feed a man of his size. Hoping to push the distant look from his eyes and repair his smile, she leaned over and offered him her apple.

His long fingers grazed the tender flesh of her hand, sending shivers across her skin. Her breath caught, knowing he must have felt it, too.

He lifted the apple to his mouth and slowly bit down. White teeth sank into the succulent fruit. Sweet liquid glistened upon his lips. She wondered if he made the apple that much sweeter.

She licked her lips, imagining what he might taste like. Sweet apple, juicy and warm, mixed with his scent and the peppermint leaves she had seen him slip into his mouth.

Flustered at her wild imagination, she turned away and wrapped the remaining food in the linen. With unsteady limbs, she moved cautiously, mindful that she was alone with a man who made her envision her own ripening fruit plucked by his lips.

She glanced out the small window. With evening closing in, she knew her position was becoming dangerous. Somehow, she would have to remind her body that this was not the time to explore the width of his shoulders, the strength of his back. No; her duty was to her father.

Ranulf said he needed proof. Well, she, too, needed proof. She had to return to Margrave Manor and speak to Maud without Robert or Annora knowing. She would find that irrefutable evidence Annora had used to threaten her.

A searing pain scored her heart. Ranulf would be furious when he learned of her betrayal. He would surely doubt anything she might ever say again, but there was no use crying over lost dreams. "At what price?" he had asked earlier. Clarice refused to accept that the price might be the warmth of his companionship.

Ranulf took another bite of the apple. She could hear the soft crunching sound of the skin and flesh. The one who had killed her father had torn away at her heart in just that manner. Would there be anything left when she was done with her quest? Would the dreams of love and happiness remain as dormant seeds, or would they grow into a life beyond this vow?

She drew up her legs, resting her chin on her knees and watching the fire in silence. A drop of water hit the top of her head.

"Come." Ranulf was quick to offer the protection of his arm. "I've a dry, warm spot in which to curl."

Clarice slid over, tucking her shoulder under the crook of his arm and silenced the growing regret. She would miss him when she left.

Despite the darkness of the gray sky, they still had a few more hours of daylight. Reluctant to ruin their peaceful existence, Ranulf knew he must gain the information he needed to protect his king and country. If Nicholas had not plotted against Henry, there were others who had set the course to ruin him and draw attention away from their own direction. 'Twas imperative he discovered their identities before the king set sail for France.

On the other hand, if Clarice was a Margrave, would she not lie to save her father's name? Or even use him to continue with the plot? It galled him that he still knew so little about her. He had no proof to save her. The Margrave name gave him the right to place her under arrest.

The vibration against his ribs tugged at his thoughts. She shivered again. The damp had begun to seep in. Sickness from exposure held no place in his plans.

Ranulf leaned over and caught the small wooden barrel with the heel of his boot. Feeling her tense with his movement, he rolled the barrel closer and offered an explanation. "I found it tucked under an eave."

A look of doubt flashed in her eyes.

"Not to worry, 'tis not so old that it survived the fire. Someone left it for their next return. As these are my lands, I confiscate it and hold it as payment for trespassing."

He pulled out the wooden cup he always carried in his pack. "Here. A toast to warm your heart and heat your toes."

She eyed the cup. "Unless 'tis vinegar, I shall accept it with relief and gratitude. But how this will warm my toes I cannot fathom, not unless we hold it over the flames."

"Haven't you sipped wine at your family's table?"

"Been drinking watered mead since I was a babe." She lifted the cup to her lips and drank deep and long. A cough erupted as soon as the burning liquid slid down her throat.

"What are you thinking?" He grabbed the cup from her hand. Leaning her over, he pounded her on her back until she swatted at him to go away.

Clarice sat up, her eyes watering. "Obviously, I wasn't thinking at all."

He let the fruit's scent drift into his nose before taking a swallow of the burgundy liquid. "It does have a bite, but it appears to be an excellent French wine."

He refilled her cup and held it out for her to try again. "Go easy."

After a tentative taste, she took another drink and wiped her mouth with the back of her hand. "How did you know 'twas French?"

He smiled and tipped the cup to his lips.

She squinted at him and then at the wooden cask at his feet. "Ah, 'tis not a trick you have. It has French markings on the outside."

"What's that? Where?" He pulled the barrel into the light of the flames and read the markings on the barrel. "God's blood, you're correct."

Carefully, he put the barrel down. Who traveled his lands without his knowledge, hiding wine that was good enough to grace the king's table?

After filling Clarice's cup and then his own, he leaned close and tapped the rims together. "To truth sought."

She tapped hers back. "To answers found."

He leaned over, took her cup again, and refilled it. Her cheeks rosy, she nodded and did not seem to notice that he no longer continued to drink his wine.

Puzzled by her story, he brushed a smudge of dirt from his leggings. "Why were you locked away that night?"

"That night? Or when the others returned to Margrave?"

"Let us begin with the last night you were with your father. Later, if you like, you may tell me about the other times."

She frowned into her wine, her heartache apparent to anyone who looked. "Anytime Annora and Robert are at Margrave, I must stay out of sight."

"But you said Nicholas kept you at Margrave because 'twas for your protection."

"He did."

"This makes little sense," Ranulf argued. "If Margrave Manor protected you, why wouldn't you be safe behind the walls at all times? No matter who arrives, you should have been safe." He lifted her empty cup. "Why would your father feel the need to protect you from your stepmother and stepbrother?"

"I don't know," she whispered.

Kneeling beside her, he pulled her into his arms. "What if you were the babe your father took from the orphanage?"

"But why would I be there to begin with?"

"Lord Nicholas's first wife. Your mother. Do you know aught of her death?"

Clarice shook her head. "We never spoke of her. 'Twas never allowed. Annora would become overwrought with grief."

"'Tis odd, don't you think?"

"When I was a small child, I found a chest of my mother's things. The sight of it nearly broke my father and set my stepmother into a rage." She picked at the hem of her gown. "The punishment came in the form of being locked in my chamber for a week while they set off for London." She looked up and grinned. "But knowing not one drop of Annora's blood flowed through my veins was well worth the price."

"'Tis a wonder you never ran away."

"And where would I go? I knew what I faced with my family. At least I had shelter. Food. 'Tis more than others can say."

At a loss for words, Ranulf rested his back against the wall. Holding out his hand, he drew her onto his lap and gathered her pliable body to his chest.

There were stories bandied about at the court. One was of love between a knight of the king's realm and that of an angel. Was there any merit to this tale?

Upon his return to Sedgewic, he would seek out Erwina. She had tried to speak with him before they rode out. If memory served him, she had arrived soon after the fire. He would learn what he could from the old woman.

Chapter 26

Clarice burrowed deeper into Ranulf's embrace. His breath came slow and deep as he drifted off. The dark shadows deepened as the night wore on. Their small fire flickered, casting wavering figures against the charred walls.

Her mind nibbled on the changes her simple life had taken. Where once she had been cold and lonely, she now sat warm and snug in this man's arms. Instead of her barren room, with little more than four walls and a locked door, she now sat upon the lap of a lord. In fact, she sat as if she belonged there, as if her whole purpose from birth was to be with him at that very moment.

But he is the king's wolf. How can I trust him to help me? To clear Father's name?

She pushed her hair out of her face with a heavy hand, blinked away the blurred vision, and looked about the blackened shelter. Firelight etched the skeleton of the building. Its meager light trickled through the seams of the walls and makeshift roof. The tension in Ranulf's arm relaxed and Clarice settled closer. She brushed her fingertips over the sprinkle of whiskers shadowing his strong jaw. His smooth cheeks rose above the chiseled wedge of bone. She marveled at his lashes. They were long enough to cause any young woman to weep with envy.

"Clarice." He mumbled her name softly, with a hint of impatience.

Her movements stilled. She waited. Rewarded with the deep rise of his chest, she began her search again. This time she spoke to settle her nerves. Hesitant to hear his answer, she whispered, "Who is this man deep inside?"

Her hand trembled as his heart beat against her palm. She needed to feel him, all the while retaining the sense that she was holding him at bay. Relief flooded her limbs when his answer was a muffled snore.

Did he not experience the same need? To have the feel of his body touching hers? What manner of man was he? Did he not wish to take advantage of their situation?

Clarice's thoughts jerked to a halt when bands of muscle hardened as he tightened his arms. His hand draped over her hip. His fingers splayed tenderly across the fabric of her gown.

Her brain fuzzy from the wine, she attempted to ignore his heat pressing through her clothing. She began to count the rise and fall of his chest. To her frustration, she found her knowledge of numbers lacking. Her mutinous body distracted her from her task. She lost her place again when Ranulf took a deep, sighing breath.

The numbers abandoned, she concentrated on the shadows as they stretched and darkened into one complete mass. The rhythm of the rain continued to beat against the building. Fat drops fell and hit the bare timbers. Nature's song, combined with the sounds Ranulf made when he slept, lulled her into a blissful fantasy.

She would tame the wolf and he would not bite her hand as she fed him sweet morsels.

Ranulf bolted awake and grabbed for his sword.

Clarice cried out again. This time it did not take long for him to realize she did not call out in passion. Her struggles escalated when Ranulf pulled her close. Placing soft kisses against the nape of her neck, the smooth flat blade of her shoulder, he whispered against her skin. "Open your eyes, sweeting."

He tried yet again to pull her from her fitful dream as she began to weep. "Come, there is nothing to fear."

Heartbreaking sobs erupted from her chest. Her body shuddered. Ranulf pulled her closer, cupping her hips against his belly. Rolling to his back, he lifted her from the hard floor. Turning her so that he might cradle her from the cold, he realized his mistake when her soft curves pressed against his thighs. He became well aware of their dangerous position when she became restless and wiggled deeper into the safe haven of his arms.

He braced for the awakening rush through his body. He was busy willing the offending member back to hibernation when he realized his efforts were for naught. Her sweet breath blew out in a soft puff. It wrapped around the endearment she called out in anticipation.

Bitter satisfaction swept through him. He pressed his chin on the top of her hair. 'Twas as he feared. He indeed heard correctly. Clarice called out for the peddler.

Birdsong floated through the cracks in the leaning rafters and escorted the sun to a new day. Rays of light peeked behind a dull gray sky, racing to be first to shine through the small window.

Blinking from the light that wedged its way between her eyelids, Clarice moved to block the bright daggers. She lay on her side, the hard ground digging into her joints. She shifted her weight and winced from the biting pain that raced through her. Her head rested on Ranulf's lap. Her hand lay tucked between his legs.

She licked her parched lips. Aware of the heat radiating from his body, she snuggled deeper into the pocket of his lap. *If this is a dream, I wish it to continue.*

"A new day is upon us," Ranulf said quietly.

Clarice flinched at the sound of his voice. *Not a dream after all.*

She did not dare lift her head and increase the pounding. Covering her ears, she made sure the top of her head would not pop off before she spoke. "Please tell me that barrel of wine has vanished."

"You care for more?"

"Lord in heaven, no," she whispered. "I pray I shall never partake of that poisonous French swill again."

"I will be certain to relay the message to the French countrymen when I stop in Calais."

Clarice groaned. "How soon until we ride for Sedgewic?"

He bent forward to see out the little window. She held her breath in anticipation of the brush of his chest against her back. His hand settled on her shoulder.

She could not stay in this spot indefinitely. One word of discomfort and he would have released her. She knew this and ignored it just as she ignored the race of desire leaping though her veins. With her conscience locked away, she decided to stay where she was to enjoy the warmth of his touch. *Just for a while longer.*

Ranulf slid his fingers into her hair, sending shivers of pleasure down her spine. If she did not do something to stop them, her arms would wrap around his neck on their own.

Thinking to forestall her body's betrayal, Clarice trapped her hands under the weight of his leg. Her fingers itched to stroke a single line along his leggings. Lightly, with the edge of her fingernail, she took purchase of the soft woolen material. The groan she had successfully held at bay purred in the back of her throat.

She shivered as he slid the neck of her gown off her shoulder. He touched her temple, pushing away the curls that covered her cheek.

"Others will ride out for us as soon as there is light to guide their mounts," he said.

"Others?" she asked. "From Sedgewic?"

"Are you expecting another? Mayhap a peddler?"

"Don't be a goose. I have no one to come for me."

He shifted and drew her to his side. "At least tell me of the peddler. Who is he to you?"

"He is no one," she said. Her neck arched, offering her nape.

"No?" He nuzzled perfect flesh. "This nothing you don't wish to speak of. Does he have a name?"

"I am sure he does, but I don't know it."

"Yet you dream of him. You call out for him. Why is that?"

Before answering, Clarice shivered under his expert caress. "Do you not dream of many things?"

"Not recently."

She snorted her rejection of his answer. "'Tis difficult to accept."

"'Tis true. Ever since I pulled you off young Hamish, my dreams have become painfully singular."

"I didn't mean to squash him. I fainted."

Ranulf stood and kissed her hand as he pulled her up. "I know you meant him no harm. You wouldn't be alive if I believed otherwise."

No matter how hard she tried, she could not tear her attention from his mouth. His lips were so inviting. She swallowed, hesitant to ask her next question. "And what is that singular dream that pains you so?"

Clarice flinched as he traced the edge of her mouth.

"I dream of you." He nipped her jaw and trailed down. "Of doing this." A shiver ran up her spine. "Touching you here." Her legs turned to liquid and she leaned in to him. "And here . . ."

She held her breath, hoping he would turn away from his questions. She wished he would stop touching her. *Liar!*

The memory of the peddler may have brought her dream to life, but the dream of the peddler was just that, a dream. He paled in comparison to the man beside her. Ranulf was alive, vibrant. He offered her more compassion than she had ever known, and yet he did not trust her. It pained her heart that she had been unable to sway him from his suspicion.

Madness. This is madness. Clarice's awakened passion was ravenous. Her lips hungered for his kiss. She ached to be touched, even with just the tip of his finger.

His strength gave her hope and caused fear in her heart. He would never believe that she and her family did not plot against the king. He would claim no knowledge of her to the king. He would turn her out. Spurn her. Leave her thirsting for the satisfaction of his touch. Once she tasted this potion, she knew she would die, withered and parched, if he never trusted her.

Clarice's reality became clear. 'Twas as if she laid a crystal stone upon her life and it clarified the daunting task her father laid before her. 'Twas no longer just his name to clear; 'twas hers as well. It would do her no good to prove her birth and then have her head chopped off. She glanced up at the man. He not only held her hand, he held her life.

Ranulf frowned, and trapped her hips to draw her closer. "Your inattention wounds me," he said.

Pushing all doubt and fear away, she ran her hands under his leather jerkin. The coarse patch of hair sprinkled on the planes of his stomach tickled her palms. Her fingers stretched and curled before splaying over the taut muscles that protected his chest. Her heart raced to match the tempo of his heartbeat. She ached for him to pull her into his arms. To her mounting frustration, he stood, still and quiet, his heart thundering under her hand. She wrapped one arm around his neck. The rigid chords strained under his control. She edged toward him.

Ranulf trapped her hands with his. Through the leather, he squeezed her fingers. "You know not what you are about."

Clarice touched her lips to his chin. The scrape of whisker stubble surprised her. She leaned back and tested the tender flesh with her tongue. Rising on tiptoe, she repositioned herself and brushed her lips across his mouth.

Their kiss deepened. His groan of pleasure rippled through her. Her breasts ached for his touch. The core of her being throbbed between her legs. Wanting more, she wriggled against his chest and hoped they would not be found for quite some time.

Chapter 27

Clarice tightened her hold on the soft leather covering Ranulf's hips. Smiling, she arched her back, offering her body, begging to be feasted upon. Need ignited the apex between her legs. Her nipples tingled, aching for the heat that came from contact.

They came together, pressing, needing, barely holding on to restraint. Another groan escaped. His. Hers. Melded into one. Then he released her, only to regain his hold. This time his magical tongue slid over her collarbone, leaving behind the promise of seduction. Her nipples pebbled. Muscles, nestled in her core, pulsed with need.

For once in her life Clarice knew the adoration of another. She lost herself in the depth of his heated gaze. Her limbs shook as his fingertip danced above the edge of her bodice. He drew her closer, sighing into the sensitive area of her neck, dipping his fingertip into the crease between her breasts before tugging her bodice and allowing his lips access.

The cooing pigeons nesting in the rafters broke the spell as they took flight in a rush overhead.

Ranulf tensed. His tongue paused in the tasting and exploration of her breast. He smoothed her hair away from her face.

"My lord—"

Clarice blinked, awakening from the passionate spell.

Hamish had elbowed his way between the barrier formed by Darrick and Nathan's knightly legs. He craned his neck, this way and that, trying to see what caught everyone's eye. After much grunting, the boy said with dismay dripping from his words. "—when you're done licking her face, mind you watch your step. Takes forever to get the bird muck off them boots—"

Realizing she still gripped Ranulf's hips, she snatched her hands away. If not for the fact that he maintained his hold, she would have fallen to the ground. Embarrassment ripped through her, heating her face, taking her breath. She twisted to hide. Her skirt caught between their feet. Ranulf's breath came in short bursts, as if he had been in a foot race. His gray eyes were dark, heated.

"—and that dress—" Hamish prattled on.

Four pairs of eyes settled on her. Hearing their collective intake of breath, she looked and saw the damage.

"—will never come clean. She's ruined it for certain."

"Steady," Ranulf whispered. He closed his eyes. His long lashes, dusted with gold, shadowed his cheeks. Taking a deep breath, he set her behind his back.

A chill filled the space that had been afire seconds before. She shook her head. As if that would ever clear the need that had consumed her from head to toe. She swallowed, fighting the urge to run.

"—been up all night, searching for you and—"

"Enough, Hamish," Ranulf ordered. He turned to look at his two friends. "I advise everyone to shut their gaping mouths before the damned birds he keeps yammering about deposit their droppings."

Ever the gallant knight, Sir Darrick turned his gaze from their faces. Unfortunately, his efforts were to no avail as his eyes darted between Ranulf and herself.

Sir Nathan, however, snapped his mouth shut, and a slow grin spread from ear to ear.

Fighting back tears, Clarice began the task of putting her shattered self back together. Keeping a safe distance from the men, she swept Ranulf's cloak from the wooden beams. The birds overhead scattered in a mad flutter of wings and Hamish yelled for everyone to duck their heads.

Clarice hunched her shoulders, scanning the group of men who rode before her. Her time with Ranulf was done. Upon the appearance of his allies, the lord of Sedgewic had returned to being his dictatorial self, ordering everyone to mount up and keep silent.

Flanked by a packhorse on one side and Hamish on the other, she sat astride Buttercup and suffered in silence. Abandoned. Had it not been for the occasional dark imperious look he cast toward her, she would believe he had forgotten she was there at all.

She shifted on Buttercup's wide back. The small matter of being ignored would have been a blessing had it occurred earlier. Instead, the three of them had come upon them with her stroking the lord of Sedgewic's backside.

Cringing, she sank her shoulders deeper into her cloak. Heaven help her, how would she ever look into Ranulf's eyes without remembering how he had pulled away from her even as she pressed against him. *Good lord! I nearly threw the man to the ground.*

Warmth rushed over her face. Her heart raced at the memory of him touching her breasts with his mouth. The heat of his hands sweeping over her waist, surrounding her hips as he drew her close. His need pressed against her, their joining barred by his chausses and the folds of her gown.

Clarice winced as she recalled the feel of Hamish's nut-brown gaze boring into her. It was as if he searched for horns sprouting from her head. *Lord, save me from eternal mortification.* The familiar sense of loneliness crept in, taking her breath with it. Oh, how she ached to be held again.

She had tried to ignore the way the knights' eyes had widened and narrowed when they came upon her, wrapped in his lordship's arms. As they rode toward Castle Sedgewic, the men expressed their concerns. Their voices carried over the creaking leather and dusty sounds of horses' hooves striking earth. She strained to hear, catching snippets of their muffled phrases floating past. 'Twas not long until she realized their anger was pointed in her direction.

She glanced over as Hamish brought his pony close to Buttercup. "Not today, imp. I am weary and must concentrate on the reins."

"Quiet. I'm guarding you," Hamish said.

"What?" Clarice snapped.

The three knights, caught in deep discussion, halted their mounts and swiveled to look at them.

Hamish waved at the three knights. "'Twas a bee," he called out. "Intent on stinging the lady."

"Clarice." Ranulf wheeled his destrier around and rode back to where they had stopped. "Are you harmed?"

"As the boy said, a bothersome bee. Nothing more."

"'Twas trying to sting her arse," Hamish added.

"You have said enough," Clarice warned.

Ranulf's gaze slid over her flushed face and dropped to below her waist. "Try to stay out of trouble." He turned to Hamish. "That warning is meant for you, too, young sprout."

Clarice wondered if Ranulf noted the hunch of the boy's shoulders. In an effort to forestall Hamish's lower lip from trembling, she made a show of shoving the hair off her face. "How soon until we reach Sedgewic? Do you suppose a peddler might have stopped by with a new assortment of ribbons? The last one who stopped at Margrave carried a supply. How wonderful it will be when I can tie my hair back."

"A peddler?" Ranulf asked.

"Last one was as skinny as a chicken bone," Hamish chimed in. "Never brought any ribbons I know of."

She glanced up at Ranulf, and was taken aback by his response to her question. 'Twas not the change in the way he held his body that caught her attention. He looked as relaxed in the saddle as always. However, his snapping gray eyes had become dark and stormy as the previous night. That and the slight tick in the muscle at his jaw gave away his irritation.

A chill ran between her shoulder blades. "Then mayhap Fat Thomas might peddle his wares at Sedgewic."

"No," Hamish said. "Nary a fat peddler around here."

Crestfallen, Clarice had to squint to see past the sun shining over Ranulf's head. "'Tis true?"

Ranulf smoothed the ends of the reins and gave a tight smile. "I'm sure the lad would know more about that than I."

"Oh," she said. Christ's blood. That one-syllable word sounded like a goose honking at its gander. Her face flushing hot, she cleared her throat to try again.

Ranulf traced her cheek before tucking a curl behind her ear. "These ribbons; do they mean so much to you? Or is it the peddler for whom you pine?" He held up a hand to silence the denial that was on her lips. "If I find him, I'll send him to you."

Clarice caught his hand. "Would you? Would you do that for me?"

"Though I cannot imagine how a scrap of material will enhance beauty when 'tis already apparent."

Confused by his flattery, she brushed off his compliment as if she received one every day of her life. Her spirit swelled. Refusing to respond to Hamish's ill-concealed snort of disgust, she pinched her leg to keep the chuckle inside.

"Hamish," Ranulf asked wickedly, "how long has it been since the garderobe has been scraped clean?"

Hamish's reply came as a loud gulp. Clarice thought he might have swallowed his tongue when his little round face turned red.

"Mayhap the peddler's travels have taken him far away from Sedgewic and Margrave. 'Tis certain," she nodded, "the poor man is still locating a brace of swans for Father."

"Swans," Ranulf ground out. He jerked his hand away and jammed it on top of the saddle's pommel. His fingers whitened as he gripped the smooth padded leather. "Enough of this chatter. I trust the swarm of one bee has passed. 'Tis time we quicken our pace and reach the safety of Sedgewic's walls."

Without waiting for their response, he wheeled Aldwyn around.

Hamish kicked his pony with his heels and swatted Buttercup on the rump as he rode by. "Come on, Clarice. I don't know what you did, but his lordship is determined to make our return quicker than usual. We'll see the top of Sedgewic's parapet before we know it."

The trestle table in Sedgewic's hall bowed from the meal Erwina and her household had prepared. Soldiers filled the great room. Their voices rang out in ribald good cheer. They ate heartily from their trenchers piled high with wild boar and freshly felled pheasant. Steam rose from a pot of thick, hearty stew. Pitchers of ale sat on a side table. The servants stood in the corners, awaiting the signal to serve the next course.

Clarice touched the crumpled parchment hidden in her pocket. A note, delivered by Hamish, led her to believe Erwina had something of great import to tell her. Anxious to hear what the woman had to say, she gobbled the thick venison stew and brown bread. She put the last chunk of meat into her mouth and pretended to choke on the bite.

Ranulf glanced her way before giving her a curt nod. Assuming he gave her his leave, she moved quietly toward the tapestry hanging behind the diners and slipped behind it.

Clarice stepped inside the solar and sagged against the door-frame. A triumphant smile formed. It appeared the men would continue their discussion on into the night. She could not imagine why she was to be left unwatched. Never had she been allowed to wander the castle without someone nearby before. No one watched her rise from the table. No one took her by the wrist and led her away. But how long would it be until someone noticed her absence?

"Come, Erwina, show yourself," she muttered.

Clarice paced over the dry rushes of lavender and sage covering the solar floor. With her every step, the pungent scent broke into the air. Someone had finished covering the hole made when she and Hamish had crashed through the wall. The scent of new plaster tickled her nose. Although showing signs of wear, tapestries of knights on horseback hung against the wall. Rows of empty shelves covered one side of the room. The bare wood reminded her of an empty, gaping mouth, hungry for books and ledgers.

A large window gracing one wall remained closed against the cool night breeze. She turned the peg that held the shutters, spread the wooden panels apart, and let the window open out to a southern exposure. The edges of the evening sun shot rays of rose-colored shadows across the flower garden. The sight was a soothing balm to the ache that remained in her heart.

Weary, she sat on the thick, padded bench beneath the window. Pulling her knees close to tuck under her chin, she listened to the sounds of life moving through the castle.

Two dogs tussled over a bone. Somewhere nearby, children sang a ditty about a lady named Mary. They squealed with delight when the words became a little naughty.

Lost in dreams of sugar-crusted almonds, Clarice nearly fell over when Nathan's booming baritone and Darrick's clipped tones joined Ranulf's deep voice. They were just outside the solar.

Jumping up, she found the darkest corner of the room and perched on a small stool hidden in the shadows of a heavy tapestry. Spying a sewing chest beside the stool, she rummaged through the contents and located an abandoned embroidery hoop.

She squinted in the shadows. What design was she about to stab with a needle? She held the hoop close to her face. Small letters, stitched with delicate bits of thread, were sewn into the edge of the linen. *M. D. Lady of Sedgewic.*

Ranulf walked into the solar and paused before moving to the open window. Something was amiss. He was certain he had closed those shutters earlier in the evening. If they were ever to rid themselves of vermin, he would need to speak with Mistress Erwina to see that it was done every night.

Darrick bent and tossed another log on the fire. He stood with his back against the heat.

"Your injuries still bothering you?" Ranulf asked.

"'Tis nothing." Darrick shrugged. "With the rain comes the pain."

Nathan lifted the jug of wine he had brought with him and motioned to fill their cups. "Well, my friends, 'tis time we discuss our concerns."

Ranulf swore he could feel Clarice standing next to him. How odd to notice the lingering scent of a lover even though they were not in the same room. He shifted, turning ever slightly, to examine the chamber. *That wench! What wild tale will she spin this time?*

Satisfied, he withdrew from the window and pulled up a chair. "Speak freely."

Darrick remained where he stood, his arms folded across his chest. The fire highlighted the streaks of gray in his coal black hair.

Nathan grinned and lifted his glass to toast his friends. "To honesty. Painful as it may be."

"So 'tis agreed?" Darrick asked.

Ranulf rubbed the back of his neck and nodded. "As I have been informed more times than I care to remember, 'tis my duty to king and brotherhood. I will stay behind while the two of you report our findings."

"As soon as the plot is stopped," Darrick said. "Then you are to join us."

"Have you learned anything, other than that which we spoke of earlier?"

Nathan lifted the jug and sloshed the liquid inside. "I think we have an interesting bit of information right here."

"The French wine?"

"We received a report that a cache of the swill was found on Margrave land," Darrick said.

"So, here is our proof. Nicholas of Margrave was a French supporter." Nathan tipped the jug.

Ranulf leaned in. "The same markings as on the cask in the monastery ruins?"

"Appears so." Darrick walked over to take the jug from Nathan's fingers. "You have a bigger problem, my friend."

"How so?" Ranulf asked.

"This wine was also found in Sedgewic's cellar. One would have to ask you, Lord Ranulf, how French wine came to be in your possession."

Ranulf jerked to his feet, his fingers curled into fists. "What are you implying?"

"Remember," Nathan reminded him. "'Tis time for truth."

"And your honor is not at stake here," Darrick said.

"If 'tis not, then I would like to know where this information is leading," Ranulf said.

Nathan set the jug down and placed a hand on Ranulf's shoulder. "While you were riding about the countryside with your prisoner, we had a moment to speak with Mistress Erwina."

"You would speak to my castellan without my leave?"

"Your castellan bade us speak with her," Nathan pointed out.

Darrick joined Nathan to stand by Ranulf. He placed his hand on Ranulf's other shoulder. "Mistress Erwina feared she could not prove her suspicions."

"Suspicions?"

Nathan gave Darrick a curt nod. With a hapless shrug, Darrick answered Ranulf's question. "While you were away on the king's business, Robert of Margrave did make nightly visits with your wife."

"Why would she do this?" Ranulf ground out. "Our marriage may not have started with love, but what arranged marriage does?"

Nathan ignored his questions and pressed on. "He was recently seen crossing through Sedgewic lands. Whether he is meeting someone here or moving on, we have to follow his whereabouts."

Ranulf cupped his head with his hands. Keeping his gaze to the floor, he took time to form the words before he spoke. "The Margraves may have been friends to King Henry, but the bastards have shown their true colors. 'Tis possible we protect his consort within our camp."

"Ranulf," Darrick said, "I heard talk of a daughter who died at childbirth. Nothing of value came of that rumor."

Ranulf nodded. "Like as not Erwina can substantiate that. She was here during that time."

"Whether Clarice is of his blood or his consort, she must be kept close," Darrick said.

"I would find that task a fitting sport." Nathan's chuckle was grim. "The little beauty is quite tempting."

Darrick returned to his spot in front of the hearth. "Either way," he said, "you miss the point. Consort or daughter, mayhap she joins Robert in seeing this plot through to the end."

"True. The fig doesn't fall far from the fig tree," Nathan said. "'Tis likely she'll see that her father's plan is fulfilled."

"Get close to her, Ranulf," Darrick added.

"I admire the cozy embrace we found you in," Nathan said. "Good work, man. Keep the wench in your arms and we'll block their plot of treason with your bed."

"All in the price of our brotherhood," Ranulf said.

"Vile miscreants! All of you!" The far from ladylike curse emanated from the corner. Ranulf jumped from his chair. In an instant, Darrick and Nathan flanked him, their daggers in their fists.

White-faced, her blue eyes glittering with anger, Clarice stood before them. The forgotten embroidery hoop clattered to the floor, spinning in drunken circles until it came to rest at her feet. "I would rather choke on pig dung than be with you in any fashion of your imagination," she said. "All of you should be ashamed of yourselves, speaking ill of the dead. My father was an honorable man. Loyal to the crown!"

Taking a step forward, Ranulf motioned for Clarice to come closer.

"How could you?" she whispered. Her skirt whirled about her ankles as she ran past the stunned men.

"No." Ranulf caught Nathan's arm before he gave chase.

Nathan shook off his grasp. "Why did you let the wench run off without an explanation of whom she follows?"

Waves of guilt washed over Ranulf. A hole opened up where a conscience should have been. But his duty to the king demanded first priority.

"Did you know she was here all the time?" Nathan asked.

Ranulf offered a quiet, slow smile as his answer to his brothers' questions.

Darrick's brown eyes widened before they narrowed. "What are you about?"

Ranulf checked the edged of the blade with his finger before tucking it into the scabbard inside his boot. He was responsible for causing Clarice heartache. A lump of regret lodged in his throat. "Just a rustling of the reeds. To see what little beasties come out."

"I believe," Nathan called out as he strode toward the door, "we are now all in agreement."

Ranulf grimaced. "I'll keep her so close, she'll not turn for fear of stumbling over me."

Chapter 28

The noise in the bailey yard rose as the men continued to gather their belongings. At day's end, more of the king's soldiers joined forces with Sir Darrick and Sir Nathan's men. The troop had increased in size as the day wore on. Men from surrounding villages sought an opportunity to find their fortune. Their price for fame would be to fight alongside the brave soldier king.

Clarice smacked her hands against the windowsill. She would not accept failure. Her efforts to convince Ranulf to take her to the king had been demolished in a single moment. The knights' small minds had twisted truths and half truths until she could not straighten out the tangled web. Her spirits sagged from the weighty knowledge that her stepbrother had indeed played a treasonous role. But had her father known?

Their last visit together, he had hinted that he had written to the king, implicating those who had plotted against him. Father's ink-stained fingers, the bit of sealing wax on his cuff, came to mind. Had Robert intercepted her father's missive? How far would Robert be willing to go to keep her father's silent?

Clarice thought again of the note Erwina had sent to her. She had yet to speak with the woman to discover anything new about her questionable background.

Despite all her efforts, she had not received a single drop of trust from Ranulf. She did not know whether she wanted him to believe she was a Margrave or not. Either way, in his eyes she was as guilty of treason as her father.

She knew better. Now, after hearing about Robert's malicious mischief, an inkling of suspicion had taken root. She did not know why he had agreed to play a role in overthrowing King Henry, but she knew he was more than capable. The task of proving Robert was the only Margrave involved in France's attempt to gain a hold on England's throne would be difficult.

The door to the bedchamber opened, tearing her thoughts from her jumbled life. Ranulf stood in the doorway. His gaze locked on her face. Heat built inside her veins. Memories of the overheard conversation reverberated in her mind. She would have no choice where to lay her head. No matter where he went, whether in a tent or the castle, she would be tied to his side.

Clarice looked past Ranulf's broad shoulders and wide chest. If she could free herself from this velvet-lined prison, she would prove to the great knotty-headed man that she and her father had had nothing in common with Robert.

Ranulf braced his back against the door, blocking her way out. He folded his arms and presented his body as a solid wall. "How long had you been spying?"

Clarice spun on him with irritation boiling in her veins. She feared her heart would jump out of her body. "Long enough to know that you, sir, have no honor. Nor do your friends."

"'Tis my home. My place to question your truthfulness."

"I've done nothing wrong," Clarice protested. "Mayhap 'tis you who should examine your actions."

"You would have me believe you just happened to slip away without escort?"

"You granted me your leave."

He remained where he stood, a human barricade to her freedom. Did that man remember nothing of their time together?

Ranulf shook his head. "You'd been told to stay within my sight."

"You cannot possibly think I have anything to do with Robert."

Ranulf pushed his back from the door. Closing the space between them, he caught her wrist as she turned. Her pulse quickened as he brought the flat of her wrist to his lips

"How long will you protect him before you accept my help?" he asked.

Clarice's breath caught as he brushed the back of his knuckles over her neck.

Stepping closer, she wondered what he would think if she wrapped her arms around him and refused to let go. Would she see the soft smile again? Or would he turn away with the suspicion he held against her emblazoned on his heart. Oh, to feel his lips dance over her skin. The longing rolled through her, leaving her awash in a sea of desire. Would he ever forget, if just for a moment, that he connected her family to treason?

Finding the courage to face his rejection yet again, she carried his hand to her lips. She uncurled his fingers and kissed his palm. With tiny bites, she nipped the creases. Emboldened, she ran the tip of her tongue across his flesh.

A groan rumbled as he pulled her tight against his body. "What shall I do with you?"

Licking her lips, she wrapped her arm around the curve of his shoulder. The corded bands of muscle along his neck felt strong and comforting under her hand. She tilted her face, so that she might taste the corners of his mouth. "Kiss me," she said.

The sound of urgent shouts tore through the window, cutting a path across their embrace. A shadow crossed Ranulf's face. He stepped away. The distance between their hearts grew.

Clarice closed her eyes and gathered up her shredded pride. She turned away to hide the emptiness that had already begun to pool. What a fool she nearly had become because of that man. Determined to defend her heart, she ignored the throbbing pain and pasted a smile on her face.

She strode past Ranulf and looked out the window to see what had caused the commotion. Men and women rushed about the bailey lawn. Saddled horses, already prepared for travel, stood waiting for their riders.

The door swung open with a resounding slam against the wall. Hamish rushed in. His face flushed with excitement as he announced with great enthusiasm, "A rider was seen coming across the lands. Sir Nathan and Sir Darrick are readying to ride."

Hamish turned to Clarice, his eyes round and innocent. "Suppose 'tis your peddler you've been wanting?"

The question cut through what was left of the fragile peace she and Ranulf had formed. She hoped that one day she would rebuild whatever they might have started. As it was, if 'twas her peddler traveling nearby, she must find a way to gain his attention. She could not wait for Ranulf's help to repair her family name. She would have to find the truth herself.

Ranulf grumbled something unintelligible and rested his hand on her shoulder. "Step away from the window."

Clarice pretended his words had not cut into her heart. "Hamish, run, see if 'tis he."

Attempting to push past Ranulf, she collided with his chest. "Excuse me, my lord. I must make myself presentable. We should ride out to meet him."

Ranulf stood in front of her, once again blocking her way. "Likely 'tis not your peddler but Robert of Margrave."

Over her head, he nodded to Hamish. "Go. Tell the men I'll join them on their ride." Ranulf pointed to Clarice. "You'll stay here."

"I thought you determined I must always be at your side."

"This time you will wait for my return."

"And if 'tis not Robert?" she asked. "What then will you blame on me?"

Ranulf muttered a curse under his breath and pulled the boy out of the room. The door slammed behind him.

Clarice followed on his heels. She waited, resting her hand on the door latch as she prepared to make her escape. With all the comings and goings, had they forgotten to lock it?

The familiar grind of the iron bolts sliding across the door was her answer.

She strode back to the window and searched the courtyard. Sitting high upon Aldwyn's back, Ranulf joined the two knights and a few of their soldiers as they rode through the gate.

Hamish entered quietly on tiny mouse feet. Clarice barely heard him until he was standing at her elbow.

"Shouldn't you be abed?" she snapped.

"S'pose that's what happens when a body gets two mothers at one time," Hamish grumbled. "Makes a person double overbearing." He looked her up and down as if she had grown an extra head before he spoke again. "Don't see the angel, but don't see the devil neither. Me—" He shoved a thumb toward the middle of his chest. "I don't have a mother or a father, but I'm doing just fine the way I am."

She watched the boy move ever so quietly. In fact, she had never thought him capable of such stealth. Thoughts that he was up to another escape danced in and about her head.

"Hamish, have you seen Erwina? I had hoped I might speak with her."

"She is busy talking to Sir Darrick's man, Sergeant Krell. I heard 'em right before I came up here." He paused before he spoke again. In a hushed voice, he said, "'Tis unfair that you have two mothers. Let alone an angel."

"Hamish, have you been listening to things you shouldn't?"

He squinted, staring into her face for the longest time. She was certain his eyes would soon cross. 'Twas when he heaved a heavy sigh that she knew he had come to an important decision.

He pressed a finger to his lips and motioned for her to follow. He opened the door and waited. "You want to leave, don't you?"

Clarice eyed him warily. *Could it be as easy as that?*

"Well?" His face flushed to a heightened shade of pink. His nostrils flared, reminding her of Ranulf. "A few days ago you did. I heard you say so many times."

Still unable to find her voice, she nodded. She watched the boy set about the room, grabbing her things, shoving them in a sack. When he was done, he flipped the bundle over his shoulder and flicked her cloak off the wall peg.

"Come. You must leave before they return."

Clarice took her cloak, pausing long enough to look around the room. She had formed memories she would cherish in her old days. She wondered if she would ever return. A part of her wished she would, another reminded her that she should not wish for what she could not have.

Chapter 29

Clarice prayed the path, with its twists and turns following the country terrain, did indeed lead toward Margrave land. She listened to the slow, rhythmic sound of Buttercup's hooves hitting the earth. Her thoughts drifted to the deep track cut into the tall grass. Who were these travelers who left behind their mark? Where did they go? Why had they never stopped at the Margrave keep to seek refuge for the night?

She blinked, ducking her head to avoid hitting a low-hanging branch. The mishap narrowly averted, she resettled her attention on her surroundings. She had long given up on measuring how much further she would have to ride. The stretching shadows had already begun to blend into the night. Soon she would not even have the sun to give her guidance. With her resolve in place, she ignored the nagging fear and kept her face pointing to the northeast.

Hamish's final instructions had become a chant that buzzed in her head like the hum of an annoying fly. "Ride until the sun sets," he had ordered as he led her through the hidden tunnel. "Find shelter when darkness falls."

How well she already knew this. Her ride from Margrave had been in the dawning hours and still she had had difficulty making her way. Had the heavy fog not addled her, she would have missed the Sedgewic lands and found herself in London. She might even have found her way to the king's court. On the other hand, now that she understood the accusations against her family, her own neck might have been stretched on the block. Indeed, the king could still demand it.

Fate had brought her to Sedgewic. This she had come to accept.

In Sedgewic, she had found a glimmer of what she always believed existed. Life was not all sugar-coated figs and sweet almonds.

'Twas a wise person to watch for a molded fig or rancid nut in a handful. Nevertheless, one hoped the sweet outweighed the bitter.

Her thoughts drifted to the last she had seen of Hamish. His eyes had danced with anticipation of adventure. Had she not held her ground and refused him, he would have found a way to join her.

She shook her head. That child gripped hope with both hands. One day he would make a grand squire for some deserving knight. If only he would learn to listen and follow orders without mishap.

Recognizing the crossroad where first she had encountered Hamish, Clarice pulled on the reins and stopped. How much had changed since she first crossed this road? With a simple tug on the reins, she could re-trace her steps back to Sedgewic and into Ranulf's arms. She yearned to do just that. But then, what would become of them afterward? He still had his duty to the king and she still had Father's good name to restore.

"Come, Buttercup." She nudged her with her heels. "We're al-most there."

High above Margrave Manor, Clarice watched for movement about the bailey. 'Twas midday and she had yet to see a single sign of life moving across the lawn.

She deposited a handful of grain on the ground and tied Buttercup to a small tree. After whispering softly in the velvet-fringed ear, she gave the horse a final pat before leaving her hiding place.

Skirting the main gate, she walked along the outer wall and fol-lowed the narrow path that led to the small passage cut into the cur-tain of stone. She bent to clear the vines covering the path tangling about her feet. A streak of white peeked out from the undergrowth. There, by the wall, lay another stone she had never noticed before. Clarice brushed the leaves away.

Curved wings and a flowing robe spanned the smooth surface.

Clarice traced the edges of the angel with a dirty fingertip. "You must be Father's angel."

A tight smile tugged at her lips. She lifted the latch, shoving against the unyielding door. Locked. Her smile slipped into a firm line of deter-mination

An oak tree grew near the wall, its gnarled branches stretched over the stone partition. One particularly sturdy branch spread out as if offer-ing a chivalrous hand to assist her.

She hitched up the hem of her skirt, tying the folds of material with the ribbon from the peddler, and began her climb up the great tree. Perched in the deep V formed by the trunk and branch, she paused, eyeing the branch. It seemed much closer when looking at it from the ground. Taking a deep breath, she swung out.

The weight of her dress was too much for the bits of ribbon and the skirt's hem dropped to her ankles. The bark bit into her flesh as her grasp slid from the limb and she hit the ground on the other side of the wall with a jolt.

Snagged by a rambling rosebush, the traitorous scarlet ribbon whipped in the wind. Clarice caught the bit of satin and stuffed it back into the pocket of her skirt.

The overgrown bushes provided cover as she crept into the neglected garden. Her steps faltered. A plain stone marked the solitary grave of a sinner. She kissed the tips of her fingers and pressed them to the marker.

"I have not forgotten my promise, Father. You will be vindicated."

Outside the threshold of Maud's room, the patch of herbs lay in disarray. Weeds grew with abandon. Vines wrapped around feathery leaves, strangling the life from the rosemary.

Heady perfume broke through the air as Clarice grabbed the vine and ripped it from the pungent plant. With a tentative turn of her wrist, she opened the door.

"Maud," she whispered to the old woman lying on the cot.

Gray strands, soft as the silk inside a milkweed pod, hung loose around her friend's face. Cheeks once smooth and round were now hardened by the edge of bone beneath her skin.

"Oh, Maud," Clarice said, "you cannot leave me now!"

Maud stirred. She caught Clarice's fingers. A single word floated up. "Child."

Clarice lifted Maud's shoulders from the thin straw mattress and pressed her to her heart. "You scared me so."

A chuckle deep inside the old woman's chest rose. "My dear, I never doubted you'd return."

Mindful of her friend's frailty, Clarice cradled her in her arms.

Maud's brow furrowed in thought before she spoke. "Did you succeed in finding the wolf?"

"I don't believe 'twas what my father intended. I fear I may have wasted so much time."

"A waste of time? Your father wouldn't have urged me to pass the message on to you if it were so."

"The wolf I came across protects no one but the king and no doubt has more secrets than my father. Was there not another message?" Clarice hesitated, gentling her question. "Mayhap you misheard?"

"These ears may be old. My mind is not."

Clarice smoothed Maud's wrinkled hand. "I had hoped I hadn't heard correctly, or that I missed a vital word or two. If I am ever to unravel this knitted pack of lies, I must first locate the threads of truth hidden in their coil."

"'Tis a difficult task you set for yourself."

"Nothing more than my father would have done for me," she said.

"You must not stay here." Maud's rheumy eyes held her gaze. "Your stepmother refuses to leave until she hears from Robert. His return is expected at any moment."

Clarice picked at a piece of thread hanging from the elbow of her sleeve. The ache in her right arm increased. Had she managed to tear open the healing flesh? She felt along the strip of linen. The bandage was dry. She pressed, just hard enough to feel the sting. The physical pain was bearable. She could manage that easier than the pain of betrayed love.

"Maud, I have need of answers that are more pressing than your silence. But one day I would hear why you never showed me my mother's grave."

Clarice rose and picked up a jug. After sniffing to see if 'twas fit for consumption, she filled the cup with wine and held it out to Maud. "Before I left, Annora swore there was irrefutable proof that I am of Margrave blood. Did she succeed in her search?"

"No. She raves at the king's thieves. Swears the soldiers took it right from under our noses."

Clarice's heart began to beat a little faster. "Have you any idea what her proof might have been?"

Maud pressed her palms against the thin woolen blanket draped over her legs. While Clarice waited, she noted how thin those birdlike legs had become. "Have you had not a morsel to eat this day?"

Maud lifted a shoulder in a shrug. "'Tis of little importance." She waved her hand to silence Clarice's protests. "I serve no purpose now."

Clarice's stomach clenched. "Lady Annora should—"

"Lady Annora doesn't believe she is required to give me food. Not unless 'tis the scraps off the trestle table. Which," Maud added with a glint in her eye, "after that woman picks the meat off the bones, is very little indeed."

"We shall remedy that."

Digging in the pouch hidden under her skirt, Clarice pulled out a small wad of cloth. She unfolded the corners to reveal the hunk of brown bread Hamish had given her and placed the gift gently on Maud's lap. With reverence, her old friend gathered the crumbs and put the morsels into her mouth.

Clarice was struck by the magnitude of how her life had changed since she'd left Margrave Manor. Not once, since awakening in Ranulf's arms, had she suffered lack. The return of loneliness echoed with his absence. Oh, how she wanted the comfort of his embrace.

Maud touched the back of her hand. "I've had a great deal of time to work out the tangle, but I don't know where to tell you to look."

"Anything will be more than what I know now."

Maud hesitated. "'Tis odd to speak of things that have been sworn to silence all these years."

Clarice glanced at the window. Time was passing. Despite her worries, she wore a calm smile and leaned in to hear Maud's words.

"I came to Margrave Manor when I was a young girl. To be your mother's chambermaid." A faraway look floated over her eyes. "So very long ago." She exhaled and began again. "Though your father was betrothed to Annora Stanford, he could not turn his eyes from her younger sister, Angelica. Their attraction reached beyond normal boundaries."

"Angelica." Clarice's heart fluttered with fragile butterfly wings.

Maud nodded. "Angelica could do no wrong in his eyes. Devotion came from all who did her bidding. Tiresome chores were made pleasant by a simple word and kind smile from her ladyship."

"I imagine Annora didn't feel such devotion."

"Lord and Lady Stanford were sore displeased as well. However, your father would not turn from his decision."

"And Annora . . . was she not pained by my father's rejection?"

Clarice pressed her cheek against the window frame and tried to envision Nicholas and Angelica. "And did my parents' love comfort them when guilt reared its head?"

Maud flicked her question away with the sweep of her hand. "Despite the problems it created, a love as great as theirs couldn't be ignored."

Turning from the view outside, Clarice sat beside Maud. "Must love always extract its price?"

"How little is the cost of hurt feelings when a blessing was on its heels?" Maud's face became radiant with sweet memories. "Soon after your parents were wed, we received news that a babe was due. The manor became a flurry of activity. Forgoing propriety, the nursery was designed so that your mother might see to your care at all times of the night."

Maud paused to take a sip of the watered wine, then cleared her throat. "'Twas right after that blessed peaceful time that Annora returned. She had been to visit once before your parents' vows. It ended terribly. Her bid to hold Lord Nicholas to his word failed. She did all she could to sway his attention but to no avail. He was enraptured with your mother. In a fit of spite, Annora cursed their marriage and all they held dear."

"Could she not see their love?"

"Annora did not stay away for long." Maud shook her head. "Soon after the news of your mother's pregnancy, Annora arrived at the gate. She, too, experienced the symptoms of motherhood."

"Robert." Clarice swallowed and nearly choked on the name.

Maud nodded. "Lady Angelica was beside herself. How could she force her sister to go out into the world disgraced? She encouraged Nicholas to invite Annora to stay until the birth of her child. A husband who would take Annora and the babe as his own would be found."

Maud patted Clarice's hand. "Before that time, blind to her sister's contempt, Angelica believed the best of everyone. As time passed, she came to suspect the mischief Annora created. But 'twas too late to mend the damage. Margrave Manor was in disarray. The reigning peace and love were about to be dethroned.

"One fateful day, the two sisters had a terrible argument. Angelica told Annora to remove herself from Margrave. Never to return. That night, you were born, and my lady . . ."

"Angelica was gone," Clarice finished.

"Yes."

"But how is this story to help me now?"

"'Tis best you understand Annora's pain. She still believed she was meant to hold your father's heart."

"And my father's pain? Why would he marry Annora after what he knew?"

"I am sorry, child. I cannot explain away your father's actions. Mayhap the loss was too great to bear alone. The day before your birth, Lord Nicholas received word there was trouble on the other side of Margrave lands. He rode hard and found nothing amiss. By the time he returned home 'twas too late. His love had been taken from his life. That same night, Annora's labors began."

"And she delivered a son," Clarice finished. "Had Angelica not interfered, Robert would have rightfully carried on the Margrave line. My father had his son."

Maud caught Clarice's hand. "'Tis always been my belief Annora forced both births to arrive early. She wouldn't have left it to chance."

"And did you tell my father this?"

"Oh, I dared not."

Outrage failed to curb Clarice's tongue. "Was your position so rare a find?"

"No!" Maud cried out. "I had lost you once before. I could not chance that fate again. Your death was proclaimed on the same night as Angelica's."

"My death?"

"Annora reported your death herself and cast out the nursery maid on the guise that the woman failed to protect you." Maud grabbed Clarice's hand and pressed it to her thin chest. "Can you not feel how it tears me to cause you this pain, but it must be said." She paused and took a deep breath. "There is more that I must tell you."

Betrayal, delivered by a friend, bent Clarice double. She gripped the edge of the mattress and waited. The dam of secrets broken, truth poured out with every agonizing word. Try as she might, she could not stop Maud's words. "Then please do so."

"Soon after his marriage to Annora, your father discovered her duplicity. I never will forget the night he brought you back to Margrave. Both of you, covered in soot and smoke. The gateman threatening to set the dogs upon the lord of the manor."

"Where had I been?" Clarice asked, afraid she already knew.

"I dared not pry. Should have been an occasion for rejoicing, but I knew the look on Lord Nicholas's face held a different story. Your father tucked you into my arms, smoke-tainted blanket and all, and charged me to watch over you with my life. Not another word was to be said about that night." Maud plucked at the blanket. "I have been trying to keep my promise ever since."

The bitterness faded. "You have done a fine job."

Maud laid her palm to Clarice's cheek. "Would that I had been a valued servant to my Lady Angelica and his lordship."

"You've been much more than that." Clarice rose to fill the cup with wine. "Is there nothing more you can think of?"

Maud tugged at her ear as she rummaged through old memories. Then a flicker of hope danced in her eyes. "Lady Angelica kept a book with her all the time. Bound in leather. 'Twas her book of prayers. 'Tis possible she wrote what happened between sisters."

Clarice stood with indecision sticking her feet to the floor. "Do you recall the trunk I found when I was a little girl?"

"How could I forget? 'Twas also the day that devil Robert fell and injured his arm. Annora was furious with Lord Nicholas for not punishing you severely. He purchased that ruby ring to quiet her."

"He was ordered to burn the trunk's contents."

Maud chuckled. "To Annora's great frustration, his lordship didn't always listen to her commands. It is still here, in the tower nursery."

Chapter 30

"Maud," Annora called out. "Why are you skulking about like a fishmonger's cat?"

The door to the tower nursery swung open. With no time to find a place to hide, Clarice pressed her back against the wall and did her best to make herself small.

Annora stepped inside the tower room. "I see you aren't so weak that you are unable to leave your bed," she snapped "'Tis time you earn your keep."

Amber light of the setting sun poked through the window slits of the barren chamber. Sensing movement, Annora swiveled on her heel. Cobwebs hanging from the rafters shifted in the wind, teasing her attention from the far corner. "Suit your own concerns," she called out. "You'll come to regret it in the end."

Her face twisted into a scowl. "Old woman, you have been nothing but a thorn in my side since the day you arrived at Margrave. I told Nicholas repeatedly to rid us of your services. But did he listen? No," Annora muttered, "that would be an affront to the memory of his precious angel."

She paused in her complaining and turned toward the cot. Nearing the edge of the bed, she sniffed the air as if she were a hound upon a coney in its warren.

Clarice's heart galloped a frantic race in her chest. She feared the woman could hear it from across the room.

"Come out, little rabbit," Annora whispered as she bent down to peer into the shadows. Her lungs squeaked against the uncomfortable position of her body, bound by a snug bodice, and fought for air.

Fingers digging into the floor, Clarice prayed her stepmother would lose interest and retreat to the hall.

"Bah." Annora rose, swatting at the sticky cobwebs. She turned and paused. A smile tugged at her lips as she turned away from the cot. She smoothed the tight material over her hips. Although the boards complained under the weight of her steps, she moved hastily over the wooden planks. The train of her skirt left a trail of smudged dust in its wake. After shuffling her bulk through the doorway, she slammed the door shut.

Relief crashed over Clarice as she pressed the heel of her palm to her eyes. She had escaped.

A rustling behind the door pulled her from her internal celebration. The voice she had come to dread scraped across her ears.

"Clarice. Clarice," her stepmother cooed. "You've been a selfish creature, worrying me as you have. Robert, too, has been most anxious to speak with you. He'll be here soon. And when King Henry learns of the army of men Robert brings him, our king will be begging for our return to court."

Clarice paced the room and found its lack of space more restrictive than ever before. But this time she did not want to leave for herself. It was imperative to find a means of escape so she might warn Ranulf and his men.

Her fingers curled in anticipation of throttling Annora's neck. *Aunt Annora!*

Strengthened by the seething anger boiling in her veins, she broke a leg off the cot. Vengeance poured out as she struck the wall. Ignoring the burning in her arms, the sweat dripping down her bodice, she did not stop until she heard a hollow thud.

In the far corner of the nursery, under the bench where her father would have her sit and say her prayers, she found the indentation. Time had begun to pull the repairs from the wall. The mortar around the false stone crumbled.

Clarice knelt down and peered inside. A leather strap was barely within reach. After wiggling her arm into the hole, she caught the strap and tugged it closer. Feet braced against the wall, she dragged the trunk through the hole.

The chest. 'Twas much smaller than she remembered. After all, she had been a girl of nine years. At that age things always seemed much larger than they really were. Time had a funny way of reducing fearful images to nothing more than faint imaginings.

Even in her short time away from Margrave, her perspective had changed. Father was not the same man she had left behind. He was a man capable of loving, though imperfectly. The mother who inhabited her dreams lay no farther than the outer wall. Most of all, Annora could no longer hurt her.

Smoothing her hand over the metal chest, Clarice's heart thrummed a cadence of joy as she contemplated the contents within. She tested her memory of that fateful day.

Pretty gowns and escaping confinement in the country were all she had been interested in at that time. The dresses did not serve her well then. She had her doubts they would do so now. Yet here she was again, still searching for her freedom.

What she needed was Angelica's prayer book.

Kneeling beside the trunk, her hands trembled as she tugged at the latch.

Locked. *Christ's wounds!*

Frustrated, she jumped up and paced the floor. She stopped at the window and looked out at the garden, locating the spot where she now knew her parents waited. "The answer must be here."

She explored the horizon. "Where are you, Ranulf? Have you returned to Sedgewic? Are you furiously angry to find me gone?"

The Southampton seaport was south and in the opposite direction from Margrave. The chance that he would ever come this way was slim indeed. She withdrew the peddler's ribbon from the pouch hidden under her skirt. It caught on something in the bottom of the purse. An impatient tug brought the metal object spinning out, clattering against the window ledge. She returned the ribbon to the pouch, gasping and lunging for the key.

The swan's head gripped in her hand, she knelt beside the trunk. Was this the reason her father had ensured she'd received it?

She inserted the key into the lock. The narrow end went in without obstruction but did not turn the spring.

Rocking back on her heels, she stared at the puzzle. "Reveal your secret," she whispered. Her heart skipped. The rhythm beat a little faster. With great care, she connected the deep marks where the escutcheon had decorated the lock. Around and around, her finger flew until the pattern appeared.

With trembling hands, she tried the key once more. This time she placed the head of the swan into the center of the missing metal plate.

She scrubbed her hands on her skirt, leaving a damp, dirty trail, and turned the key. A sound as quick as a cricket's chirp clicked into place. The spring turned the small bolt and the latch gave way.

She wiped her mouth with her sleeve. Sunlight was fading. Soon the chamber would be thrown into darkness. Carefully, she raised the lid.

"Christ's holy blood."

The golden gown that had once reminded her of moonbeams lay on top. She put it aside and picked up a pair of leather riding gloves that were the color of doves. Although time had taken away their sheen, they would have protected soft hands as they held the reins. Folded beneath the gloves lay a garnet cloak made of velvet. She buried her face in the satin-lined hood and inhaled. *Angelica.*

"Would you smell of the garden?" Clarice wondered aloud. "Of roses, lavender, and rosemary?"

Tears scored her cheeks. The cloak draped over her shoulders, she pulled the folds close, and for the first time in her life she was enveloped in her mother's embrace. With renewed determination singing through her veins, Clarice searched until the trunk lay on its side, empty of its contents.

Nothing. I've wasted time on a wild-goose chase.

Dejected, she rubbed her cheek with the velvet hood. Not only hadn't she found the proof of her birth, she had failed to find a clue about her father's death.

The growing shadows of nightfall had shifted, making it harder to see. Clarice tipped her head and squinted. The shadows outlined an uneven edge along the interior of the trunk.

She caught a piece of the rose-colored lining and pulled until it ripped open. Underneath was hardened brown leather. She rapped the bottom with her knuckles.

"What have we here? A secret compartment?"

She ran a shaking hand over the leather and felt the hard-edged spine of a book. Grasping the lining, she yanked harder. The opening ripped a little more and the small book slipped out.

"Angelica's prayer book!"

Bound in soft brown leather, the gilded lettering on the cover read *Book of Hours.* On each corner was a flower-shaped medallion. Each medallion, topped with a precious stone, surrounded by smaller, similar stones.

Reverently, she opened the small book where it had been marked with a delicate chain. The chain poured from the book, landing softly at her feet.

Clarice picked it up and held it to the dwindling light. A necklace. An emerald stone swung from a teardrop pendant. Several damaged links altered the filigree pattern. It pooled in her palm, warming her skin until she hid the necklace in the pouch under her skirt. Why would her mother hide it in the prayer book?

She moved to the window to catch the last of the sun. One by one, she searched the pages for clues that would lead her to answers. Page after page was a prayer for the day. On some pages were short verses. One for every hour of the day.

Moments later, she was still no more certain of why her father would give her a key that would fit this chest.

A cool breeze rose to the window. Thankful for Angelica's cloak, she lifted the hood and wrapped the folds tight around her body. On the verge of giving up hope, she turned the last few remaining pages. A few had been cut from the inner seam. Now, free of their moorings, the parchment fell to her feet.

As Clarice bent to pick up the loose sheets of vellum, the clatter of horses' hooves crossing over the wooden bridge broke through the silence. Whoever rode through the gate did so without thought for their safety or that of their horses. Before she could see who the careless riders were, the door swung open.

Maud's small frame tumbled into the darkened chamber. The flame from the candle she carried wavered but held to the wick.

"For the love of all that is good," Clarice scolded. "You will harm yourself so you cannot travel when we're ready. Return to your chamber before they know you are up and about."

The glazed look swept from Maud's eyes. Her mouth opened and snapped shut and opened again. "Dear Lord, I thought 'twas my lady Angelica, come back from the grave." She swept her hand over Clarice's head and smoothed the hood. "You found it."

"Come." Clarice led Maud to the mattress on the floor. "Tell me. Who rides through our gates?"

"'Tis him! Robert has returned."

"And has he many men, as Annora swore he would?"

"No, but he has a small man riding by his side."

The two women jumped up as the door struck the wall.

"I knew it," Annora exclaimed. "I knew I would find the two of you when I saw candlelight shining from the window." She stumbled back. "Angelica. It . . . it cannot be."

Clarice let the candle cast shadows across her face and stood so that Annora could clearly see Angelica's cloak.

The clatter of hobnailed boots striking against the stairway moved closer. Robert skidded to a halt before slamming into his mother's back. He wiped the clump of hair plastered against his cheekbone. The overgrown patch of beard on his jaw was spotty from the constant rubbing of his helmet. His eyes were red-rimmed and swollen. "Shite! Cease your pathetic sobbing. 'Tis Clarice."

Clarice ignored Maud's plea for silence and stepped forward. "Why, Annora? Is there reason for Angelica's restless spirit to visit you?"

Annora arched her back like a cat's. "You'll not speak of the dead."

"Angelica." Robert limped past Annora and moved to grab Clarice's arm. "I know not of this Angelica. Who is she to you?"

Clarice jerked her arm from his grasp. "My mother. Angelica Stanford. The true lady of Margrave. Is that not correct, *Aunt* Annora?"

"Aunt—" Robert began.

A howl of anguish stretched across the room as Annora lunged for Clarice. Robert grabbed his mother and pushed her toward the mattress.

"No! He loved me! He did!" Annora cried out. "Then she spoiled everything." Her sobs grew heavier. "He married my sister instead of me."

Robert caught Clarice, his relentless grasp digging into her flesh. "Mother," he said, "the past is gone. You are lady of Margrave. No one but the king can take that away, and even that I am seeking to rectify."

Annora shook her head and buried her face in her hands. "She'll ruin us," she cried.

His lips twisted. "Then we shall have to see that she doesn't spread falsities. It has been done for another. This time her words shall be silenced. Just like Father's."

Chapter 31

Annora pushed her rump off the mattress and propelled herself forward. "What do you mean?"

"Silenced." Robert's grip tightened around Clarice's arm. His blunt nails dug deep into her skin. Turning to Annora, he responded, his mouth forming a cruel arch. "As in the dead shall never speak their tales."

Annora's eyes widened. They were like twin moons in the shadow-cast chamber. "What are you saying?"

"Mother," he said in soothing tones, "distress your heart no more. I have taken care of everything."

He turned his back on Annora and searched Clarice's face. Shadows danced across his twisted face. He released her arm, snaking his hand around her wrist before she could make her escape. His warm breath scraped across her flesh. "Such pale skin. You simply glow."

Clarice swallowed a terse response. Her pulse, pumped under the pressure of his thumb. The pain increased and her bones threatened to snap. She tested his resistance, trying to free herself from the trap.

"But your hands." He jerked her close. "They are as cold as your heart." He tapped the ridge of her collarbone. "I have my doubts it beats within your chest."

Clarice pulled back so that she might meet his eyes. "I never intended—"

Robert tightened his hold, jerking her close again. His lips pressed into the crown of her head as he spoke. "Ah, my precious Clarice. What it must cost you to return to your tower."

"I-I-I am sorry."

"Sorry." He chuckled. "You expect that all can be made well with a single word?"

Clarice settled her fingers on his forearm. She prayed he did not feel the tremble that shook her core. "I suggest a truce."

He smoothed the strands of hair that stuck to the damp side of her throat. His slack arm moved around her shoulders, sliding up to her neck. Laughter rumbled where he pressed her ear against his chest. "A truce, you say?"

Her lungs burned. Unexpected relief came when Robert adjusted his hold. Clarice gulped in air as if she were drowning.

"My darling . . . sister . . . or is it cousin?" He gripped her chin and pressed another kiss on the top of her crown. Turning, he acknowledged Annora, who whimpered beside him. "What say you, Mother? Shall it be a truce?"

Clarice's eyes watered as his fingers dug into her jaw. She clawed at his hands, his chest. The leather jerkin slid under her nails.

"What?" he exclaimed. "No answer from the lady of the manor?"

His voice rose over the pounding in Clarice's ears. "What say you, Annora? 'Tis obvious to me that we cannot have a truce between siblings. Why is that, d'you suppose?"

Robert bent his head to Clarice. He mouthed the word, his lips hovering over her as he whispered the single word. The pressure on Clarice's jaw increased. "Say it!" Robert said. "Say it again. So everyone can hear."

He dragged Clarice with him and cast a pointed look at Maud. "Say it loud enough that the deaf one hears you. Say it one more time. Your last time," he goaded.

Her throat ached from the pressure. Her tongue pressed against the prison of her lips. "Bastard," she croaked through gritted teeth. "You are a bastard."

Released, Clarice dropped to her knees. She clutched her throat, dragging in a breath.

"No," Annora cried. "Not true."

His dagger drawn, Robert pointed it toward Maud. "Stay rooted to that spot, old woman. Don't move until I take my leave."

Without a sound, Maud bent her shoulders in submission.

"Robert. Wait." Annora rushed toward the door. Her departure stalled by the razor-sharp edge pointed in her direction, her footsteps slowed. "Put that thing away," she snapped. "Let me pass."

"Afraid the bastard child might disgrace himself or the Margrave name?"

Annora snorted. "Rubbish. The stench of your accusation fills my nostrils." She tried pushing past, but Robert continued to block her way. The point of his blade never wavered far from her face.

"And the knowledge I am a by-blow smells as fetid as a dung heap."

"Your father—"

"Was not Nicholas of Margrave."

"'Tis not true! He—"

"Admit it. You know not who my father was."

Annora's eyes widened. Her lips pursed. "Whether you are his son or not, it matters little. He accepted you as his. Besides, who is to prove otherwise? No one of any consequence is among us." She pressed closer toward the door. "That one over there?" She tilted her head. "The old woman has ears like two stones."

"And the other one? Nicholas of Margrave's daughter," Robert said. "Exactly."

A slow smile drifted across Annora's face. "Silence it will be."

"See, Mother?" He stroked her cheek with the back of his hand. "You are not of a simple mind. Those who know must be removed so they won't tell tales in their sleep."

Annora opened her arms to draw him into her embrace. "My son."

Robert stepped away.

Her breath sucked in as she stared at the empty space between her arms.

The door locked behind him, he called through the surrounding cracks, "Think you I would lose my hold on Margrave Manor now that I have inherited the title? Think on your own silence, Mother. Ponder how you'll prove your allegiance to me. Keep your silence. Keep your neck."

Clarice tucked the velvet riding cloak around Maud's thin back. She swore she could see each indentation where her joints attached like a string of pearls.

Annora shuffled past the cot and sniffed loudly. For the hundredth time since Robert's exit, she asked, "What will he do? Who will care for him?" Gaining their silent response, she continued, "He needs me. He must know he needs me."

Clarice could not listen to another whimper. "God's blessed bones,

Annora, you'll find that no matter how long you pace, your journey won't take you through that door."

Annora glared back and refused to stop. "'Tis your fault. Had you bedded the king as I instructed, we would be dining on roast pheasant and wild boar."

"What purpose would it serve for me to go to the king?" Clarice spat the words at the woman. "Thanks to my family's machinations, I could have shouted from the rooftops that I was a Margrave and no one would have believed me."

"Selfish girl," Annora snarled. "You could have warmed his cock. Bent his mind to forget the problems of Margrave."

"And when I found out you murdered my mother, I would have shouted it from his bed."

Annora's face blanched in the early morning light. Her knees buckled. She caught her weight on the prayer bench and sat down.

Angelica's book of prayers fell. The jeweled stones clicked, dancing over the floor. The pages fluttered before settling at the center.

Annora read the words aloud. "'A prayer for justice.'" A low keening came from deep within her as she swayed from side to side. "It cannot be."

"Why?" Clarice came to stand in front of her. She fisted her hands to keep from striking the woman. "Why did you have to do it?"

Annora looked up, her eyes filled with fear. "I was his chosen one. He was mine to have."

"They were in love."

"And so was I," Annora cried. "Does not my heart matter?"

Clarice bent to pick up the book, keeping it out of her aunt's reach. "And what of the lives you have destroyed with your love?"

"Lives?"

"My mother and father."

"I was to be the lady of Margrave." Annora waved her hand at Clarice as if sweeping her away. "You were a complication."

"And Robert?'

"Robert? He is the lord of Margrave now. Just as he was meant to be."

"Meant to be?" Clarice scrubbed her fingers through the tangled knots in her hair. "Can you be so dull-witted? Without Father to prove his innocence, we have nothing but our word. To claim heritage to a man believed of treason . . . what madwomen we would seem."

"Robert will repair the damage. You heard him; even now he is turning Henry's mind from our ruination."

"How will Robert fare better than my father? All I see is that his claim to Margrave improved upon my father's death."

"He promised he would set everything aright. 'Twas even Robert's idea to return to Margrave."

Clarice scoured over Annora's face. "His idea? It was not my father's decision to come here?"

"Your father," Annora said, "sought a private meeting with the king, and when he was turned away, he hadn't the stomach to demand that scoundrel king see his error. Robert is certain he can correct Margrave's relationship with the crown."

Clarice's temper flared. "So Robert set about ridding himself of those who got in his path."

Annora bolted from the prayer bench. Her hand clutched the amulet swinging between her breasts. "How dare you speak foul lies?"

"Like from like." Clarice crossed her arms. "Son and mother, using the same means to obtain what they want. You wanted to be the lady of Margrave. Robert wants to be lord. Remove that which stands in your path. You removed your sister. He removed my father."

Annora's face paled. "More lies!"

Clarice glanced out the window. There was a small flicker of light near the gate. Nothing more than a flash. Then 'twas gone.

She blinked, resisting the urge to rub her eyes. Hope began to build within her heart. She combed the horizon for movement, for a bit of light, an unexplained shadow.

"Believe what you will, Annora. The truth will win out this time."

Chapter 32

The scrape of the bolt sliding in the lock echoed amid the snuffles and snorts coming from the corner where Annora slept. Clarice scrubbed the grit from her weary eyes and rose from the prayer bench. Had she not heard that sound more times than she cared to recall? Yet recall it she did.

She gripped the necklace she had found in her mother's prayer book. The smooth surface of the teardrop stone warmed her palm. The gold filigree links, some bent and broken, bit into her skin. Yet her grip did not lessen. She had read the pages in her mother's prayer book. Memorized each scribbled word from Angelica's failing hand.

The radiance of a new day broke behind her. Crimson light infused the room with an early morning glow. A halo radiated around her as if a deity from the heavens had come to visit. Save the soft breeze floating through the window, nothing moved.

The three women kept to their spots. Held their breath. Waited.

Then Annora rushed to the door. "Robert, my darling, your mother forgives you." Unable to believe her pleas went unnoticed, she crumpled to her knees in despair.

No longer able to ignore the woman's apparent shock, Clarice deserted her sanctuary. If nothing else, there must be support among women. The door opened as she gently touched Annora's thickly formed shoulder.

A man with a face wide at the forehead and narrow at the chin stood in the doorway. His eyes were small and black. A mustache wiggled as he spoke. "Lord Robert has told me to convey his wish that you enjoy your stay in the tower."

Annora untangled her feet from the folds of her skirt and squared her girth before the rat-faced man. "From under what dung heap were you plucked? What gives you the right to address me thus?"

"Name's Harald." His mustache twitched, and a slow smile spread under the whiskers. "You're his mother, are ya? His lordship said you'd be right put out. Was to ignore your arguments of any style."

Annora attempted to rush through the doorway. Her foot came down hard, narrowly missing his toes. Without a word, he drew his sword. The metal hissed through the air.

"How dare you?" Annora's voice broke over the tension of the three women in the room.

"Said you'd do that, too." The red from the sun reflected in his gaze, giving him a demonlike glow. "You," the rat-faced man said, pointing the tip of his blade at Annora. "Take the wench to the old master's bedchamber."

Clarice pushed toward Annora and their guard. "I shall not leave without Maud."

The man shook his head. "She stays here."

Clarice glanced at Maud, wagering the outcome of their escape. Together they would not make it past the gate. Nevertheless, if she were no longer locked behind the door, escape would be possible.

Maud pushed at the mattress, struggling to stand and defend her charge.

Clarice met her gaze. "No," she mouthed.

"Lift your skirts," Harald, their rat-faced jailor, called out. "Get moving down them stairs."

While Annora sputtered her outrage, Clarice walked to Maud. She bent to kiss the top of her grizzled head. Annora gripped Clarice's arm, her fingers digging into the wound. The neat stitches Erwina had placed earlier began to pull away.

Pain radiated from shoulder to fingertips. Clarice buckled forward and fell.

"Hand me that book," Annora snapped.

"'Tis not yours." Clarice slipped the prayer book into the pocket under her skirt before rising.

"Here now," Robert's guard called out again. "His lordship's an impatient man."

He propelled them forward, his blade poking their backs as he prodded them in the direction of the stairs.

Clarice planted her feet in his path, refusing to follow like a lamb to the slaughter. She braced her arms, barring him from moving down the stairs. "Wait. There must be something—"

Her world exploded in pain.

Clarice slumped on a rickety stool. Her head ached as if the roof had caved in upon her skull. It did not take long for her to realize how the wobbly bit of furniture had escaped the kings' men. The telltale signs of cow dung and half-chewed hay stuck to the legs.

She closed her eyes again, fearing she would see more than hardened manure. Her heart twisted. The conjured image of her father's blood smeared on the stool was enough to force them open. Better to see what was than to imagine what was not.

Annora claimed the high-backed chair. She sewed at a bit of embroidery as if it were an everyday occurrence to guard someone with their hands tied behind their back. Clarice noted that in her absence furnishings had begun their return. 'Twould not be long before Robert had refilled the manor house. Whether by fair means or foul, he would gain that which he desired. 'Twas obvious he thought he had beaten the king and his men.

Annora looked up. A tiny gasp escaped and she nearly dropped the hoop on which she worked. Robert's name was sewn in erratic stitches on the fabric.

"You awaken," Annora said.

Clarice blinked. If her hands were not tied behind her back, she would have tried to feel the growing lump on the side of her head. As it was, she escaped the self-inflicted torture by knowing the throbbing location must be where she had been struck.

Annora shook her head. "'Twas not my fault. I believe you tripped."

Clarice worked to moisten her parched throat. "As your sister did?" she croaked.

Annora's knuckles whitened. She held the hoop as if it were her salvation from being dragged to hell. Her words were cool. "Angelica was a stumbling fool. She was probably dreaming of Nicholas. Wantonly throwing herself at his feet. Like as not, she forgot to look where she was going."

"I know what happened that night," Clarice said.

Annora's cheeks paled. "You don't know anything."

"She spoke to me from the grave."

The forgotten hoop spun to the floor. "Rubbish."

"You sent Nicholas away. Tricked him with a rumor of rebellion on our lands."

"No!"

"You argued with your sister."

"No!"

"Angelica fell. Her labor began."

"Don't you see? Your own words prove I did not kill her."

"Not then. Later. What was the argument about, Annora?"

"Nothing."

"Nothing?" Clarice pushed.

Annora played with the cuffs of her dress. "Not that I recall."

"You fought with my mother because you, too, had found my father's bed. He did lie between your legs and plant his seed. His devoted love, a sham to the both of you," Clarice pressed. "'Twas a race to the finish. And you were losing."

Annora lurched from the chair, growling as if she were a wild boar protecting her meal. "That birthing bed should have been mine. I was not about to see my perfect sister steal from me one more time." She shrugged. "I took an herbal brew that started the cramping. We labored, my sister and I, as if our lives depended on it. And they did."

"Angelica delivered a daughter."

"And, within seconds, I delivered a boy."

"But he was not a legitimate heir to Margrave."

Annora's chest lowered and rose with each dragging breath. "Your birth was of no consequence. The male always wins out, I told myself. Yet I had to know 'twas certain. I had to see. I went looking for Nicholas when he did not visit my bedchamber to speak with me and see our son."

Annora lifted strands of Clarice's hair and let it run through her fingers as she spoke. "I walked into the master chamber and there was my sister and my lover. The perfect family. He kissed you and called you his other angel. I just stood there. My heart filled with regret and a baby everyone believed to be a bastard from the stables. What else could I do?"

"You made certain my mother did not survive the birthing bed. The bleeding would not stop."

Annora's gentle hand hardened against Clarice's head. "I gave Angelica an herbal infusion. One that draws a babe from the womb. Too much and 'tis the harlot's life that joins the babe's descent into the beyond."

"You made her bleed to death."

"Later that night you were to die, too," Annora said. "But I couldn't do it. I sent you away instead. Convinced everyone that you were dead, wrapping a slaughtered piglet in swaddling. But the nursery maid disobeyed my orders and ran. Took you with her to the monastery to hide."

"You used my father's loss. His mistakes. All, against him." Clarice swallowed the boiling rage. Her arms were beginning to deaden from their bent position. Even if she could break free, she would not be able to mount an attack.

"What have you to complain of?" Annora asked. "'Twas I who suffered. You were returned. A constant reminder of my loss."

"You stole my mother's life," Clarice cried out.

"I took back what was mine. Nicholas needed an heir. He needed to fulfill a promise to Angelica to ensure her dear sister's future was secure."

"So he married you."

"Do not charge all deeds unto me. 'Twas he who plowed my fields and planted his seed. He made promises to love me and protect me." Annora bent, her face nearly touching Clarice's. "I, too, had been called his angel."

Applause erupted from the doorway.

Annora swiveled on her heel and ran to Robert, her arms stretched wide. "My darling boy!"

He swaggered into the room as if he had not a care in the world. Until Clarice looked closer, and saw his eyes glistening with enough fire to put the North Star to shame. Over his shoulder he carried a rope, its end looped and knotted.

"I cannot decide whether to kill you or kiss you." He lifted Annora's hand to his lips and pressed a kiss against her knuckles. "This shall have to do. For now."

Annora winced as Robert squeezed her hand. The ring on her finger cut into the skin and began to bleed.

"Robert, my son," her voice quavered. "What have I done that vexes you?"

"Lies, dear Mother. Lies you have spun ever since I dandled on your knee."

"Small tales." Annora reached out to caress his cheek. "Only to protect you."

"Your protection," he said, "cost me my father's life. Had I known, I would have taken his death less lightly."

"Stop." Annora tugged on her fingers, trapped in his grip. "You are beginning to frighten me."

"I have just begun." Smiling, he snapped the edge of his riding cloak behind him.

He was dressed to ride at a moment's notice. Tall boots covered his legs from toe to knee. The thick protective leather tunic covered his padded gambeson.

He flipped the rope from his shoulder. It landed with a deadened thud next to Annora's feet. "Don't you love it, Mother? Just as you desired. An end to young Clarice's life."

Annora stared at the rope as if it was a snake with two heads writhing at her feet. "I cannot do it."

"You must. You have no choice." Robert spread his arms wide and looked up at the beam overhead. "Don't you see? How fitting I have made this gift for you. Angelica died for me. Nicholas died for you. Now Clarice shall die for both of us."

Annora gripped the back of the chair, the shape of her knuckles showing through her skin. "You killed your father?"

A smile worthy of a proud boy with his first prize at the fair stretched Robert's mouth. "I suppose I did."

"H-h-h-how could you do this?" Annora sputtered. "You jeopardized all I have given my soul to."

She strode up to Robert as if he were still the little boy who cowered from her stern voice and struck out.

He caught her wrist in his grip. "Do not force my hand. Attempt to block my path and I shall remove you as I did Nicholas." He lifted her knuckles to his lips. "Now Mother, prove to me that you are worthy of my trust."

Chapter 33

Annora picked up the rope. Her hands trembled as she slid it between her fingers. Her countenance, which Clarice had never seen without an expression of impatience, was tarnished with remorse. Her lips quivered. Her attention remained on Robert's weapon of choice.

Clarice strained against the strips of leather that bound her wrists. "Annora," she said, ignoring the fear that welled inside her chest, "don't do this. We will go to the king. You and I. Together. We can stop this mad plot. The king will reward you for your duty. Think of your sacrifice. All you desired will be returned to you."

"Must I do everything?" Robert yanked the drooping noose from Annora and shoved her to one side. Her yelp of pain when she landed on the floor went unnoticed.

"Better to have my murder staining your soul rather than Annora's," Clarice said. "Not that you would mind having my death added to our father's when your soul is accounted for at St. Peter's gates."

Robert ignored her and pulled Annora to stand at his side. "Hush, Mother, weep no more. Let me show you how 'tis done." He wrapped an arm around her shoulder and placed her hands on the rope. Together, they lifted the noose over Clarice's head.

Woven threads of hemp scratched against her neck. The weight of the rope pressed her flesh. She gulped the air trapped in her throat.

"Not to fear," he said. "Unlike the gallows men, I have ensured the noose is one that brings you a quick death."

He spoke softly to Annora as he pointed to the beam in the ceiling. "There."

The door to the bedchamber swung open without a knock for permission to enter, interrupting his instructions.

Robert's impatience exploded over Harald. "Must I guide you with a boot up your arse? I will let you know when I am ready."

With their attention diverted, Clarice renewed her efforts against the leather bindings. Robert may know how to tie variations of the gallows knot, but his rat-faced man did not. The leather's bite began to slacken.

Robert turned, his ire reverting to a sanguine smile. His hand trembled, as if fighting to contain the boiling within his soul. In a matter of a few short breaths, he had forgotten the man at the door and returned to scrutinize his handiwork.

"This is much neater than other ways to die. Poison is too slow and untrustworthy. The blade makes a mess. This we know from personal experience, do we not, Clarice? And a pretty lady should not be covered in blood at her death."

"Sweet Mary, save us," whispered Clarice.

His hand brushed across her brow. "I knew a Mary. She did slay me when she withdrew her love. And as God's word does say, 'an eye for an eye.'"

The rat-faced man cleared his throat. "Sir . . ."

Clarice looked up, willing to plead with anyone who filled the doorway. Even Robert's own man.

"'Tis a peddler," Harald said, thumbing to the man standing behind him. When Robert did not reduce his glare, he added, "We have need of supplies before we take our leave."

Robert smiled a tight thin line that never reached his eyes. "A peddler, you say?" He strode across the room. "Why do you keep your face covered with that hood? Reveal yourself!"

"My lord, 'tis scars that would turn the bile in your stomach."

"From the plague?" Robert took a half step back.

"Just returned to me health. Don't fear, m'lord, the fever has passed." The peddler hesitated for a brief moment. "If you still wish to witness my discomfort, I shall obey your wishes."

Robert's cheeks flared red and held up his hand. "We've met. I recognize your stature and voice. You served my father."

Clarice twisted to see who stood outside the chamber. Her eyes watered when Annora dug her fingers into her shoulder.

"Yes, m'lord. I regret I did not fulfill his last request before his death," the peddler murmured.

"You serve the new lord of Margrave now," Robert ground out. "Show me your wares. I warn you, I will not be trifled with. Ladies, I shall return to finish our discussion." He flicked the chamber door shut.

Clarice flinched at the thump of the rope as it swung over the rafter. Her breath caught, her body rebelling against her efforts to control the fear. *Please God, let that be my peddler.*

Ranulf dropped another bag of wheat into the wagon. The thought of Clarice in danger made his vision redden with rage. If only they would have let him enter the room, see if she was there. The need to strangle Robert prancing in front of him was encompassing. Carving an extra hole in the rat-faced man's gullet would be a pleasure, too.

Gods! He wanted to toss everything out of his cart and run to Clarice. Yet how was he to be in two places at once?

Although violently aware Clarice needed him, he kept within his role. He must maintain the most important reason for being at the manor. 'Twas his duty. To stop the plot against his king, he must find the ringleader. In all that he had seen in his time as a knight, he had never seen one more unsuited to lead a revolt. Robert was unstable.

Ranulf had worked with venomous, clay-brained men before. Those without morals. No conscience to contend with at the end of the day. He had even enjoyed their company at times. Knowing what they were capable of, he had not been dealt surprises. Until now.

This one standing beside him, treating him as if he was offal stuck to the bottom of his boot, had no idea what consequences would soon befall him. Ranulf would find pleasure in seeing this one receive the king's justice.

Robert began his complaints anew. "I won't pay a penny more for your goods."

"Have you nothing on which we can barter?"

Ranulf recognized the smallish man standing beside Robert. He had been the one to bring news of Clarice's attack against Robert.

The man nudged Robert with his elbow. "Offer him what's below in the cellar, my lord. You cannot carry it all with you, no how."

Robert glanced up at the sun as if to tell the time of day. "My man has a point. We have a cask or two of wine to trade."

"English wine?" Ranulf pursed his lips and shook his head. "'Tis no good to me. Now French wine . . ." He rubbed his hands together. "For that I'd give you all in my cart."

Before he knew it, he was standing before a cart filled with casks of wine. The markings were identical to the one found in the remnants of the orphanage. He rapped his knuckles on a few of the wooden barrels. His suspicions were confirmed. The first few casks were filled with wine; the rest were empty.

His thoughts raced to Clarice as he hastened to take his leave. His return must go unnoticed if he was to free her from Robert's hold.

Less than ten paces outside the gate, he drew his cart behind the wall. He turned at the sound of cracking twigs. Darrick and Nathan led their horses through the dry brush. Hamish sat on Nathan's horse, his short legs bent in an angle as he clung to his perch. To Ranulf's surprise, Erwina rode behind the boy. Her bony white knees stuck out from under her skirt as she lifted her leg to slide off Darrick's mount. She stopped when she caught his glare. She understood his meaning and stayed where she was.

They drew close enough for them to whisper.

Hamish searched the wooded area. "Where is she?"

"I think they keep her in the master's bedchamber," Ranulf said.

He cast a pointed look at Darrick and Nathan. "I had no idea you meant to bring the whole of Sedgewic with you."

"Settle your ire," Nathan said. "We found Mistress Erwina walking the trail. We couldn't let the poor woman wander the countryside unescorted. What of her virtue?"

Ranulf snorted. He should have known she, too, would not heed his orders to stay behind. She had worried herself into a frenzy by the time he and his men had returned from their search for Robert. It wasn't until he swore he would form a party to look for the wayward lady that she broke her silence regarding Clarice's past.

He lifted the castellan of Sedgewic off the horse, motioning her to keep silent. He pointed in the direction of the manor. "I wager they aim to leave within the hour. Stay here until they do. Follow them until you discover the ringleader's identity."

"Think you 'tis not our Robert?" Darrick asked.

"His mind may be pockmarked with evil, but he hasn't the fortitude to lead men into battle."

"Many a madman has led lost souls to the devil," said Darrick.

"I don't think this one can think for himself, let alone for others. Follow him. Keep him close. He may circle back if he fears Annora has not done his bidding."

Nathan's green eyes glittered as they bore into the shadows of the manor. "Your lady?"

"She remains. But I fear not for long."

Hamish nudged the horse closer. "How could you leave her?"

Ranulf excused his brash tongue. He understood his concern. Had the boy not listened to his inner voice, they would never know what had befallen Clarice. Hamish had followed her and found her horse tied in a grove of great oak trees. Waiting all through the night for a sign, when he saw the light in the tower he knew she needed their help. For once the boy made a well-thought decision. He rode his little pony hard until he met their party.

Ranulf reached out and squeezed Hamish's ankle. "'Tis a good friend she has in you."

Darrick motioned for Ranulf to head back to the manor. "We'll keep the lad with us. He'll be safe until we meet again."

Erwina placed a hand on his forearm. "I shall come with you. There may be some who require my skill."

Saluting the men and child, Ranulf made his way back to the gate. This time he would not make a sound. Erwina followed suit, joining him in the shadow of his footsteps.

Just as they were nearing the gate, a single rider, along with a horse and cart, raced out. The cart creaked and rattled with its heavy load. Ranulf smiled. Darrick and Nathan would have no problem in following those two.

His resolve bolstered, he retraced his steps to the master's chamber. He and Erwina stopped at an alcove off the hall. "Stay put."

Erwina nodded, waving him on.

He opened the door to the chamber and his heart lurched to a halt.

The dung-coated stool lay toppled on its side. The rope dangled from the rafters. The empty noose swayed in the breeze.

Ranulf staggered under the weight of the catapult launched at his head. With the hood of his cloak pressed to his ears, his hearing muffled, he barely understood the words that flew about his head.

"I knew you'd come back," Clarice cried. "I knew I could depend on you for my rescue. You, of all people, would never leave me to this vermin. Ah, my darling peddler, how shall I repay you?"

Ranulf lifted her hands from his ears. How could she entrust her life to her bloody peddler? Damn, but he would not play court jester to that character, even if it were he who played the role. His need to have her clinging to him with desire roared inside his head. *Unfair* his heart raged. *'Tis the peddler she clings to, not me.*

Until Clarice pressed her cheek to his chest, he had every intention of scolding her for running way. Now, with her heart beating against his, he was capable of nothing more than holding her tight. His heart nearly burst when her tears dampened his jerkin. Her body shook as if she were about to shatter.

He tilted her chin so that he might have access to her lips. He drenched the salt-laced mouth with his love and then pulled away. It pained him to know her kisses were not for him. Nor was her offer of love. How she must hate him. She had run from him. Would she run again if she knew 'twas he who held her?

He smoothed her hair and let the silken strands wrap around his fingers. He gently pried her from his chest and placed her out of reach. Keeping his face in the shadows of his hood, he whispered in a falsetto voice, "Annora of Margrave. Where is she, my lady?"

Ranulf knelt beside Annora. She rocked back and forth, mumbling a prayer. Beside her lay an open book of hours. He lifted the woman's balled fist. One by one, he pried open the fingers until a gold chain slid from her hand.

Clarice knelt beside him. Tears glistened and slid down her cheeks. "'Tis my fault," she said. "In an act of desperation, I gave her the necklace."

Ranulf lifted an auburn brow in puzzlement.

"'Twas hers. I thought to return it. To make amends for the past."

Clarice smoothed a strand of hair out of Annora's face. "My mother, Angelica, pulled it and broke it as she fell down the stairs. She had put it in her prayer book on the day of my birth, which was the day she died. It, combined with all other revelations, must have been Annora's undoing." Clarice paused to wipe a tear from her jaw. "Robert murdered our father."

Ranulf started to draw Clarice into his embrace. Before he touched her, though, he hesitated, as if scrambling for a safe footing. For the first time since his childhood, he was unsure of himself. Even in his unhappy marriage, he had known he had a right to fulfill his wedding vows. He had a right to demand access to the wedding bed. With Clarice, he wanted more. He wanted her to demand he love her until the end of time. Yet how could she, when she did not know him?

Ranulf stood and looked out the narrow slit in the wall. How was he to untangle the knot of intrigue his own hand had made of this predicament? Frustrated, filled with jealousy of his own making, he struck the windowsill.

Behind him, he heard a rustle of skirts, but he did not turn. How was he to expose his identity and keep her trust intact?

Clarice tugged on the hood of his cloak. His joints stiffened, then went to liquid when she wrapped her arms around his waist. His muscles heated with each soft word she pressed into his back. Turning slowly, Ranulf could no longer deny himself the answer.

"What did you say?" he asked, surprised to hear his own voice, hoarse with emotion.

She reached up and moved the hood of his cloak out of the way. "I was saying a prayer, thanking my father for sending me to find my red wolf."

She tugged at the auburn hair that had escaped his cloak. "I much prefer seeing where to place my lips, Ranulf, Lord of Sedgewic."

He lifted her off her feet and spun her around, raining kisses on her lips.

Erwina ran into the chamber with a candlestick raised over her head. "Oh! I beg your pardon." Her weapon dropped to her side. "Oh, dear, 'tis Annora?"

Ranulf nodded in answer to Erwina.

Holding Clarice close, he turned her so that she might never have to look upon the broken woman lying on the floor. He kissed the top of Clarice's head. "I would spend an eternity holding you as we are now. But we must prepare to join the others."

Clarice gasped and grabbed Ranulf's cloak. "The king! Robert must be stopped."

"We'll stop him before he can end another life. The others are looking for him now."

"Others?"

"Hamish rides with Darrick and Nathan. None could be persuaded to stay at Sedgewic and await word of your return."

Awakened from her trembling, Annora pushed up from the floor.

Her eyes blazed with hatred. "Harlot! I won't let you take my love from me again, Angelica."

Erwina called out Ranulf's name as he caught sight of a blurred shape flying across the room. He tucked Clarice behind him as Annora launched forward.

A scramble of legs and arms ensued. Ranulf positioned his arms across Annora's back and pressed her face into the floor. He looked up from where he lay across the bucking woman. "It seems we must find our quarry before he finds us."

Chapter 34

Clarice knelt before the small stone marking her father's grave. The shadows from the trees overhead deepened her weariness. Her heavy heart made it difficult to breathe. Never in all her dark imaginings of revenge could she have guessed there would be pain in exacting justice. They had taken Annora to the chamber in the tower. Her sorrow echoed down the stairway, giving Clarice pause. She could not help wondering why the people of Margrave never had broken from their ranks and helped Clarice escape her own prison.

She told herself and all who would listen that she preferred the silence and solitude of the garden. But its beauty was lost. Now all she wished for was the comfort she found in Ranulf's embrace. That, too, however, had shadows that haunted her in the solace of the garden.

She heard the snap of twigs breaking underfoot. The roll of pebbles scattered with each step. She was unafraid. Those who walked the garden path did not mean her harm.

"Forgive me, my lady, but I thought we might speak while the men are busy."

Clarice smiled up at Mistress Erwina. She motioned for the woman to join her. "Come. Sit, if you will."

Erwina glanced at the ground. A reluctant grimace flashed, immediately replaced with a smile as she gathered her skirts.

Clarice noticed her hesitation. For the first time she realized Erwina's age was not much less than Maud's. "Stop," she said. "I have a need to move my legs. Mayhap we shall stroll through the garden."

Erwina eyed the weed-strewn path. "I would like to clean this area as soon as I am able." Her eyes keen on the disarray, she appeared to be taking in every flaw in the garden. "'Tis time."

Clarice motioned to the stone. "My father—"

"And your mother is over there," Erwina finished for her."

"When first we met, you knew my face. How is that so?" Clarice asked. "And no games this time," she warned. "Speak only truth to me."

Erwina's fingers bunched the apron hanging from her waist. Her reddened knuckles whitened as she searched for words. "'Tis I who failed you. I did not protect you as I vowed." Her body shuddered as she drew in quick, halting breaths. "I failed my lady Angelica, too."

"You were the nursery maid who took me to the monastery," Clarice said. She touched Erwina's knuckles with the tip of her finger and covered the work-worn flesh with her hand. "Don't you see? You did not fail me. You protected me until my father learned the truth."

Erwina's eyes filled with tears. "I should have sent a message to your father."

"You did all you could."

A shadow of a smile tugged at Erwina's mouth. "Can you find forgiveness, my lady?"

"'Tis certain I can."

"But your mother . . ."

"Lady Angelica would have been proud of your efforts."

Erwina bent her knees to curtsy. The cracking of old joints sounded as if crickets had taken residence under her skirts.

Clarice shook her head. "No need for this. You no longer serve a Margrave. You serve Lord Ranulf."

The meager smile on Erwina's face stretched. "Quite a job indeed. His lordship has certainly come into his own as a fine, strapping young man."

Curious, Clarice could not help asking, "You knew him when he was a child?"

"For a time."

She glanced at Erwina. "The tale of my father is true?"

"His lordship would not be turned away until he tore down the place that hid his angel. I fear his soul paid a hefty price for destroying the Lord's place of worship. But I understood his anger."

"And Ranulf?"

"Your father did Lord Ranulf a kindness by arranging his position with the young prince. One never knows what he might have come to be without that opportunity."

"And the children who come to Sedgewic now?" In the distance, Clarice could see a little one approach. "Hamish?"

At Erwina's silent nod, Clarice motioned him closer. "Then I shall see that he, too, has the same opportunities to advance his station."

Hamish ran toward them, ignoring Erwina's scolding to mind his dirty fingers and face. His pudgy arms wrapped around Clarice's waist and held her tight.

"Lord Ranulf says you are to join him in the great hall at once."

Clarice arched a brow at Erwina and grinned. "If you will excuse us, Mistress Erwina, our presence is required." Their hands clasped together, she hitched up the skirt of her gown so as not to rip the hem.

"One, two, three," she counted. "Go!"

They raced to the hall. Their laughter rang throughout the bailey yard as they ran on. Breathless, they skittered over the doorway.

Three stern faces, masked in cold indifference, turned from the weeping man they were questioning. Harald's whole body quaked with fear.

Ranulf's harsh gaze ripped the laugher from their throats.

"Where is Robert?" Clarice asked the men.

The silence that followed crackled as if ice were underfoot.

"I cannot comprehend why 'tis necessary for me to stay at Margrave." Clarice pointed a finger into Ranulf's chest. "In truth, 'tis a command I refuse to heed."

He caught her finger and kissed it. He smiled as if he had licked the last drop of milk from the saucer. "For the hundredth time, 'tis not safe for you to ride with us. You would make yourself a target."

"But that is what I want."

"And I won't allow it."

Nathan pushed away from the great hearth's mantel. "Hear the woman out, Ranulf."

Clarice grinned and bobbed a slight curtsy. "My thanks, good sir."

"Then we can stop wasting time and move on as we planned," Nathan said.

Before she could launch into another tirade, Darrick left the corner where he had been standing. "Let the lady speak."

Incredulous, Nathan turned to Darrick. "You agree with her?"

"I think I do." Darrick bent a knee to Clarice. "Excuse the inter-
ference, Ranulf, but it has to be said." He paused until the lord of
Sedgewic granted him allowance to speak. "She cannot be left alone.
She is a Margrave. No disrespect intended," he added,

"None taken," she replied.

"And you'll not be at your best if she's out of your sight," Darrick
said. "Besides, what better way to draw out our prey than to have two
tasty morsels in front of his nose?"

"Damn, but I have to admit he has a point," Nathan acknowledged.
" 'Tis better to have Robert's mind set on you than on the king."

Clarice looked at her hand trapped against Ranulf's chest. His
heart raced when they spoke of her family's name tied to her own. His
fingers tightened and released. Now they lay lightly. Disconnected
from emotion. The rhythm in his chest matched his calm breath. Indifference had returned to his eyes. Yet he could not contain the
growl deep in his throat. "I protect what is mine."

"Silence, my wolf. I've no fear of your ability to protect me."

Clarice rode beside Ranulf. Buttercup's steady pace carried her
through the Margrave gates. She turned back to look at the tower
spire. The tip of its gray point could be seen over the trees.

"Maud and Erwina are like birds of a feather," he assured her.
"Before you know it, Maud will have her fill of Erwina's meat pies.
And Erwina will be satisfied that Maud's health is returning."

"Do you think they'll be safe?"

"Sergeant Krell will see the ladies are protected."

"And Hamish?"

"He rides with two of the king's most trusted men."

A firm line formed Ranulf's mouth. "Nathan and Hamish will
alert our men to break camp."

"And Robert—"

"Robert's man, Harald, said he would be heading for Southampton. He intends to stop the king's fleet before they set sail for France.
Darrick rides ahead to alert them." Ranulf reined in Aldwyn and
drew beside her. "We must be wary, Clarice. Harald believes Robert
may delay his plan if it means capturing you."

An uncomfortable silence hung between them like a heavy, wet
cloak.

"If 'tis I Robert cannot resist, then let us entice the beast into our lair. Stake me out like a goat for the taking."

Ranulf groaned. "I swore you would be safe in my care."

Sliding his hand up Clarice's arm, he cupped the back of her neck and drew her face to his. The lines around her mouth softened as his lips sought hers.

He smoothed the hair that always seemed to escape whatever confines she created. "This beast wants us both."

"Mary?" she whispered.

A pained look, one of haunted guilt flickered over his face as if marked by her ghost. "My wife," Ranulf said. "Erwina admitted she had seen him visit her while I was away on Henry's business."

"Then let's see that his hunger is satisfied."

Ranulf eased her off Buttercup and onto his lap. She handed him her reins and settled her head against his chest. Aware of his desire, she pressed her back deeper into the angle of his thighs.

He bent his head, nipping the hinge of her jaw. "Keep your eyes open, Clarice."

"Shall we ride much farther? I—" She groaned and rocked back as he slipped his hand between the folds of her cloak.

"Watch the horizon for me." His hand roamed to her breasts.

"Ranulf," she whispered. "I don't think I can do this."

Her eyes snapped open the moment he withdrew his touch. She shivered. Where heat once flamed, the trail was cold. A wall of ice slid between their bodies. She tried to turn to see his face.

"What is it? Is it Robert?"

"Quiet," he hissed.

They rode in silence. The distance between them grew with every step away from Margrave. Clarice could not understand why he would pull away. Was it not she who said she could wait no longer?

Her heart skipped. Dread leaped in. That was not what she had said. Had he misunderstood?

His loins continued to press against her. She was aware of the life that throbbed in his veins. His hand settled at her waist and rested there, as if she were the pommel of a saddle. Her nerves jangled with every step. Need blossomed, pouring through her body, threatening to ignite like dry tinder.

By the time the stars had begun to form overhead, frustration whispered on her skin. It hid just barely below the surface until she realized she was rubbing her back against his chest and taking deeper breaths so that his thumb might touch the base of her breasts. She turned her face to feign sleep and found her arousal increasing when she smelled his scent. Yet, despite her hunger, they rode on in silent agony.

Chapter 35

Clarice let her gaze sweep over the horizon as she smoothed Aldwyn's slick, dark shoulder. "I don't understand why we must stop so soon. The sun hasn't moved position since the last time."

Receiving a nudge with his hand, she ignored his offer to lift her from the saddle. "We shall never make it to Southampton at this pace."

She arched a brow at Ranulf's grunted response and continued with her examination of his face. "That is where we are headed, is it not? Or won't you admit our destination?" Her lips pursed. She found his silence most distasteful. "Is it because I am a Margrave?"

She pushed his hand away, slid off Aldwyn, and walked into the grove of oak trees. She would have preferred the long walk back to the manor house than spend another moment sitting next to such an unbearable man. Her wobbly knees had a different notion altogether and refused to budge another step past a group of felled trees. Although she heard Ranulf call to her, she decided to keep her back to him and continued to scan the shadows dancing under the canopy of green vegetation.

Ranulf ran to her and caught her elbow. "You are not to take yourself out of my sight." He pointed to a fallen log. "Stay here. Without argument."

Hiding a grimace, her back straight and rigid, she turned from the tree and chose a different one. After straightening her skirts, she folded her hands as if she had been waiting for his presence all day. She drew a long-suffering sigh that would have made Annora cringe.

"'Tis ridiculous," she snapped. "All that I have been through to prove I am who I say I am, and now I am punished because of it."

Ranulf's shoulders bunched as he cared for their horses.

Guilt nipped at her conscience. 'Twas unlike her to act the petty fool. However, he was not helping the matter. If he chose to treat her with disregard, then she would be obliged to show him disdain, too.

Despite her vow to dispatch all her feeling for this man, she watched him move about the clearing and wondered what had put him in such a bilious mood. She had to find a way to breach the wall he had erected between them.

Even though the warmth of the sun penetrated the canopy of leaves, she shivered, aching for what they had shared in times past. She could not retreat from the passion he kept hidden. 'Twas a rare sight to behold in this man. Indeed, she had discovered he cared with alarming passion. *I ache for those brief, breathless moments.*

Ranulf tied off the horses and began to gather dry sticks. Clarice's concern grew with each addition of kindling. He intended they stop for the remainder of the evening. They would not arrive in time to speak with the king.

He smiled and motioned for her to join him by the fire. When she did not heed his request, he gave up on his self-imposed silence. "You cannot intend to keep your perch all night."

She pulled her spine erect. "I find this location much to my liking."

Ranulf threw the gnarled log into the meager fire. The dry wood ignited, snapping and crackling. Flames danced, entwining their tips like embracing lovers. Sparks shot out as the kindling erupted into a roaring blaze.

Enraptured by the instant combustion, Clarice glanced up. Ranulf stood before the flames, surrounded by its ginger-colored glow. Smoke swirled above his head. Scorching heat radiated past him as if it were coming from his soul. His face remained in the shadows, but she could feel his eyes. They poured into her being, seeking the answers to his questions. Clarice tore her gaze from his. She cleared her throat before she could speak again. "Does it not worry you that someone will see the fire?"

Ranulf massaged the muscles of his neck. Agitated fingers ruffled the ends of his hair, where they curled against his damp skin. "Have you already forgotten your offer to be the lure for our prey?" He threw down the stick he had been holding. "Please, I beseech you, Clarice. Allow me to return you to Sedgewic before you are harmed."

"You of all people understand vows."

"But not at the cost of your life."

Clarice shook her head. "I cannot turn from my vow."

He moved to stand beside her. Worry marked his gaze. "You think it easy for me to offer you up as bait?" He lifted a strand of her hair, tucking it behind her ear.

Clarice leaned into his caress. "My safety is a small sacrifice for the king's."

His finger swooped down to the nape of her neck. He tipped her head and sought her lips. "I would that you were tucked out of harm's way."

A soft sigh escaped before she nipped the corner of his mouth. "We must snare him before he harms another."

"I cannot stand idly by if he lays a hand upon you."

She raked her teeth over his jaw and down the band of muscle leading to his shoulders. "This I know," she whispered. "I would that our snare was tripped quickly."

Ranulf found her lower lip with his teeth. He nipped the edges, letting his kiss dance over her flesh. Slowly, he lifted his head. "I thought you craved distance between us."

"A foolish misunderstanding." She captured his shoulders with her arms. "I would that we were joined for eternity, my darling wolf."

Growling, he drew her to his chest.

She gripped his hair and gave a quick tug to his auburn curls. "Dismiss that worried look on your face."

"Robert . . ."

Grinning wickedly, she slid her fingers under his tunic. "'Tis also possible that devil is far from here."

He trapped her hand in his and shook his head. "We dare not let down our guard."

Clarice sighed, molding her body to his.

"Rest." He led her to the blanket spread between the logs. "The night may prove to be eternally long for both of us."

Despite the sleepless nights and never-ending travel, sleep refused to come when Ranulf called it. Rest had officially deserted him after the partaking of their meal of roast hare. He was left to count the stars as they appeared.

One by one, they blossomed. Their singular illumination spread across the night. Beams of light streaked across the cobalt backdrop, making a ceiling of winking diamonds. He traced the lines between the stars, forming pictures in his mind. One group of stars reminded him of Clarice's beautiful face. He was certain he could see the laughter in her eyes.

He resisted the urge to look to see if she really did rest her head beside him. He knew her arm would be nestled under her ear, her other hand fisted under her chin. Even in sleep 'twas as if she dared someone to try to oppose her chosen path.

He smoothed the velvet cloak that covered her shoulders. She moved to snuggle closer. Folds of material entwined her legs.

He shifted his seat by the fire. Worries for his king were erased by the vision at his side. He glanced up again to the sky for help. The picture of lovers traced in stars winked back as if they laughed at his efforts to push Clarice away. But how could he press his interest under these circumstances? What would she think? Would she turn him away as Mary had?

He looked down, and Clarice pulled his head near so she might whisper in his ear. "Hold me," she said.

Ranulf closed his eyes, enjoying the pleasure of her bold tongue as it danced across his lips. A purr vibrated against his chest. His breath caught. He dared not lose her precious smile. It pained him when he thought of the possibility. He had given Mary everything that was his: his name, his home, his hopes for the future. He had even thought one day to give her his heart.

Clarice pressed his palm against her breasts. Her twin mounds strained against the bodice, stretching the seams taut. "Love me," she urged. "Love me."

Unsure if he had heard correctly, Ranulf lifted his head and looked into her face. "We must keep our wits about us."

She arched her back, searching for his touch. Warmth poured through him as she stroked his core.

His blood drummed in his ears, drawing all his senses to focus on the passionate woman spread out for his pleasure.

Ah, but to taste her. He nuzzled her breast and watched the nipple pebble into a bud.

To touch her. He lifted the folds of her gown, sliding his hand up her satiny thigh, exploring the apex of her legs.

To hear her sweet pants of pleasure. His cock swelled when she moaned softly, wiggling until he held her in his palm.

Praising the fates that had brought this blue-eyed maiden into his life, Ranulf feasted. Nipping, then licking, he grazed his teeth over sensitive flesh. He renewed his attention to her legs, her hips, her mons. He returned to her, forearms braced, to cradle her head in his palms.

When her grip tightened around his rod, all coherent thought left him. He drew his tunic over his head and closed his eyes, letting the heat from her hand draw him over the edge.

"Ranulf," she whispered against his neck. "Now."

Heart to heart, they scattered the moonbeams with their passion. The stars nodded and laughed overhead.

"And what is that star over there?"

Clarice nestled into the crook of Ranulf's arm. The velvet cloak angled over their legs. The blanket lay, bunched and rumpled. Her bodice hung carelessly at her waist. The hem of her skirt pillowed around her thighs. Ranulf's bare chest and shoulders glistened under the glow of the fire.

Ranulf placed a lingering kiss on her temple. His fingers traveled down to her breast. "North Star," he murmured.

"And that one?"

She snuggled deeper into the cleft between his legs. The thrill of discovering each other still hummed through her veins. Though tender, her core was heated, wanting more of his skilled attention.

He wrapped his arms around her waist, pulled her closer and kissed the sensitive hollow by her collarbone.

"Ranulf?"

"Hmm?"

"What is it? I fear you are drawing away."

Life returned to his burgeoning flesh, demanding she take notice. "I'm right here, love," he whispered as he pressed another kiss to her neck. His tongue danced across her skin until he found her cleavage. There, he lingered over each breast.

She squeezed her thighs together, testing the tenderness, wanting more. She had heard women talk of their first time with a man. Some had complained of pain. Others winked to one another, sharing the secrets of lovemaking.

Clarice's face flushed with desire. She recalled the smooth texture of his skin stretched taut over the layers of muscle and sinew that formed his body. It was all she could do to tamp down the urgent need to have him once again fill her completely. Her body hummed with the recent memory of their joining.

Yet she could not let the niggling feeling that uncertainty erected a wall between them. She would not let him think she looked to force his protection.

"Ranulf, please know that I do not ask you to sacrifice your freedom for me." She turned in his arms and held his face when he began to deny her words. "What you have given me, I shall treasure as no other gift." She pressed her fingers to his lips, silencing his protests. "I vow I shall not demand a price from you."

"Clarice," Ranulf crushed her to his chest. "I cannot—"

She could not bear to hear him turn her away and covered his mouth with her lips. Their heat renewed, growing with their shared kiss. The knowledge that it might be their last left a bittersweet taste on her tongue. But try as she might, she could not let him go.

Ranulf was the first to pull away. Tension rushed through his thick-banded arms, his strong hands, his long fingers. "Dress quickly."

Clarice's heart ached with the rush of his cold disregard. Rearing back to argue her case, she stopped when he trapped her shoulders between his powerful hands.

The stern look had returned to his eyes. "Obey me on this."

Clarice swept her hands up, separating her shoulders from his hold. Pain so deep, the like of which she had never known before, tore through her. Wide-eyed, she grasped the bodice to her chest.

"Why?" she whispered. "Why must you . . ."

Ranulf's skin had paled. His eyes, fierce and strong, scoured the trees.

Chapter 36

Robert stepped out from the trees, a gentleman of the royal court no more. His unkempt hair stood out to the sides in a wild mess. Perspiration covered his forehead and dark streaks slashed across his face as if, in his haste, he had been whipped by tree branches and thorny brambles. In a silent twist, his jaw thrust forward.

Clarice drew his attention. The menacing force of his hatred spread through the camp, covered the air with the scent of death. Ranulf's hands tightened as he tried to shove her behind him.

"No," she hissed, digging in her heels.

Ranulf shifted to retrieve his sword where they had been laying.

Firelight flickered on Robert's outstretched arm. "Hold!" He pointed his blade toward Ranulf as he moved closer. "Do you think to hide behind a woman? Don your hose so that I don't have to look upon your filth."

Robert kept his distance from Ranulf as he moved closer to the rumpled blankets. He turned the edge with the toe of his boot, uncovering Ranulf's blade. A smile twitched under Robert's beard as he stood on the weapon. "I see that I find you at a disadvantage."

"That is where you are incorrect," Ranulf said, pulling up his chausses and tying off the leather string at his waist. "I am never at a disadvantage where you are concerned."

"Such bravado! A courageous face indeed. Henry would be proud of his swan knight."

"What knowledge of courage have you, Robert?" Clarice asked.

Robert withdrew his attention from Ranulf to pin his glare on her. "I wouldn't hide behind a harlot's skirts."

"Is that not what you did by hiding behind your mother?" she shot back. "Look where it has taken you. What more shall you think to do to the Margrave name? You are now its lord and yet you strive to destroy it."

"I was forced to take my vengeance against king and swan." His rage thundered over Clarice and Ranulf. "They took everything. Henry took my Mary and gave her to another."

"Our king united Sedgewic and the Dunley family by our marriage," Ranulf said.

Robert sneered, pointing to Ranulf. "This one took what was not his. He knew how she despised his touch, yet he stole her away from the court. And still he could not stop us."

"Bastard." Ranulf shot Clarice a warning glance before pushing her behind him.

"Look at you, Clarice," Robert persisted. "Why do you hide when 'tis you I am saving from this wretch's touch? I may have failed Mary, but I shall not fail you." Desperation gleamed in his eyes. "I realize I was wrong to threaten your life. Come with me. I shall shower you with the wealth of France."

"I'll never leave with you."

"'Tis where you belong. By my side. The two of us together."

"Not while there is life within me, Robert of Margrave." Ranulf shifted his position and, despite her entreaty, he became her shield. "You've taken on a battle you will never win."

"You can be nothing more than a brother to me." Clarice stepped out, laying her hand atop the crook of Ranulf's elbow. "'Tis him I love. Not you."

"Knight's whore." Robert wiped his mouth with the back of a trembling hand. "Soon," he said, "you, too, will be breeding with his spawn. Will I have to cut it out as I did the other one? Another bastard of his in the world? Won't repeat my mother's mistake. I'll make certain 'tis dead before its first breath."

"A plague on your rotting soul," Ranulf shouted. "Mary was my wife in the eyes of God and king."

"She was mine."

Ranulf stepped forward, shortening the distance between them. "If you loved her as you say, she didn't have to die."

"Your empty promises turned her head." Robert reared back, as if clarity blinded his eyes. "You don't know what her last words were to me." He tapped his lips with the tip of his finger. "I must have a moment to ponder what would cause you more pain: to know that she spread her thighs and shared your bed with me or that her foolishness had to be stopped when she thought to go to you and beg your forgiveness?"

"Devil's spawn," Ranulf growled. "I will cut out your liver and feed it to you."

Robert blinked in response, but the tip of his sword did not waver. "Found her in the stables. Said she had a change of heart. Selfish bitch didn't care that it didn't sit well with my plans. She needed a rough wooing to correct her thinking. Yes, she did." He paused, pointing to Ranulf's scar. "That night. Unfortunate timing. You arrived earlier than expected. The damage to our sweet Mary had already been done. Milk spilt. Eggs broken." He stroked his temple. "A parting gift from me to you. Something to help you remember your failure in protecting those you love."

Robert's smile widened. "Soon you and King Henry will know firsthand of loss. France and I will defeat you. You and your Knights of the Swan will exist no more. Worms will feast upon your flesh. England will be another jewel in the crown of France."

Clarice's fingers tightened around Ranulf's arm. She pressed into his side to gain his attention. He did not heed her touch and tried to shake her loose. He stepped toward the tip of Robert's blade.

"You will have to go through me before you can lay your hand on Clarice or England."

Robert's sword arm trembled as if it wearied from the weight. The blade dipped and shivered before he could right it again. He took a half step back as Ranulf pressed his advantage. "Think you that since you are a Knight of the Swan you can defeat a blade?"

"No," Ranulf said. "I believe that I, a common man, will defeat you."

Robert's eyes widened as he realized he had become the prey. "Advance no more," he cautioned. "Or I shall end your life here and now."

Ranulf took another step closer. His teeth flashed in the firelight for an instant before he struck out, trapping the steel between the palms of his hands. "Lay down your weapon."

Robert renewed his grip and held the hilt with both hands. He strained to escape Ranulf's hold. "You shall not block my path."

"Don't be a fool. Look around you. Your bridges of retreat are burned."

Robert's sword arm sagged as he turned his head to the left and then to the right. "'Tis a lie."

Darrick and Nathan stood at the edge of the camp. They held their swords at the ready.

She did not dare distract the knights from their quarry and quashed the need to ask where they had hidden young Hamish.

"Robert of Margrave," Darrick called out.

Nathan's grin stretched as wide as a feral cat's with a basket of fish. "Your man Harald sings a pretty tune. We apprehended your French contacts before they left Southampton."

"Consider yourself warned," Darrick said. With a jerk of his chin, he pointed to the surrounding trees. "The king's finest archers have stretched their bows. They await your slightest movement."

Ranulf took the sword from Robert's grasp and announced, with finality in his tone, "In the name of King Henry V, you are under arrest."

Relieved Robert could do no harm, Clarice bent down and picked up Ranulf's sword. She heard Robert's roar as he barreled past Ranulf, a dagger clutched in his hand. Her eye caught the flash of a small form hiding in the bushes, directly in Robert's path. The familiar round face and tousled hair. *Hamish!*

Clarice fisted the hilt of the sword. With all her might, she arched the heavy weapon and slashed it through the air. The pounding in her ears muffled the sound of men yelling for someone to stop. Her arms jerked from the impact of blade against body. Fire raced up her arms and into her shoulders.

Her fingers uncurled. The sword dropped to the ground. A cloud of dirt billowed up from the impact. Robert's knees crumpled. His confused gaze caught hers and held before he fell to the earth.

Chapter 37

Smoke lifted and swirled overhead, filling the tavern. The smell of sweat and salted meats pinched Clarice's nostrils. Voluptuous women, breasts clinging to their gaping bodices, fisted tankards of ale and maneuvered through the throng of boisterous men. Female squeals carried over the din of merrymaking. A round rump pinched, a breast fondled, and the sound of coin hitting the table rattled the senses.

Clarice shifted her legs and remained seated on the bench. The wide planks bent and bounced as men came and went. She leaned her forearms on the surface of the rough wooden table and examined her hands in the dim light. It had taken hours of scrubbing to remove all traces of Robert's blood. Had she done the right thing? Even now, the man who commanded all of England to do his bidding was deciding her fate.

King Henry had barely acknowledged her when he came marching through as if he were a wandering soldier. Had Ranulf not motioned her to keep silent, she would never have known the king had passed with a simple nod of his head.

No groveling of men. No kissing his feet. No bending of the knee. The king commanded honor and allegiance from his countrymen. His people of England. His Knights of the Swan.

She fidgeted while she waited for Ranulf's return. She leaned to one side and peeked around the edges of the drawn curtain. The king's men filled the alcove. Men, both short and tall, stood shoulder to shoulder as they bent over the table. Ranulf's head of auburn curls lifted, as if he had heard his named called. He smiled, his gaze reaching out to her, and then returned his attention to the man who spoke at his side.

Clarice found the courage to sit and await her fate. She had not seen Darrick or Nathan since they'd taken Robert away in manacles. He was barely able to walk under his own power, yet he had enough hatred in his spirit to curse her and spit on the dirt by her feet. She prayed King Henry would grant her protection, even though his patience with her family had been destroyed at Robert's hand.

Clarice grasped the small amount of peace she had gained from their journey and held it to her heart as if it were a priceless jewel. In her father's truth, she had found lies amid reality. In searching for her past, she had not found perfection but a mother's love nonetheless. In her desire to leave Margrave and make a life of her own, she had discovered a strength she never had known she possessed. And she had found someone to love.

Her newly found knowledge was bittersweet. She had found a life, though 'twas not hers to hold. Plans were being made that might soon carry her love out of her life. Mayhap forever.

She readied a smile and lifted her head at the sound of familiar footsteps. A sense of urgency bubbled in her veins. If Ranulf were to leave her side, she would not let him go without his knowing where her heart resided. She took hold of his hand, pressing it to her cheek, breathing in his scent of juniper and mint.

Ranulf cleared his throat. "Clarice, come with me."

She stood and bravely matched his purposeful strides. Her thoughts scattered as she tried to form the words to express her love. To keep him by her side as long as the king would allow.

Ranulf drew back the curtain and led her into the alcove. Clarice curtsied deeply before her king.

With boyish charm and a soldier's grace, King Henry rose to meet her. Curling his fingers around her fingertips, he bent over the back of her hand. "Not here." Henry gave a slow, lazy wink. "Too many watching eyes."

Clarice's knees trembled. The imagined noose tightened around her neck. "Sire—"

"My gratitude is immense. Sir Ranulf has informed me that you were instrumental in unearthing the culprit of this plot against England. 'Tis within my power to grant you a boon." He smiled playfully. "Just do not damage my coffers with your request.

"And you," he said as he turned to Ranulf. "You, too, may request a favor from your king."

Clarice's heart thundered within her chest as Ranulf wrapped his hand around her waist. "My king, I would ask of the lady a boon in place of yours."

Henry's brows arched and he rose. He braced his feet, his hands behind his back. "State your boon from the lady of Margrave," he commanded.

Clarice's breath caught. "In truth, sire?"

"Upon my honor." Henry flicked his hand through the air. "Now, Ranulf, be quick about it. If the weather holds I must prepare to set sail."

A pink stain streaked Ranulf's cheeks. He cleared his throat to form the words that would not come with ease. "Clarice . . ."

She could not watch her love struggle any longer and answered before he finished. "I will."

"How can you agree when you haven't given me a chance to ask?"

Clarice reached up and smoothed the wave of auburn from his face. She traced the healing scar that ran into his hair. She smiled back at the man who had proved to her that she really could touch the stars.

"I am listening," she said.

Ranulf ignored the men who remained around the table. He ignored the king, who watched and listened. He kissed her as if they were the only two people in the crowded tavern.

Then he raised his head and grinned as he paused long enough to let her catch her breath. "Clarice of Margrave, I ask you to accept my love and become my lady of Sedgewic."

"Here, now," King Henry said. "'Tis within my means to join your names together."

Ranulf shook his head. "Sire, I would have a marriage of love or none at all."

Releasing his hold, he closed his eyes as if he were afraid he would see denial in her gaze. "Clarice, I place it in your hands to deny me or grant my desire."

"Well, my lady, what say you?" King Henry asked. "First, your request of me?"

Clarice prayed she would not know the king's ire. "I would ask that you allow this Knight of the Swan to stay here in England and watch over the protection of her people." She glanced up and swallowed. "You did give your word upon your honor that you would hear my request."

King Henry's face flushed, his eyes twinkling with restraint. "So I did." A ghost of a smile washed over his face before he went on. "And what of your boon to Ranulf? I must hear it before I make my decision."

Desperate to let Ranulf know that her heart would forever remain his, she pulled out the oddly shaped key from her pocket and held it out for all to see. The swan's emerald eye winked at all who stood around the table.

With Ranulf's rapt attention, she began, "Once, I believed this was the key to my freedom. Now I know 'twas meant to lead me to the keeper of my heart." She placed the key in his palm, curling his fingers around it. "My heart is yours. Care for it, wherever you may be."

Ranulf pulled her into his arms again. The boisterous voices quieted as one by one they turned to look at the pair. The tavern's silence broke as Ranulf and Clarice were pulled from their weaving of moonbeams.

King Henry cleared his voice so that all could hear. "It appears your lady has given you her answer."

Ranulf wrapped his arms around Clarice's waist and held her as if he were afraid he would have to let go too soon.

"And now I will give you my decision." King Henry paused, letting the moment drag. Grinning wickedly, he said, "It seems to me that I don't have the time or coin to spare for the rebuilding and cultivation of the Margrave lands. Ranulf of Sedgewic, make it profitable and I will grant the manor to you upon my return. Watch over my people of England. Ensure 'tis a place where her sons and daughters can lift their heads high and proud."

Henry kissed the back of Clarice's hand. "No more word of the Knights of the Swan, my lady." He dropped a brooch shaped like a swan into her hand. "Unless you need assistance from your king's elite."

King Henry lifted his mug of ale. "A toast to eternal love!"

As their cups were raised, the king held Clarice and Ranulf in his gaze and he added, "May there be someone to hold 'til the wee hours of the morn. Someone to love us, despite our faults. Someone to care whether we live or die. And may that someone be ours to love throughout eternity."

Cheers rang out after the mugs were drained and slammed down on the wooden table.

King Henry winked, then worked his way past the mass of bodies crammed in the room.

Clarice looked up at Ranulf. "Do you regret your decision to stay?"

"Don't be swayed by our king's easy charm. He knows that my eyes and ears will be alert to any news, be it evil or good, while he is away."

"Forever a Knight of the Swan?"

"You have captured my heart, my lady." Ranulf caressed his lips against the nape of her neck. "I will be a Knight of the Swan all the days of my life, but my love shall forever be yours."

Clarice wrapped her arms around his waist, leaning into his embrace. "'Tis all I have ever desired."

Historical and contemporary romance author **C.C. Wiley** is a farm girl at heart and now lives in Utah. She tried the city life but soon discovered she likes wide-open spaces, rolling hills, fresh air, blue skies, and a little quiet. It just feels right.

C.C. states that one of the wisest steps she took as a writer with a dream was to join the Romance Writers of America. Soon after joining that organization, she began the arduous task of learning all she could about writing a story. Those lessons continue every day,

She believes there are wonderful, courageous characters waiting for someone to tell their story. It is her hope that each adventurous romance she writes will touch her readers and carry them away to another place and time, where hopes and dreams abound.